Has to Be Love

Has to Be Love

JOLENE PERRY

Albert Whitman & Company
Chicago, Illinois

Library of Congress Cataloging-in-Publication data
is on file with the publisher.

Text copyright © 2015 by Jolene Perry
Published in 2015 by Albert Whitman & Company
ISBN 978-0-8075-6557-5
Printed in the United States of America
10 9 8 7 6 5 4 3 2 1 LB 20 19 18 17 16 15

Design by Jordan Kost
Cover image © Cindy Clarissa Tanudjaja/Getty Images

For more information about Albert Whitman & Company,
visit our web site at www.albertwhitman.com.

To Emma,
because I will never really understand

Poems are measured in meters, which are sort of like rhythms,
The way our tongues and lips come together
As we read someone's carefully crafted words.
Our bodies and minds operate in rhythms too,

I think.

Shifting from one kind of beat to another,
There are times when I'm perfectly in sync with one person,
Or even with myself, and then...

I'm not.

1

My hair flies out behind me as I race on my four-wheeler toward the hardware store. The cool spring air bites my cheeks, but there's actual warmth from the sun and the faintest hint of green at the tips of the tree branches. Any day the leaves will burst. Every spring in Alaska moves from snowy to green in about two weeks, and I can't wait to get rid of this ugly brown in between.

The large log storefront and old metal warehouse of Motter Construction come into view through the thick trees along the river, and I hit the gas, making the lugged tires kick out mud behind me.

The lumberyard, hardware store, and construction office is my once-a-week job, or whenever my boyfriend's mother calls and asks me for help, like today. I slide to a stop in the gravel parking lot just in time to see Elias toss a bundle of lumber over his shoulder.

I stand on the wheeler for a moment longer, watching him with the customer, all perfect smiles and strong shoulders. He jogs back into the warehouse from the lumberyard, and I head for the front door. My body and brain are still buzzing from the acceptance letter I got today. I'm not going to do anything about it yet, so there's no point in saying anything.

Tapping my back pocket, I double-check for my small notebook. Nothing's worse than knowing exactly what to write and having nothing to write it on. It's there, like always.

"Clara Fielding." Mrs. Motter sighs over her laptop. "Have you come to save me from inventory again?"

The relief on her face bubbles a short laugh up my throat. "Yep."

Her gaze doesn't even pause on my scars as she watches me walk toward her. She's known me since long before the attack that marred the right side of my face just over five years ago.

I step around the store counter. "Let me see what we have going on here today." I flip her laptop toward me and know immediately it has everything to do with technology and very little to do with actual inventory taking. "Why is all this red?"

"I don't know." She shakes her head as she sighs again. "I thought I was *adding* inventory, but—"

"You subtracted it." I smile again, and this time she does glance at my face for just a moment too long. I tilt my head forward so my blond hair gives me some coverage. No matter how often I smooth my bangs down and keep my head forward, I'm still known as the girl with the scars. Or, more often, the girl who was attacked by a bear and survived.

"Now I'm worried I don't have the numbers right." Her shoulders fall. For Mrs. Motter, computers are still voodoo magic. Almost anywhere but in small-town Knik, Alaska, this would be a problem.

"Let me go in the back and get the drop-off receipts, okay?" In reality I'm looking for an excuse to see Elias and maybe sneak a kiss in the warehouse.

"Thank you, Clara." She stares at the screen like she can somehow *will* all the numbers to do what she wants.

I jog through the doors into the back and slow to a walk, wondering how long it'll take me to find him in the floor-to-ceiling maze of metal shelving.

"Saw your girl is here." One of the guys laughs, but I can't see anyone over the high racks of tubing, lumber, trim, and insulation.

"Her face, man…She must make it up to you in other ways, huh?" A different voice, but the twisting in my stomach is familiar.

"Don't be a dick, Kev," someone says. "Grow up."

I'm used to this—I am. But it still takes my breath away. Elias mutters a few things I can't understand, and I flatten myself against a row of doors.

*Breathe, Clara. It's not a big deal. You don't even know the warehouse guys that well. They're older…*But I know that guy voiced what everyone probably thinks. He was just rude enough to say it out loud.

Pressing my hand over my heart, I close my eyes and take in a deep breath. I need to find a smile before I see Elias. I catch a glimpse of his faded red Motter Construction T-shirt between two rows. I sprint toward him and grab his belt loop.

His smile is wide as he spins around. "Hey, beautiful."

I've always thought of Elias as a haiku—all simple, gorgeous perfection.

His hands slide around my waist and his fingertips tap my pocket. "Been writing?"

I kiss his cheek. "Always." Maybe I'll write even more now that I know it could actually get me somewhere.

"Do I get to see?" He kisses my cheek back.

"I could be persuaded." I step back wanting him to follow, but he doesn't. Elias never does. At least not here. He wants to seem professional to the crew and his dad, who has brought Elias into the company almost full time now.

I want a kiss. I always want a kiss. There's something about connecting with someone that way that makes the rest of the world matter a little less.

He shakes his head with the teasing smile I love so much. "Not here, Clara."

"Please?" I step closer.

He clears his throat as his gaze dances on everything but me. He forgets I know when he's trying to hold in a smile. "So, when is Cecily back?" he asks. "You two withering away without each other yet?"

I stick my finger in his dimple. "She's back a couple weeks before we graduate." I lean closer. "You already know when my friend returns, and you're ignoring what I want."

"And is the trip to Seattle before or after that?"

"Before." This time I kiss his dimple. "You already knew that too."

His near-smile just makes his dimples deeper. "Incorrigible."

"Irresistible?" I turn my head a little to the right. It's automatic to always turn my scars away from people. Even him. Even after knowing him since long before my scars and dating him for close to two years.

He leans back and does a quick scan both ways. The look on his face as he steps closer says "all clear" so I move in for my kiss.

He rests his calloused hands on my shoulders and leans in, pressing his lips to mine and sending the fluttering tingles through me that seem to be fiercer every day. The comments from the warehouse guys start to slip away. I part my lips a little and am leaning forward when someone clears his throat behind me.

Elias and I jump, and his dad gives us a frown.

"Elias, we have another load."

Elias's jaw tightens slightly as he steps around me and takes the slip from his dad so he can collect the order. He gives me one quick look over his shoulder, tilting his head toward the back of the warehouse where the river is—meaning, *I'll meet you there in a few.*

I hate it when Elias is right and we're caught. He warns me every time, and every time I ignore him. If I'm being honest, we're caught more often than not because once I start kissing Elias, I'm not good at stopping. He has the stopping part of kissing me down to an art.

"I'm getting the new inventory sheets," I say to his dad, even though we both know I'm back here for Elias. His dad shares the same view as his son. Work is work. Dates are dates. No need to confuse the two. I want them all smashed together. All the time.

I quickly snatch the drop-off sheets from the office and run back to the store so I can get this mess sorted out. The second I sit down, Elias is next to me, taking my hand and tugging me back to my feet. Unlike his dad, his mom gives us a smile as we walk for the door.

"Five minutes," I tell her, but she waves us away.

Elias leads me out the door, and I follow him to the small bench near the river. The river runs brown and thick and muddy this time of year, matching the brownness of everything else.

When we were kids we made mud pies behind this warehouse. When my mom died and my scars were new, Elias built this bench for me. When I turned sixteen and my dad said I could date, Elias gave me my first kiss on this bench. Now we still come here sometimes to kiss.

I slip my arms around his neck, his hands touch my lower back, and I think we might end up in the middle of a very nice make-out session. It's probably good that we're out in the open like this because kissing Elias tends to turn off my moral compass and makes me want all of him.

Being raised with strict standards where boys are concerned—no dating until sixteen, no sex until marriage—should mean that I'm the cautious one with Elias. But it seems like I'm never the more careful one.

Elias breaks our kiss and taps my notebook in his hands. He won't open it without my okay though. He never would.

I start to tell him my writing got me into Columbia, but then we'd be in the middle of a conversation about futures, which I'm not sure I'm ready to have. Columbia is my mother's school. She'd be so fiercely proud of me. My chest feels like it both caves and swells, like most times when I think about Mom.

"Hey," Elias whispers as he touches my cheek—the unscarred one. "You okay?"

"Mom moment." I shake my head before plopping my arms around his neck again. A "mom moment" is a lot easier to explain than admission to a college he doesn't know I applied to. "But I'm ready for my next kiss."

He shifts just slightly away again. Just enough that I start to feel weird for being so forward. "I just have a minute."

I lean toward him. His kiss is soft but closed mouth.

"I get off in an hour and a half," he says, our lips still touching.

My shoulders sag. "I have a family dinner tonight."

He sits back before holding my notebook out between us.

I fold my arms. "It's okay."

"You still start at the back, right?" he asks.

"It's the only way to preserve my writing mojo," I tease. *The mojo that got me into freaking Columbia.* But I'm not going this year, maybe not even next year. My plan with Cecily was to stay was to stay in Alaska for freshman year, at least until my face is fixed, and then figure out what to do for school. Besides, Cecily's going to University of Alaska with me so we can share our freshman year—Anchorage or Fairbanks is something we'll figure out later.

Elias opens my notebook carefully, and I bite my lip. I still can't believe I got *in*. It was stupid to apply a year early, but curiosity got the better of me. I had to know if I was good enough.

I am.

His callused hands flip from the back to my most recent, and he reads aloud. His cheeks turn pink.

My body suddenly feels hot from bottom to top, because I remember exactly how I felt writing those words.

His low voice echoes my thoughts back to me:
"Fuzzy brains and stupid scars,
Trips to barns and backs of cars.
Lightning flashes, sight of blue
Coming back to haunt me. You…"

Before giving him a chance to react to the rest of the poem, I grab his face in my hands and kiss him. For real. Mouth open. Tongues moving together. I really wish he'd put his hands on me. Everywhere.

And then our kissing is just over. No fingers sliding under my shirt or bending me over backward on the small wooden bench or…any one of a million other things I might like to be doing but probably should stop myself from doing.

"You're amazing." He gives me another soft kiss. "Your words *and* your mouth." His cheeks are pink again. Elias reaches around my lower back, but I know it's just to slip my notebook back into my pocket. Kissing is done. "Have a good dinner."

"Good luck with work," I say. And the same weird feeling of *wanting* I felt while writing that poem comes back to me.

2

Not only is tonight a family dinner, but it's a dinner with a stranger. I need to brace myself. The old plaid couch helps my body relax. Meeting new people isn't one of my strong suits.

I know what it's like to have people see my scars before they see me. Even in Knik, where pretty much everyone knows me, it happens. In New York? Probably a million times worse. I shouldn't have applied so early.

Tucking Mom's book onto my knees, I begin to read. Again.

She never finished her degree at Columbia, but she did manage to write a book of short stories. And every time I open *Alaskan Paths*, a tiny part of me hopes that my name will be on a cover one day too. It's a fragile dream, but I never feel more connected to Mom than when I find myself wanting the same things as her.

Dad pauses at the edge of the living room. "We'll need to get started cooking soon," he says in his gravelly voice.

I tap my finger across the cover of Mom's book—a cheesy mountain picture that looks painted. Small Alaskan press, but still a thrill.

"Clara?" Dad calls again.

"Coming!"

Dad's already set the massive table, and my heart skips again because I don't *want* to meet the guy who is subbing for Ms. Bellings for a couple months.

"I've opened a standing invitation for Rhodes Kennedy to eat with us," Dad says as he starts browning the meat, holding the spatula out to me before he burns it or something.

"Why?" The word comes out a bit snottier than I mean for it to. It's that English is *my* subject and having a sub for the end of senior year feels cruel. I take the spatula and dump in some tomato sauce and the onions he's chopped up. The smell of marinara sauce begins to fill the kitchen, and some of the tension dissipates.

Dad turns toward the fridge. "Because he's a guy who has never been here before, and I think a young college student might appreciate a couple home-cooked meals a week. Especially considering he's going to be student teaching for the first time."

His voice is so methodical and matter-of-fact that I really can't argue. It's exactly the kind of thing he'd do anyway—welcoming the new face into our little town.

And we're definitely a little town—probably microscopic for someone coming from college. The grocery store is mostly canned and frozen stuff, and the produce is an hour away, along with the Walmart.

I go to the private Christian school in Knik because Dad and the principal of the high school have some feud over…I think it's that the principal's husband is the only other accountant in town and is a "money-grubbing crook." Apparently I should not be in a school that is run by the wife of a crook. Never mind the fact that both schools only have a couple hundred students total, and that we all hang out and know each other outside of school.

"Where's he from?" I ask. I'm sure he's said before, but Dad's chatter about the school board generally floats in one ear and out the other.

"New York."

My heart gives a few thumps. "Which school?"

Dad pauses and scratches his chin. "Columbia? I think that's the one.

You applied there, right? Like your mom?"

I take a hard swallow. I could go. I mean, not this fall. Too soon. Not enough time to get my face fixed. But *Columbia*. J. D. Salinger went to Columbia. So did Federico García Lorca, Hunter S. Thompson, Eudora Welty, Jack Kerouac, Langston Hughes…Allen freaking Ginsberg. My hands shake a little at the thought of how something so far out of reach feels oddly closer now that someone from *there* is *here*. And now that my acceptance letter is *in my drawer*. Like Columbia used to be a foreign country and now…isn't.

"Good school."

I think about the acceptance I have stashed away. What it means. How we'd even pay for it if I did decide to go. Well…when I decide to go. Or maybe they won't have room for me in a year, and that decision won't need to be made.

There's a beat of silence where Dad stares at me because he's way, way too good at reading me.

"What's on your mind?" he asks.

I widen my eyes and give him a smile as I stir the sauce. "Dinner."

Dad shakes his head and watches me for a moment longer. "How are you feeling about going to Seattle?" he asks.

"Good." I shrug like it's just another trip, but I've been thinking about it at least as much as Columbia. The trip to Seattle is going to change my life. That's when the plastic surgeon will work on my scars. Then the world will open up.

"We could put it off just a little longer if you want. Sometime over the summer or next winter or…"

I stop stirring and face Dad. "We have our tickets. The appointment is in two weeks. How can you even *ask* that?" New York isn't an option this fall, but if I don't get my face fixed, it won't be an option for next fall either.

He scratches his thinning hair, leaving pieces of it up in wisps. "We were always told that there might not be a fix for your scars. I pray there is for your sake. I just don't want you to be disappoi—"

"And times change," I insist as my neck heats up, spreading embarrassment and anger far too quickly for me to hide my reaction. Even Elias's kiss couldn't totally dissolve the comments I heard today. "And that's not what we were told. We were told we needed to wait until I was older and the scars were fully healed."

Dad and I have looked over the website of the plastic surgeon a million times. It's amazing what he's done for scarring on other people. And then I wouldn't have to leave for college until my face looked… normal. That has always been part of my plan.

Right now I'm an ugly mess.

My eyebrow is half gone. I'm missing a bit off the corner of my upper lip. Four welted lines mark from the corner of my eye, the edge of my nostril, the top part of my lip and chin. The angry purply-red scars almost touch my eye and have messed up part of my hairline. Only doctors have ever asked me if the scars feel funny, but they do. Both to my fingers and to my face.

Dad and I stare at one another for a moment longer, both knowing we'll go, both knowing I won't relent, and Dad in his dream world thinking I'll somehow wake up one day okay with looking so freakish.

I won't.

"I understand you wanting them gone," he says. "I just want to make sure you're happy now too."

Right.

The doorbell rings. I'm off the hook for this conversation.

But as Dad goes to answer the door, my stomach rolls over. When I meet new people, there's always staring and then subtle (or not-so-subtle) glances over my face, and sometimes there are questions. Most often are quick, guilty glances followed by avoidance.

I can't imagine strangers' reactions changing so, according to Dad, that puts the burden on me to decide how I feel about their reaction. It's one of many things I have yet to master. The reality is that it's really hard to tell myself they're thinking anything different than the random comments I overhear at school. *She'd be maybe even pretty if... It's the one at the edge of her eye that freaks me out...Wonder if they feel as gross as they look...*

I shove out a breath and pour a half cup of red wine into the spaghetti sauce. The tangy smell of grape and alcohol tickles my nose, and I take a whiff right off the top of the bottle. Dad doesn't drink, and I've never had a drop, but I breathe in deeply again.

There's chatter from the entryway, and the new guy says something about the woodwork on the walls and ceiling. I swear I can feel Dad beam from here. He built this house and loves talking about it. In seconds he's launched into the story about the people who milled the wood from trees my dad cut down himself. I've heard this story about a *million* times.

"Clara?" Dad steps into the kitchen, and I shove the old cork into the bottle of wine. "This is Ms. Bellings's nephew, Rhodes Kennedy. Though he'll be 'Mr. Kennedy' to you."

I brace myself for the stare and turn from the stove to meet with... My heart does some sort of fantastic leap because...brain fuzzing...just wow.

Blond, curly hair in serious need of a cut (if you're my dad) or just perfect (if you're me), relaxed smile, sparkling blue eyes.

And then his eyes do the predictable scan across my face. A quick frown is followed by a hard swallow (I note by his very manly Adam's apple) and then a forced smile. This is the point when my brain checks out of the moment because his reaction makes my neck heat up and my stomach tighten. I will never meet someone face-to-face without getting some kind of stare or nervousness—at least not until I'm rid of my scars.

I tilt my head down enough that my hair cascades like a shield.

Rhodes Kennedy reaches his hand out and shakes mine. Any weird expression on his face is gone. I'm not so lucky because the tension's going to stick with me for a while.

"Need help finishing up?" he asks.

"No, I…"

Dad gives him a friendly slap on the shoulder. "Come sit down, Rhodes. Clara loves to cook."

And I do love to cook, but in this moment I'm ready to be alone in the kitchen, even though a million questions about Columbia rest on the tip of my tongue.

I give Mr. Kennedy a quick smile through my hair, carefully not watching his reaction. But instead of following Dad, he helps himself to a fork and pulls out a noodle.

"They might be ready," I say, even though I'm supposed to want him gone. He's just…I don't know. There's something about how his hair is perfectly messy and how his jeans are a little too skinny and his shoes a little too trendy and his glasses a little funky. It reminds me of how I imagined going to college out of state would feel. Like beat poetry and unexpected rhythms and quirky rhymes…like everyone would be more like him and less like me, whose jeans are stained from playing with horses and riding four-wheelers.

The stupidity of wanting a school so far out of my reach hits me again. I desperately want to be there. To be one of the too-cool people with smart opinions and term papers with deadlines. I just…It's overwhelming. And it's so *far*. And I'm so horribly ugly. I have just over a month to give them my yay or nay on the acceptance, and the thought of answering either way makes air hard to breathe.

Mr. Kennedy tosses the noodle onto a cabinet just like Dad and I do.

"Looks like it." His brows dance up once as he pulls the noodle from the cabinet and slides it in his mouth.

Dad chuckles. "We've tested noodles that way for ages."

"Best way." Mr. Kennedy gives Dad a smile.

"You, um…go…um…to…Columbia?" I ask, only my voice catches like three times during the *four-word* sentence.

"It's the best."

I nod, wanting details. Smells. Sights. Feels. Rhythms.

"I've read your writing," Mr. Kennedy says.

Dad's beaming again. I can feel it, like his pride is something that floats in the room. "I'm definitely proud of my Clara."

I stare at the spaghetti sauce as I stir, once again tilting my chin down so my hair falls forward. Ms. Bellings raves about my stories, essays, and poems, but her praise has never felt like a big deal to me because again, small town, small school. But the tone of Mr. Kennedy's voice makes it sound like my words could be a big deal.

"Oh," I say because I can be eloquent like that.

His head tilts to the side. "Small town…no real training…You're lucky to have some natural talent to work with."

"Oh. Thanks." I want to look up at him again, but I'd rather enjoy the compliment without any kind of pity stare from him about my face.

"You read a lot?"

"All the time," Dad interrupts. "I mean…unless she's writing."

Mr. Kennedy chuckles, and the doorbell rings.

"You'll have to excuse me." Dad gives me a wink before leaving the kitchen.

Mr. Kennedy leans against the counter like he lives here. "So. I'll make sure *you* get a chance to answer my question. Read a lot?"

"I've read Thoreau an embarrassing number of times, and I could read Coleridge every day." I tap the spoon on the edge of the pot before sliding it through the sauce again. "Lorca's poems are basically words to live by."

"At least you're on the right track." He smiles.

Is he *flirting* with me? I mean, he's a student teacher and not a *teacher* teacher, but still…It's sort of scandalous, I think. I shake off the ridiculous thought of his possible interest but glance through my curtain of hair again to see his smiling profile. Maybe I'm reading too much into him being nice.

"Tell me you don't like Dickinson." He rolls his eyes. "Because I think every incoming college freshman girl likes Dickinson."

"Sexist much?" I ask instead of telling him how much I *love* Emily Dickinson. *Love*, love. So very much.

Mr. Kennedy shrugs. "Didn't mean it that way. Just seems to be the case."

Dad steps back into the kitchen followed by his long-time friend, Suki.

"Clara!" Suki's smile accentuates her large teeth and the bright pink lipstick that seems to be her trademark, as she also steps into the galley kitchen. I sometimes wonder what her history students think of this overly happy but intense Native Alaskan woman whose black hair is strikingly striped with blond and whose lips are always a few shades of bright.

Dad invites her over a lot, and I keep wondering whether he'll move forward with this weird friendship they have, or if he'll pine away for Mom for the rest of his life.

"Hi, Suki." I smile back at her from the stove, but the right side of my mouth feels funny today, so I'm sure my smile is extra weird.

"Oh, this tastes like heaven." She groans as she licks the finger she just stuck in my sauce. "You have a talent, girl. I keep saying this... Probably one of the few blessings of being such an independent girl."

My cheeks warm, even though I was sort of forced into independence. First, because Mom was trying to finish her degree online. Second, because she was writing. Third, because she died. And fourth, because Dad works a *lot*.

"Glad you made it tonight." Dad smiles widely as he rolls up the sleeves of his plaid flannel shirt and leans against the kitchen door.

"Me too." Suki turns toward Dad, resting a hand on his arm and touching the edges of his gray hair, smoothing over the strays.

The touching is new, so I watch out of the corner of my eye to see how far they're going to go.

I half expect Dad to jump away, but he holds his own until he clears his throat and turns back to the table.

"Thank you, Sukiniq. I think I've got it all set." Dad's inability to use the short version of her name is just...so very *him*.

"Dinner's in five." I reach for the noodles, but Mr. Kennedy is already draining them in the sink, holding the pot with a surprisingly muscular set of arms for an English teacher.

I glance away before he sees me staring, pour the sauce into a serving bowl, and hope I'm able to relax at some point during dinner. And then Mr. Kennedy does what I do and tosses the noodles with olive oil, salt, pepper, and garlic. I mean, I had them set out, but he's totally encroaching on *my* thing.

"Oh. Sorry." He stops and stares at the bowl. "I saw the ingredients, and I just did that, and—"

"It's how I make them too. It's fine." Our eyes catch again—and "catch" is the absolute perfect word because I was going for a quick glance across his face, but I got stuck at the blue. My heart skips and

16

acts in a ridiculous manner for an organ that's supposed to be keeping me alive. My mind is racing, going over my totally bizarre reaction to someone I've barely spoken ten words to. This is so…weird. He's a teacher and someone I don't know.

I start for the bowl to take it to the table, but I'm stopped by Mr. Kennedy.

"I got it." He reaches through my arms to take the dish. I'm stuck with what is probably an odd expression. It must be odd because I can't feel my face in this moment. "I like to be in the kitchen. No worries."

"I'll…" But my throat still isn't working so I cough a few times. "Be there in a sec," I croak as I spin around to get the sauce. Seriously, what is with me? He's just a *person*.

Voices carry from the dining room—Dad, Suki, and Ms. Bellings.

I pick up the bowl of bread in one hand and the sauce in the other and walk slowly toward the table. I set down the food, and my eyes hit Mr. Kennedy's again. He gives me a relaxed smile, and I think my lips twitch as I *try* to smile, but I'm not positive.

When I take my seat, Dad asks us to stop for a moment of thanks before dishing up.

He might be a little overzealously religious since Mom died, but when we have guests over, he's really nice about just giving us all a moment of silence instead of going through the long list of people and things he likes to include in his prayers.

Dad knows he'll see Mom again after this life because we believe in forever-marriages instead of just-for-this-life marriages, so Dad clings to every part of religion he can. I have to admire his dedication, even when it gets in the way of my appetite. Or my sanity.

I close my eyes and start a prayer, *Dear Heavenly Father*…but nothing comes. I'm all nerves over having a Columbia student here and from worrying about whether or not I did a good job with the spaghetti and wishing Elias could have come.

When Dad says thank you, everyone digs in at once, which is how he likes things in our house, and he gives me a wink from the opposite side of the table. Rhodes Kennedy is across from me and Ms. Bellings is to my left, putting Suki very close to Dad at the end of the table.

Mr. Kennedy pulls out spaghetti noodles with two forks, his eyes on his food. "So what do you want to do with your writing?" He spoons out sauce, licks his fingers, and shoves a large bite of spaghetti into his mouth.

"Oh, I'm…" I trail off. My dream of dreams is too big to be spoken out loud.

"She's full of talent." Dad smiles wide. "I have no doubt she'll put it to good use."

I look down again because I have no idea how to take compliments—even when they come from such a biased source.

"Some of her poems I don't quite get, but I think that has to do with age more than anything else." Dad gives me another wink.

"I think they're fantastic." Suki smiles.

Ms. Bellings shifts in her seat. "I meant to ask you if I could send some of your writing to Rhodes, but I figured it was okay when I knew you wanted to apply to Colum—"

"It's fine," I interrupt. "Totally fine."

Dad knows I applied to Columbia, but he doesn't know it's *the* school. He thought it was more of an exercise to see if I could get in. It was more than that. And I made it. My heart speeds up in nervous anticipation of what that acceptance means. I'm not ready to make decisions that big—not until I can't think past my scars. And not until I can figure out if it's even possible for Dad to send me to one of the most expensive schools in the country.

"Well." Dad wipes his mouth. "You nailed it again, honey. Worth keeping a little red wine around the house just for this."

I nod, trying to relax my throat to swallow and to push away the nerves of too many big decisions about school and scars and life.

Mr. Kennedy's eyes find mine again and I stop breathing.

Dear Heavenly Father: Why did you have to make his eyes so perfectly blue? You've put him at a totally unfair advantage and me at a severe disadvantage because I'm bound to say something stupid tonight. He's a teacher. Teachers aren't supposed to mess with my head this way. I'm also not supposed to notice someone who isn't Elias.

"This is the best spaghetti I've ever had," Mr. Kennedy says.

"Just like her momma." Dad spins his fork on his plate. "Don't know what I'd do without my girl."

Five years since Mom died, and I really think he'll be okay. Me? I'm still on the fence.

Ms. Bellings starts to talk, and I really do try to listen, but I'm staring at Dad and Suki. I watch them for a moment—or more than a moment since the wooden walls in the background come in and out of focus as they exchange smiles. The lingering smile exchange is maybe new too. Huh.

"So, Clara will be a big help to you there as well," Ms. Bellings finishes with a smile.

"What?" I sputter.

Mr. Kennedy's clear blues are on me. "The production?"

"Oh." I'm still staring. This is definitely too much staring at his eyes. I can't seem to stop. "Yeah. I'm the stage manager."

He smirks. "We covered that."

Oh. Brilliant.

His gaze is still on me, unflinching.

I'm convinced in this moment that he knows everything about me.

That I stole gum from the store once and never told. And if my bra and panties don't match in some way, I feel weird all day. And I have to have a pillow under my arm to sleep. I miss my mom more than I've told Elias or Dad or anyone, even though there are days when I can barely remember her face. He sees me. The depths, the…everything. I can't remember the last time I felt so exposed.

Get your head back on, Clara. Seriously.

"So, Mr. Kennedy," I start, having zero idea how to finish, but knowing I do not want to just sit and stare like the village idiot.

"When we're not at school, you can call me Rhodes. I'm young. Only sort of a teacher. It's short-lived, and your dad has already told me I'm required to eat at least two meals a week with you while I'm here." He gives me a half smile as he twirls the spaghetti onto his fork. "Also, it's still weird to be called Mr. Kennedy."

"Oh." That's all I can manage right now.

"You were going to ask me something?"

"I don't remember." I shove another large bite in my mouth.

Rhodes looks over my shoulder out the large window. "I thought it was light all the time."

"It's only April," I say, glancing behind me at the slowly dimming light. "By May it'll be light enough to read all night, just not yet."

He rests his elbows on the table. "And it gets warmer, right? Because if your days don't get warmer than forty-five, I'm going to need to buy a few more sweaters." He chuckles.

I nod. "A little, yeah."

"Probably depends a bit on my definition of warm, eh?" He shoves another large bite into his mouth.

"And the wind, because when it blows down from the glacier, our warm days cool down fast."

"And get dusty," Dad adds. "That glacial silt gets into everything."

Rhodes blinks a few times, and I wonder if he had any idea what he was getting into when he decided to teach here.

"Dinner was good. I'm impressed"—Ms. Bellings sets down her napkin—"but not surprised."

"My mom was a good cook." I stand, clear off the sauté pan, head for the kitchen, and set it next to the sink. Little things like my cooking and spending time in our barn make me feel like Mom could walk around the corner any moment, even though she won't. And when I talk about Mom or think about Mom, my heart feels like someone's shoved it in a box that's a size too small.

"Clara?" Dad sits back in his chair. "I'll handle the dishes tonight. Why don't you show Mr. Kennedy the barn before he heads for home?"

I glance toward Ms. Bellings, sort of hoping she seems interested, but she and Suki are totally absorbed in a conversation revolving around the university where Suki teaches.

"Sure." I pull in a breath, stretching out my chest so nothing feels squeezed or pinched anymore. I need to feed the horses anyway, so all I have to do is try to keep focused. *Focus. Focus.* I should be able to manage that.

3

Rhodes follows me up the trail at the edge of the forest to the wooden barn behind the house. I wipe my sweaty palms on my pants and try to take a deep breath. I'm seriously being ridiculous. *Totally* ridiculous. Like girls who swoon over boy bands ridiculous. He's an older guy that I just met. That's all.

"So, do you guys stay up all night in the summer?" he asks. "Because of the light?"

"Sometimes." I'm not sure how different our nights could possibly be just because it's light.

His gaze scans the tall trees around us. The path to the barn is wide enough for two cars to go side by side, but it cuts through the trees, giving the trail a kind of private feeling.

"Do you worry about bears?"

My answer gets stuck in my throat before I cough it out. "Yep. Especially this time of year."

His eyes scan the woods more thoroughly.

"Where are you from?" I ask. Totally safe question.

"Everywhere. My dad is career Air Force. I was born in Germany and spent most of my childhood there. We were in Italy for a while and then moved back to the States when I was in high school. California."

So many places. In seventeen years, I've been here and to Seattle. "Wow."

"It's given me a severe case of wanderlust, which is why I'm up here."

Wanderlust is something I only half understand. Going to Seattle still feels like another world. "Oh."

I tap my back pocket. Notebook still there. But the double check gives me something to do while we walk.

After I slide open the large barn door and step inside, Snoopy sticks his black and white head over the stall door, shoving his nose into my face.

"So, is everyone up here into the outdoorsy stuff?" Rhodes asks. "Do you have a raft? Or do you know someone who could take me down the river? Is it too cold to swim? Can we fish on the river, or is that just certain times of the year?"

I let out a slight laugh. "I'm not really sure what to answer first."

"Sorry," he says as he follows me into the barn. "I really want to experience being here, you know?"

No, I don't know. "Yes, tons of people have rafts. Elias has a really nice one. We only jump into the river briefly. The current is strong enough to keep you under with or without a lifejacket. The water will also give you hypothermia in minutes because the river is glacier fed. And fishing doesn't open on our river until sometime in July, I think, but lakes are always open."

"The canyon here is deep," he says. "I guess I should have expected the glacier thing."

"We can hike that too, if you want." What am I saying? Did I just offer to take my teacher out?

"The *glacier*?" he asks.

"The glacier isn't nearly as cool as it sounds. It's about a four-mile hike from the road, and most of where you can hike on the glacier is covered in dirt. We can hike up to where the snow and ice are clean, so I guess it's a little cool, but the crevasses get dangerous fast. There's a zip-line place up the highway too. It's pretty fun unless you're afraid of heights."

"So. Wild. Hiking on a glacier. And a definite yes to zip-lining." His smile widens and his eyes are on me for another moment before he looks around the inside of the barn. Rhodes's eyes follow the same trail that everyone's do. Over the horse stalls and tack room. Then his gaze travels up to the loft, which is half open to below. He looks a lot more like a student than a teacher in this moment.

"This is cool," he says. "I'm sorry. My thoughts are all over the place. I love being somewhere new."

I can't imagine loving to travel the way he does, but maybe with a fixed face, traveling won't feel so out of reach.

I shove the measuring can into the large bin of oats and dump a canful into each of the feed buckets. Keeping busy around someone my body's reacting to is probably smart. "Dad built it with Mom when I was a baby. Just after building the house."

"You've lived here a long time."

"My whole life."

"You're going to college, right?" He leans against Snoopy's stall, and my horse immediately shoves his nose in Rhodes's hand. He grabs Snoopy's upper lip and tugs, playing my horse's favorite game.

"Why do you ask?" I grab a few flakes of hay and start tossing them over the tops of the stalls, wondering where Rhodes was when he got acquainted with horses.

"Everybody should get out of their comfort zone once in a while. And if you want to be a writer, like my aunt said, I don't think you'll get the teaching you need up here."

I want to be a writer.

But that want feels fragile—like if I talk about writing as a career too much or hope for it too much, that future will shatter before I have a chance for it to begin.

"I might go up to UAF for my freshman year," I say as I toss the last load of hay over the partition and lean against the stall next to Rhodes. University of Alaska is a massive compromise, but it's one I'm willing to make to stay close to home—at least until my scars are fixed. After that, the world might seem less like a cliff I've been asked to climb with no gear. That's when I'll maybe leave for New York, but not before. I'm still not sure how to manage the idea of leaving Elias behind for Columbia. I shove the thought away.

Rhodes's brow furrows. "You might want to think about somewhere else. See the world a little. I fully believe in current opportunity."

"What does that mean?" I ask.

"It means that life is too short to wait for things to come to you." He gives me a purposefully crooked smile, like he thinks he's cute or something. "Sometimes you have to reach out and try for what you want. Sometimes you don't know what you want until it's right in front of you. I had no idea I wanted to go to Alaska until my aunt suggested it, and now here I am, experiencing Alaska."

I'm self-aware enough to know I hide in my bubble, but that's as temporary as my scars.

I trace the welts coming off my upper lip as I lean against Snoopy's stall.

Rhodes's eyes are on me. Something in me should be squirming under his gaze because we just met, but the relaxed way he's talking to me and playing with my horse, makes me feel like I've known him longer than I have.

People don't normally warm up to me like this. They always keep their distance for a while, watch me, and wait to feel comfortable before they talk. It's one of the things I love about Knik—everyone here knows me and the story of my scars. I get second glances, but not the stares I get when I'm somewhere new.

Rhodes keeps watching and my gaze flits to the ground. I drop the hand from my face.

"Do they hurt?" he asks.

"No." I shake my head, wishing I hadn't touched my scars in front of him.

"Do they feel strange?" He steps forward, his voice completely relaxed as his fingers slide over the scar on my eyebrow, his face more inquisitive than anything else.

I jump back, and he drops his arm.

"Sorry." He shakes his head. "That was probably rude. I was curious."

My heart's like a hummingbird—fast and out of control.

"Umm…yeah. The scars are sort of numb. And sort of funny, tingly, weird down deep."

"Sorry." His brows twitch, but he's still just leaning against the stall like we're out here together every night instead of him being someone I just met.

"It's fine." I'm more flattered with the relaxed way he's hanging out in the barn with me—he's a teacher *and* someone who attends an Ivy League school. "No one asks, but I know they want to know the story of how it happened." *I hear them whisper about it in school.* I turn toward Tori in her stall as her nose hits the back of my head, her mouth full of hay.

"So…" He rubs under Snoopy's ears and for the first time is pointedly not looking at me. "Do you have a simple version of the story?"

"Yep." I swallow once, rubbing my hand over Tori's forehead until she starts bobbing her head up and down, using me as a scratching post. "I don't remember the bear coming at us or Mom screaming for help or anything." I swear though, the *feeling* of the memory is still there, digging into my stomach and heart, tearing up my insides worse than anything marking my face. "I don't remember leaving for our morning walk. I know nothing about that day until I woke up in the hospital."

Tears stream down my face before I realize how deeply my chest aches. It's been so long since I've cried about Mom that the loss of her hits hard, like it does once in a while. *How do I not remember losing my mother?* I was twelve. Not three. I should remember. She should be here.

"Clara. I'm sorry. That's…crazy."

I swipe my hands over my face again and again; my right hand slides over the bumps of my scars. Rhodes reaches for my face, and his fingers brush just under my eye, shocking me into jumping back.

He raises his arms in the air in a gesture of surrender. "I'm so sorry. I'm an idiot. I wasn't thinking. A girl cries, and I react."

I take another step back, my heart pounding again. "I should go help Dad with the dishes."

"No. Clara. Wait." Rhodes presses his fingers to his forehead before running his hand over his head. "I'm not exactly sure what just happened, but I feel like I did something wrong. What I wanted to say is that I think it's amazing that you—"

I frown and he stops talking, but he steps close enough that his breath hits my face. My heart does a crazy *thump-thump-thump* over this stranger I'm reacting so…strangely to, and I feel myself flip into frustration to avoid the strangeness. "What's amazing? That I happen to walk around with scars on my face?" I snap. "Like I somehow have a choice?"

He leans back. "No that's not what I meant. I just wanted to—"

"Good night, Mr. Kennedy." *Maybe now when I see you at school, it won't send my stomach into a flurry.*

"Good night."

I head to the house, go through the back door, and run up the stairs to my attic bedroom. I'm sure he thinks I'm insane, but he probably wouldn't be the first.

* * *

The second I'm surrounded by my wooden, slanted walls, I grab *A Worn Path* by Eudora Welty. As I kick my shoes off and flop on my bed, Welty's words dance in my brain. The words Mom introduced me to the year before she died. One day I will write as perfectly as this story is written.

The problem is that the words aren't sticking. I'm reading, but my brain is spinning instead of following the lines.

I pick up my phone and pause before texting Cecily. She's four hours ahead, so it's like 1:00 a.m. in Georgia. Suck. I scroll to Elias's name.

You up?

Yep ☺

I'm not sure how to shake the story of Mom and the bear, or share what it was like to talk to someone from Columbia.

Miss you tonight, I type.

Maybe we should try to find some time to do a real date? Take a drive?

Immediately I relax into my mattress.

I'd love that

Being around Elias almost always seems to reset me. A night together should be perfect. I need to shake off the skittering, frantic feeling of Rhodes.

You wanna talk? he asks.

His voice might help me relax more. But then my mind jumps to Rhodes Kennedy, to how I reacted to Rhodes Kennedy, and to the letter in my drawer with my acceptance by an out-of-state school. **Nah. See you tomorrow.**

Tomorrow

I set the alarm on my phone before leaving it on my nightstand. If I can't talk to Cecily or Elias about all the new uneasiness running around inside me, what do I do about it?

4

"Clara!" Dad hollers up the stairs. "Time for seminary!"

I roll over and wish to live somewhere that I could have my once-a-day religious class during the school day and not *before* school in Sister McEntyre's living room with four other students as sleepy as me. I also sometimes wish that Elias and I belonged to the same church so he'd pick me up. I could sleep in his truck for a few extra minutes as we drove to seminary together.

Some days I'm grateful we have these morning sessions because they help me focus on being a better person than I tend to be, and other mornings I want to stab out Sister McEntyre's eyes with a spoon. I'm having one of those mornings. Should be an interesting day.

"Clara!" Dad calls again. "I'm going to go feed the horses. You need to be walking out the door in five minutes!"

I let out a sigh as I flip on my hair straightener and grab a pair of jeans from my closet. At least uniforms aren't part of my private school. After straightening my bangs over my face and double-checking the battery on my phone because my scriptures are there, I head out to my truck.

The two-lane, bendy highway that runs through Knik is quiet at six fifteen in the morning because all the smart people are still in bed. The river runs fast and muddy on one side, and the mountain stretches up almost as high as I can see on the other.

I reach the log-cabin-looking mailbox that signals Sister McEntyre's driveway and turn off, climbing the steep, gravel driveway until it levels off in front of her log home.

Two other cars I recognize are there, belonging to kids who go to the public school.

Sister McEntyre is on the porch steps and smiles an even, teacher smile. "Morning, Sister Fielding."

I give her a mumble and a nod, trying to force myself to *wake up* already. I used to think it was so cool when I became a teenager and everyone referred to me as "Sister Fielding" instead of just Clara, but in my church, calling someone Brother or Sister isn't really a distinction. I'm more and more convinced it's just a nice way of saying, "We're going to ask you to teach soon or do some kind of work for the people you go to church with." Or maybe that perception is just my cynicism.

I manage to survive seminary without nodding off once. But by the time I get to first period, I wish for a tool to keep my eyes propped open.

"Dear Baby Jesus..." Mrs. Apple begins as she says the morning prayer. Because my private school doesn't care that I've already had my once-a-day religious class and because we always start the school day with a prayer.

I never understood praying to "baby" Jesus. Wherever He might be, if she thinks He's a baby, why would she bother? What is a baby possibly going to be able to do for her? I asked her once, and she said it was blasphemous for me to question Jesus's power. And then she just gave me a weird look like of course this is something the *Mormon* girl wouldn't understand, because she somehow thinks I don't get who Jesus is. Mostly I don't think anyone gets who He is, whether they believe in Him or not.

The second problem is that as she says the words "baby Jesus" for like the fifth time since starting the prayer, I picture a really alien-looking infant with a magic wand. Not really an image conducive to prayer time, but awesome for entertainment.

Elias murmurs his own prayer like he has since elementary. A few bits of stubble dot his cheeks and chin, which means he probably worked late again last night. I stare for a moment, hoping he can sense me staring and will end his prayer early.

No luck.

I scan the room for intruders. Okay, not intruders. For people like me who still think the separation of religion from the school system was probably a good thing. I find none.

Instead of following along with the baby Jesus prayer, I think back to Dr. Breckman's website. To the people whose scars he made disappear. Only a couple more weeks before I'll get to talk to him about mine.

* * *

Elias clasps our hands together while we wait for the few theater people to gather after school. I'm not onstage, I'm the stage manager, which means I'm in charge of sets, lights, pulling the curtain, and sound. Small school.

Esther, a girl I've known on the periphery for years, glances over her shoulder but looks away the second our eyes meet. Normal, but it still gives me twinges in my stomach.

"Wanna get together after play practice?" Elias asks. "I'm finally not working tonight."

"Dad says we had company last night, so tonight's not a good night." I tilt my face forward. I'm usually much more careful about making sure Elias is on my left side instead of my right. But he's used to me, so maybe he can be my buffer today—spare the rest of the room having to look at that side of my face.

Elias shrugs like it's no big deal that "family time" interrupts time we could spend together. I don't know if I should be angry about this and want him to fight to spend more time with me or if I should just be happy we don't argue.

"We'll find another night then." He gives me a squeeze.

For sure he wouldn't be dating me if we went to a bigger school. He probably would have found someone without a messed-up face. So, really, I'm relieved I never feel torn and a bit amazed we're together.

Elias tucks my hair behind my ear. "Are you hiding from me?" he whispers.

I stare at my lap. "I don't know."

"I'm excited for you to get these fixed because you want it, but you know I don't care, right?" He softly kisses my cheek between the scar that starts on my nose and the one that starts at the edge of my eye.

No. No I don't know that he doesn't care. Maybe I should. Maybe I'm just afraid to trust him with this. He's known me for long enough that he knows how I'd feel if I thought the scars grossed him out the way they do me.

My breathing stops when Mr. Kennedy steps onto the stage with his clipboard.

I slide my hands through my hair, untucking the strands on my right side.

Esther and Abby (drama queens in more ways than one) are staring at Mr. Kennedy—their nearly identical brown, wavy hair bobbing together as they talk in each other's ears.

"I'm Mr. Kennedy, and I'll be here for the rest of the year. Ms. Bellings's daughter is sick, and she'll be spending the final month and a half of the school year in New Mexico to be with her." His eyes find mine.

Elias gives me a scrunchy eyebrow look that means he's asking what's up.

"I met him last night. Long story," I whisper. *One I probably won't give you the full version of.*

"So, that means *you'll* be here?" Abby bats her lashes at Mr. Kennedy. She's like a pro at this. Lots of practice.

He blinks and scans the clipboard before meeting her too-eager eyes. "I'll be here, yes."

"Why weren't you here for English?" I ask because I can be stupid and open my mouth when I shouldn't. I sat in class expecting his blond hair, but Ms. Bellings was there instead. I should have been relieved, not disappointed.

We make eye contact again, and I wait for him to scan my face like last night, but his eyes don't leave mine. I'm locked in this weird moment. With Mr. Kennedy.

He clears this throat. Moment broken. "She wanted a couple more days in the classroom before leaving. Any other questions?"

Elias shifts his weight forward, his grip on my hand tightening. "Are you old enough for this?"

"I graduate with my teaching degree after summer semester, and I'm halfway through my MFA at Columbia. I took this semester off aside from student teaching when my aunt said she might need my help, which is why I got the chance to be here with you. So yes." He releases a breath. "I'm old enough for this."

"You look too young." Elias's accusing tone is so totally out of character.

Mr. Kennedy's jaw tenses, but then his shoulders relax. "I graduated from high school early. I got permission to take more credits a semester than normal, and I've done summer school since I graduated from high school. That's all."

"So, how old are you?"

I push Elias's shoulder. "What is this, twenty questions? Interrogation of the new guy?"

Elias shrugs.

"Not important." Mr. Kennedy stands up a little taller.

I try not to notice him. I really, really do. I try not to see he's wearing worn Chucks with his fitted khakis. That his tie is perfectly skinny cool. That his plaid shirt looks like it was tailored to his waist and sides, and I also try not to notice how his shoulders are just slightly too wide for his shirt, even though he's a slender guy. And I even work not to stare at the sinews in his forearms exposed by the way he has his shirt rolled up or the worn, orange band on his watch.

"Clara?" Mr. Kennedy asks as he raises his brows.

"Sorry, what?" I'm reeling, wondering how long I was lost in an imagined world I should not have been in.

"Ms. Bellings said that we were walking through Act II of *Arsenic and Old Lace*, and you know all the staging."

My cheeks heat up as I frantically flip through my script. I can feel Elias staring at me, practically boring holes in my temple, which nearly makes me rip a page out when I forget to let go of it. I'm sure the whole theater group of ten is staring at me, which is exactly what I don't need. My reactions to Rhodes make no sense.

Just a guy. Too old. Too grown up. *Just a guy. Just a guy. Just a guy.* And I *have* a guy. A great one. A nearly perfect one.

"Yes. I'm ready, but we've walked through it quite a few times, so hopefully everyone remembers where to be."

"Thank you."

When I look up, Mr. Kennedy's leaning back on his stool, holding his book with his very nice, strong hands, watching me and waiting...

Crap.

For me to get people in places and start.

Yeah. Maybe if I could concentrate while he was in the same room.

I make it through rehearsals without sounding like an idiot and even remembering to correct staging as we walk through Act II. One day down, too many to go…

* * *

"What's with you today?" Elias asks as he walks me to his truck. "And Mr. Kennedy? He was like…staring at you."

"Dad invited him and Ms. Bellings over last night, so I'm probably the only person here he knows. Also, maybe he was staring at my face. I'm sure that's all." But is that all? The butterflies in my stomach are seriously messing with my head.

I kick the small rocks that were slowly dumped on our parking lot during the winter to help with the ice. There are so many that the paved surface is practically a dirt road right now.

"And you can't get out of family dinner tonight?" Elias asks as his fingers tighten around mine.

"What?" I poke him in the side. "We just talked about this. You *never* try to get me out of family dinner."

He jumps away smiling. That easy smile is what drew me in so fully to begin with. Elias really is gorgeous. He doesn't look like a guy who would be in a small town—he's more cologne ad than hick town, but he'd never think that about himself. He loves it here too much. I love it here too, just not in a forever way. We'll work out that part of being together…when we get to the point that I'm leaving.

"You just seem distracted today." He stops by the passenger's side door of his truck, and I lean my back against it instead of standing aside for him to open it. I scatter some of the small rocks with my foot.

And I *am* distracted. I got into *the* school and have no idea what to do about it. My stupid heart is doing backflips over our new teacher. I want to find a way to get some time alone with Elias. That's a lot to keep track of.

I tug on his letter jacket with a grin, bringing our bodies together.

35

"Do I seem distracted now?"

He smiles, but his gaze pauses over the right side of my face. That twisty, sharp pang in my stomach is more familiar every day, so I shove it down, needing to be in the moment. Needing to feel loved. Needing to feel the safety and relaxed heat of Elias against me.

"In a good way." His kiss is soft and sweet, but when I pull on his coat harder, his kiss gets deeper. I will myself to fall into feeling him, but instead I wonder again if it feels weird to kiss a girl who's missing part of her lip.

How can I be wondering that when I'm getting exactly what I want? He's finally pressing against me and kissing me, and I'm…My brain isn't here. This kind of touching is supposed to shut off the noise in my head, not turn it on.

An idea for another poem taps into my brain, and I slip my hand from Elias's waist to touch my back pocket. Still there.

"Okay." Elias chuckles before pecking my cheek. "Your mind is somewhere else. You go do your thing. I'll maybe go pick up a few hours of work in hope of taking some time off when you can."

I blink, my fingers sliding over the notebook in my pocket. When was the last time *I* was the one who broke our kiss? Have I ever?

"Yeah," I whisper before clearing my throat. "Yeah. Okay."

5

My phone screaming *Welcome to New York* by Taylor Swift signals Cecily, and my smile is complete before I answer.

"Tell me you've downloaded the pictures," Cecily demands.

"Oh. Crap. Just a sec." I snatch the laptop off my desk, knocking down a collection of Salinger. I can't seem to stop obsessing about the list of famous Columbia grads, which is probably not great for the pressure that comes from the envelope in my desk. I flip the laptop open on my bed, tapping into email.

She scoffs in mock indignation, and I picture her thin brows on her dark skin and smirky smile at my ineptness. "How do you not remember to download? You know I send you pictures every time we talk so we can discuss. *And* we always talk on Wednesdays."

I don't answer. Cecily is bound to be a famous photographer at some point. For now, she sells her photos on stock photo sites and does wicked things with Photoshop and some other photo-editing software she probably pirated. Cecily is the perfect best friend—aside from the fact she only lives close to me for half the year.

"So?" she urges. "There yet?"

"Almost…almost…*here!*"

Wow.

She's done four pictures of a guy's face, but there's a colored pattern on all of them that I know is going to turn into some sort of image...

"See it yet?" She sucks in a breath, and I know she'll hold it until I figure it out.

The guy's face is in dark blues and it looks like she took like five other pictures and put them over each other. Sort of Andy Warhol looking. Oh! "It's the Chuck Taylor star! Well done."

A rush of air means she was, in fact, holding her breath. "You like?"

"I love. As always. I do not get how you can put this stuff together. You need to start selling posters on one of those arty sites."

"I totally *should*."

I flip my laptop closed and roll onto my back to stare at the slanted wooden walls that come to a peak just above my bed.

"How long before you're back in town?" I whine.

"You know the deal. One semester with Mom, one with Dad. I'll be back just in time to watch y'all graduate, because my school ends earlier than yours." Her Southern accent comes back a week after she leaves Alaska for Louisiana and never totally disappears while she's here.

"That's forever away. There's too much going on for you not to be here." I cross my legs as I lie on my back in the tiny room.

"Liiiike...?" She draws out the word, needing details.

"Like we got this new substitute..."

And I tell Cecily everything. I tell her about how Elias got weird over him and how Mr. Kennedy came over and touched my face in the barn, and how he's crazy attractive to the point that my brain stops functioning when he's around. And how she really needs to be here because someone's going to have to start pinching me when I act moronic, which I do every. Time. I'm. Around him.

And then I tell her he goes to Columbia.

She's laughing by the time I finish. "So, is this the end of Elias?"

My heart does a weird *ka-thump, leap*, making me cough. "What? *No!*" I can't imagine not being with Elias. He's been part of me for way too long.

"But aren't you the girl who keeps telling me you're not going to marry him, even though I keep telling you that's exactly what he'll want from you?"

She does say this a lot. Elias's parents got married when his mom was seventeen and his dad was nineteen. His older brother got married at nineteen. Elias is exactly the kind of super-faithful guy who would jump into being married as part of his life plan of stability. Even though I know this about him, I still argue against it because my brain just can't go there right now.

"Nah. He's going to be working to take over so his dad can retire, and he already knows I'm going to school."

"Does he think you'll still be in Alaska?" Cecily lowers her voice.

Crap. Having her understand everything about me doesn't work in my favor when I don't want her to say things I don't want to hear. "He might. We don't really talk about it. Nothing's set in stone yet anyway."

"No. You just change the subject when he brings it up. Like you think that when you graduate, something's going to magically change and make your life decisions easier." I'm sure her forehead is wrinkled and the corners of her mouth are turned down.

"No. That's ridiculous." But as I think about her words, I'm wondering if part of me does feel that way. "I have a plan."

Cecily snorts. "Your plan can barely be considered a plan, Clara."

"What are you talking about?"

"Your plan is to bum around Alaska while you get your scars removed and to not talk to Elias about what you really want in your life until the last possible moment. Did I leave anything out?"

I don't answer. She'll jump into something different like she does when I don't have words for her.

"So…" Cecily starts slowly, and I know we're jumping into the subject change I hoped for. But she doesn't say anything, so maybe *she's* hesitant about something.

"Oh, man." I cringe. "Did you have news this whole time and we've been talking about me?"

"Yeah, but I've been avoiding."

My stomach twists.

"I heard from Tisch. When I said I was putting off for a year to go to an in-state school, they upped my scholarship."

New York. *This year?* My legs fall flat on my mattress, and the phone slips before I grasp it tighter.

"Clara?"

My heart pounds so loudly that I'm not sure I'll be able to hear. "But…but we were going to be freshman together…in Alaska."

Cecily pulls in a long breath. "I haven't given them my final word, but…"

"But you're going." As weak as I felt a moment ago, now every part of me feels weighted and tight. "Of course you're going." This sucks. So hard. I kick my foot against the slanted roof-wall as if the kicking will somehow make this all different.

"Have you heard back from Columbia yet?" Cecily asks. "It's weird that you haven't heard. I think you're supposed to get that stuff the end of March or beginning of April or something, right?"

I hold my breath. Close my eyes. Switch my phone from one hand to another. Picture the letter in my drawer.

"Holy crap, you got in, didn't you?" she squeals.

"I did."

Cecily's screech vibrates my phone, and I jerk it from my ear.

"I'm not going, Cee. I can't. I'm going to defer until next year, just like I planned. And even then…who knows." Like *we* planned.

"What? How can you not go? This is like…your dream. And now we'll get to be freshmen in *New York*! You cannot say no to this! Your plan is barely a plan. *Readjust!*"

"Next year is my year of—" But I close my mouth before letting my hope slide out in the words I desperately want to be true.

"Your year of getting your scars fixed. I totally get that, but…*pleeeeease*."

"I can't leave Alaska looking like this, Cee!"

"What are you talking about?" Her voice is slowly and genuinely incredulous. "I mean, I get it. I guess. I just think you see the scars in a very different way than I do. They're just part of who you are to me, Clara. They're not a big deal—"

"They are not part of me!" I yell. "They're so gross I can barely look at myself in the mirror, and they're going to get fixed before I even *think* about leaving for New York."

The phone is quiet for so long that I check the clock.

I rub my forehead, wishing I could rub the tension out of the rest of my body. "I'm sorry."

"Nah," Cecily says. "It's okay. I just meant that—"

"Can we just…Can we not talk about my face?"

There's another long pause. How do she and my dad not understand that I don't want to put myself through the torture of going anywhere but my hometown when I don't have to?

"Okay. It's late here. Like ten. At the very least, I think you should try to extend the time Columbia needs for your final answer. Just give yourself more time to think before saying no."

I feel my lower lip push out in a pout. "Maybe." But there's no point in asking for a week or more to help me decide. Deferring for a year, I can do. Or ask for.

"So, I'm gonna get my beauty sleep, but I need a text if anything weird goes down tomorrow, okay?"

"Weird?" I ask.

"Just text me." She chuckles, and with that one reaction from her, I know we're still okay.

I close my eyes, relief relaxing my limbs until guilt at that relief tugs at my heart. I should feel guilty for yelling at Cecily when I know she's trying to help. "Night."

"Night."

I roll off my bed and slide open the pocket door of my mini-bathroom.

New York. So soon. *Too* soon. I'm not sure I even know how I'd tell Elias if I were leaving in a few months—our relationship would change so much.

The gray-blue walls reflect the fluorescent light, and my pale skin looks almost ghostly in the mirror. Instead of keeping my long bangs halfway over my eyes, I push the strands off my face.

My finger hovers over the scar that's destroyed the upper part of my lip. My stomach rolls. How could anyone touch this? I trace the scar that nearly touches my eye—another thing I've been told I'm "lucky" for. *I* rarely touch the purply-red slashes. I can't imagine someone else wanting to.

Sliding my special cream off the shelf, I smooth the white paste over the raised edges even though I'm pretty sure it's never done anything to help. A definition of insanity runs through my head—doing the same thing over and over and expecting a different result.

I set the cream down, turn off the light, and start downstairs for dinner.

6

All through class, Mr. Kennedy glances my way as he makes notes or something on his clipboard. It's only been two days since dinner at my house, and I've managed to avoid him almost completely.

I flip my pencil over a few times and glance at Elias, who immediately smiles back. He's doodled a few floor plans on a blank sheet of paper—obsessed with getting as much as he can into the smallest space he can. Always has been. His focus goes back to his paper as he starts marking doorways, and I stare at the wall.

My short essay is long finished, and I'm so ready to be out of class. Only five more minutes...

"Clara, I need you to stay after class, please. I won't keep you long." Mr. Kennedy doesn't look up from the desk as he asks. He just continues to scribble on a sheet of paper.

What? Why? "Uh..." My heart beats faster, like I need an announcement that I'm in another incredibly awkward situation. "Okay."

The bell rings two seconds later, which really isn't fair because most days it takes *eons* for that minute hand to get where I want it to go.

Elias stands with me as I step up to Mr. Kennedy's desk, following like he always does. In case I need him. Or want him.

"We'll just be a minute, Elias." Mr. Kennedy does look up this time. At my boyfriend. To excuse him.

I haven't been able to look in Rhodes's eyes for days because of how I reacted to him and how fluttery I've felt being anywhere near him since then. Is it because I know he *shouldn't* feel good? Because he's older? Goes to Columbia? Willing to talk about my writing? Is it because of the teenage hormones the school nurse always tells us could lead straight to hell?

"Um…" I start, but then remember Mr. Kennedy called this little chat, so *he* can figure out what to say.

"About the production." I swear it's almost as painful for him to talk as it is for me right now. "Can you look down this list and tell me if I've got it right? Or if another time is better, we can talk later."

He clears his throat as he turns his clipboard for me to see, and his eyes get stuck for just a moment too long on the right side of my face. My stomach twists again, and I look at the clipboard because it is infinitely safer than his stare.

> *I get that this is weird of me, but I'm not sure the best way to go about talking to you or apologizing. I'm sorry about the other night in the barn after dinner. Things were awkward. Maybe I shouldn't have asked about your scars. I'm sure I shouldn't have touched your face. I'm sorry. I really want us to get along, and I need for things to not be weird because Ms. Bellings said to rely on you. And because I don't want to offend your dad by offending you. Can the awkwardness fall behind us? Because there's no way things aren't weird right now.*

Heat rushes up my neck because I'm probably acting juvenile or something about that very brief situation in the barn.

"I just want to get along. Okay?" he asks quietly.

"That all looks fine." I slide back and manage not to look at him, and I readjust my books and manage not to look at him, and I stand up and manage not to look at him, but then our eyes meet, and I think we're both stuck in the moment. Not only that, but I almost feel on equal footing with this teacher who goes to *my* university and who wants us to get along. Are we…friends? Do I have a friend in New York? That adventure feels closer again, and I'm not ready for it to feel closer. The only reason I applied a year early was just to see…I didn't want extra decisions.

A corner of his mouth quirks up in a partial smile.

In this second my world gets bigger and makes me feel smaller, and my heart races because when I start to feel how big the world is, and how many people are out there and how many places there are to see, half of me is thrilled and the other half begs to shut it out. Why did I have to meet Rhodes now? The guy who wants to travel the world and goes to my school?

"So, we good?" he asks, his voice sounding more hopeful and back to normal volume.

He's serious. He actually *cares* about what I think. My chest does that swelling thing again. Pride? Happiness? "Yeah." My mouth is pulling into a smile, and I don't remember willing that to happen. "We're good."

"Okay then." He lets out a breath, and shuffles the papers, but we're each still looking at the other. "Sorry if this is weird timing."

"It's fine." Oh crap. Elias is waiting. "See ya," I say before spinning on my heel and walking out of the classroom.

I suck in a breath, but I still feel weird over…whatever that just was.

"Hey." Elias slides his arm around my waist as soon as I step out of the room, and now the written note makes even more sense. Mr. Kennedy knew we'd be eavesdropped on, and I should have known too. But was it that big of a deal? Why didn't he just wait until the next dinner? Or pull me aside after school? Maybe the weirdness really was bothering him.

"So?" Elias asks.

I swallow the lump in my throat and stare at the floor, knowing I'm about to lie. "About play stuff."

"Oh." He gives me a squeeze. "That's all? I feel like…" He trails off.

Like what? I nearly ask but don't because I'm pretty sure I don't want to hear his question.

"I feel like he looks at you a lot, or…"

I try to shrug, but I think my body just jerks weird. One conversation with a student-teacher shouldn't affect me so fully. "I still say it's probably my messed-up face."

He frowns. "It's not messed up, Clara. You're beautiful."

Elias thinks everyone is beautiful, I'm sure.

"Are you okay?" He rests a hand on my shoulder. "You seem jumpy."

I'm not sure how to answer. I just stare at this guy who I've known since I was a kid.

"Clara?" he asks again.

I shake my head, wishing the action would jumble the loose parts of my thoughts together. "I really want out of here. Do you think we could get out of here?"

His head rests to the side and his brow furrows in worry.

I know he won't want to skip because he never does, but maybe… "Please?"

"Yeah…okay." He puts his arm around me, tucking me in to his side. "We can go."

* * *

We're five cars behind the stupid speaker at the McDonald's drive-through because it's the only fast-food restaurant in town. Despite the wait, it feels delightfully scandalous to be here instead of at school.

One day I'll be living somewhere with small, trendy cafés and corner vendors, and…My gaze floats toward Elias. The guy who I'm sure will wait for me if I ask him to. It's just a conversation I'm not ready to have, and one I can put off for another year. An uneasy feeling spreads through me in a sort of spidery way.

"The house you were designing looked cool," I say, trying to focus on something normal, but maybe we should be pushing past our normal.

He taps the steering wheel. "Thanks. Drawing plans for homes that small isn't really practical up here. But it's like when you step into a motor home and there's not an inch of wasted space. I like the idea of that."

"Hmm."

I stare out the window at the ravens gathered at the garbage bins and listen to the complex language as they talk to each other. They used to scare me, but not anymore. Even their beady, too-knowing eyes don't send creepers up my spine the way they did when I was a kid. So much has changed. I glance at Elias briefly, wondering what's going to change for us as we get older.

My small notebook rests on my leg, and I scribble a few random sentences about the birds.

Suddenly, Elias pulls away from the speaker toward the window.

I turn to face him. "I didn't tell you what I want." How did we get so far up in line?

His brows rise a bit. "In the two years I've been coming through this drive-through with you, it's been the same thing."

"Not *always*," I protest.

"Always." A corner of his mouth pulls up like I'm adorable, but I don't want to be adorable; I wanted to order.

"No." I can feel myself pouting, and I know it's ridiculous, but I can't seem to stop it.

Elias sighs. "I'm sorry then. You were watching those nuisance birds like always. You had your notebook out, and I thought I was doing a nice thing by ordering without interrupting your train of thought." His voice turns quiet. "What's going on with you?"

I want him to sound irritated or angry. I want him to give me something to push against, but there's no pushing against someone who is genuinely concerned about what I'm thinking. What's wrong with me?

"Why aren't you frustrated?" I ask.

He touches my cheek. The one closest to him. The one without the scars. I sometimes think he avoids touching that side of my face, but I can't be sure because it just sort of happens that he's on my left side a lot. He drives a lot. The deeper his eyes look at me and the more his hand touches my cheek and then my hair and then his fingertips slide up and down my neck, the less I think about wanting to be frustrated and the more I think about where else I'd like his hands.

Knowing the importance of not going too far with Elias is much easier when I'm not sitting next to him. Reconciling what I believe I *should* do around him and what I *want* to do with him is a near-constant struggle.

"I love you, Clara. If you're having a hard time, I want to help. If that means leaving school and going to McDonald's, then that's what I'm going to do. If it means being patient while you deal with what you need to, then I'll do that too." Every breath and every part of his eyes show that he's telling the truth. "You've been a little distracted over the past few days, and that's fine, but if you want to talk, I want to listen."

In a million lifetimes I could not hope to deserve this kind of devotion. And after the other night in the barn with Rhodes (the one I didn't tell Elias about) and the crazy thoughts I've been having since then, I deserve a very confused or angry boyfriend. Instead I'm getting this.

Elias's eyes are so deep that it always makes me think of the scripture about how the eyes are the windows to the soul. Elias's eyes have nothing but goodness in them—even down deep where I'm spiteful and petty.

Because instead of remarking on his awesome eyes or how good he is for me, I jump into the one conversation we tiptoe around more often than any other. "At what point do you think it'll be weird that we go to different churches?" I ask.

He shakes his head. "Why are you looking for a fight today?"

"I'm not, but we don't always agree." We've never actually fought, because one or the other of us always shrugs off the disagreement. Elias thinks my church overdoes meetings, and I know all of our forever-family stuff bothers him. He thinks we'll love everyone the same after this life, and I can't imagine that. At some point, if we stay together, our different views are going to cause problems. "Maybe that's something we should start talking about."

Elias lets out a slow breath. "I don't understand why you believe some of the things you do, but in the end, it's made you who you are. And I love you."

He always says something like this, and I think part of him is putting off having this conversation for real, just like I'm putting off having the conversation when I tell him I might want to go to New York.

"My house?" I ask and he nods.

"Your shake." Elias passes it to me with a smile. "And fries."

I stare at Elias for a moment, trying to shove away my totally unjustified irritation. "Thanks." I slide down in the seat relieved that the hard part of my day is over and having no idea what comes next. Not in the next hour or…for the rest of my life, really.

7

My house is blissfully silent. Dad should be at work for hours more, and neither Elias nor I have anywhere to be. This is his day off at the construction company, I barely work any hours at his dad's hardware store and lumberyard, and since he signed us out of school (our parents trust us way too much), neither of us is expected at play rehearsal.

I wrap my arms around his neck as soon as we're inside and slide my lips across his. Maybe this will make up for my moodiness today.

Elias matches my soft kiss before gently grasping my arms, taking them from around his neck, and stepping away. "I don't know, Clara." This is how he always handles us being alone—way too carefully. Neither of us believes in sex before marriage, and both of us have watched our friends slip off that path. There are times when I definitely want to slip. I generally feel really bad about that…after Elias has gone home.

"What?" Even though I totally know.

He rests his head to the side, like he's conflicted. He probably is. I don't know that anyone could be as good, deep down, as he is. Good parents, structured life, beliefs that run deep…"This is a lot of time to be alone."

"You mean a lot of time to get into trouble?" I'm not sure if I'm hurt or annoyed or neither, or both.

"I don't think you realize how hard it is for me. How easy it would be for me to go too far with you, and I don't...I don't want to be that guy." The way his weight shifts and his brow wrinkles, he looks honestly tortured.

"How far is too far?" I ask, wondering how much closeness I can get.

He flushes a little and looks away, moving into my living room instead of standing by the door. I immediately follow.

"I'm serious," I say. "Where do you draw the line? Where do you want to?" Because for me, that line is getting closer to sex every time we're together—at least lately. Maybe if we talk, I'll remember why I don't want to go too far even when we're together. And I actually feel this huge light-headed kind of relief that we're *talking* about this instead of avoiding.

He sits, folding his hands, his elbows resting on his knees. "Where do you?"

Where *do* I? "What? Do you want to know Mormon standards?" I ask.

He shrugs. "I think I know, but...um...yeah." And then he swallows.

"This shouldn't make you so nervous. We're not talking about having sex before my dad gets home." And it's not something we've really talked about before. *Before*, we've been polite and careful. I sorta feel like we're moving past that now, and it feels amazing—like maybe we *will* beat the odds and stay together.

"Clara." His eyes widen and he shifts on the couch, rubbing his palms on his thighs.

"*No touching shoulders to knees and everything in between* is the joke or guideline or whatever. We have youth dances at our church and we hold each other around the neck or on the waist, so the shoulders to knees thing is for under clothes, I think." The guideline is totally for both under and over clothes, aside from where we touch to dance.

His eyes are floating between my shoulders and my knees and

everything in between and there's an ache in wanting to be closer to him that pushes me forward.

He licks his lips a few times as I stand in front of him. "Probably smart."

I kneel, resting my hands on his legs and my butt on my feet, nervous energy racing through me and tightening my insides as I rub my palms up the top of his thighs. Maybe all those energy strings will tighten further if we touch more. I'm not supposed to want him this way.

"But over clothes…" It's my turn to take a hard swallow. "There might be wiggle room." There's totally not.

"Clara." His voice is pleading, but I don't know if he wants me to go away or come closer. I'm guessing he's feeling whatever I'm feeling so I scoot closer, which pushes his knees apart a little, and I lean toward him. There's no careful kissing before his tongue slides in my mouth. We kiss so desperately that we can't find a rhythm. My college decisions don't matter, my appointment in Seattle doesn't matter, the weirdness around Rhodes doesn't matter.

I pull on him and he lays me down on the floor, resting his weight on top of me. This time my legs spread a little for him and he lets out a moan as we keep kissing, still frantic. As his body rocks against mine, once, gently, I realize he seriously has a hard-on, and it's pressing into me, and I arch into him as our tongues slide together. I'm wondering if I should feel as good about it as I do, but the pressure of him feels so amazing that I find myself rocking a little with him. And even though our clothes are on and his hands haven't run over anything they shouldn't, I'm pretty sure this isn't something we should be doing.

If he asked me right now if I'd let him take me upstairs to my bed, I'd maybe tell him yes.

My scars don't matter.

His hands press into my sides as they slide down to the top of my pants, and my body is screaming, *Yes! There! Unbutton! More touching!* Maybe I'll get some release from all the tension jumping around inside me lately.

His fingers slide up my shirt, just a little. And even though we've been together for a year and a half, this is easily the furthest we've gone. If not in actual touching, then in mood. Because I don't care about breathing or eating or my dad or school or that we shouldn't be alone in my house. I care about feeling more of him against more of me.

My hands run up the back of his shirt, tracing my fingers over all the muscles he gets from working so hard.

His thumbs run slightly underneath the top of my jeans, flushing every part of my body with heat.

"Clara." His hands hit the floor as he shoves off me, holding himself in push-up position so we don't touch.

His hair is disheveled, and his eyes are wild. I arch my hips up toward him and then he's gone. He's jumped four feet away, where he's lying with his stomach on the floor and breathing hard, still watching me.

The loss of warmth trips up my brain and body, rocketing me back into the present. It takes me a second to catch my breath, and I now have an ache I'm not sure how to make go away.

His hand reaches toward mine, and I roll over to lie on my stomach, still staring.

"That was..." he starts.

My heart and breathing nearly drown out his words. "Yeah. Me too."

"I could have..." He trails off, but I don't need him to finish.

"I could have too. All the way."

Elias frowns, and a nagging tug in my chest says I did this to him.

"I'm sorry." It's all I can think of to say. I have no idea what's going on with me. I was annoyed with Elias for being over nice, I had been staring at Mr. Kennedy in a very more-than-friend way, and now this, which sort of seems like the opposite of how I was feeling about Elias in the drive-through.

"No." He shakes his head. "It's my responsibility to make sure we don't go too far. *I'm* the one who's sorry."

I sit, letting our hands fall apart. "Why would you be more responsible than me?"

"It's just…" Elias sits up. "We get these lectures from our youth pastor all the time about being a gentleman, and right now I don't feel like…I'm the guy, you know?"

"And I'm the girl." I'm not even sure what he's trying to say.

He licks his lips and stares at the carpet. We won't discuss this any further because it would turn into an argument, and apparently Elias's method of avoiding an argument on a subject is to avoid the subject. Though, with my unwillingness to really discuss plans after scars, maybe that's my method of not arguing too.

I wonder how long that'll last.

"We've been friends a long time," he says.

"Yeah."

"We both know we want to wait…until we're married."

Unease begins sucking in my stomach because I just made Elias uncomfortable. "Yeah…we've always known that."

"I'm…" He presses both palms into his forehead as he stares at the floor. "I never thought that I'd want different."

"And"—I swallow hard, terrified of his answer, not matter what it is—"you do?"

He chuckles. "I did a minute ago."

I laugh a little with him as the tension between us shifts to something easier to deal with and breathe around.

"So, I don't want to be away from you, but maybe I should go"—Elias stands and chuckles a little again—"you know…cool off."

I find myself smiling with him, grateful again that traces of our easy friendship followed us into what we have now. "Yeah. Okay."

"Oh." His face lightens. "You have mutual tonight, right?"

"Every Tuesday." All the youth at my church gather for an activity of some kind every week on Tuesday.

"What are you guys up to tonight? Maybe I'll join in."

"The boys are in charge, so…" He'll know what this means because of our small town. We know all the same people.

"Dodgeball?" he asks.

"You got it."

"I'll meet you there, okay?" He takes my hand and gives it a squeeze, his dark eyes searching mine. "I love you, Clara. So much."

There's so much feeling in his voice, and it hits me like it probably should have hit me the first time he said it. Elias means it. For real. He's not just telling me he loves me because he likes me more than any other girl he's dated. Elias really does love me. And I love him too, just maybe not in quite the same way. I don't move from my spot on the floor. I don't talk about me being Mormon or him being unsure, or how we really could have had sex this afternoon and I'm not sorry.

Instead I just say, "I love you too."

8

The church parking lot is chaotic as half the teens in town pull in for our youth night. I slide my truck into park just as Elias pulls in next to me.

I grin at him through our windows, and he smiles back. The second I slip out of my truck, Sister McEntyre gives me the one-quirked-eyebrow look that means one of two things: you're being too serious with that boy, or we need to get that boy properly baptized. "Elias came with you again?"

"Yep." Neither of those things are something I want to discuss with Sister McEntyre. Elias is happy at his own church, and the last thing I want to do is to talk about my boyfriend with anyone who is not Cecily. Well, or Elias.

"Hey." Elias walks around the front of my truck, and I let out a breath as Sister McEntyre walks toward the front door of the plain, brick church building. Sometimes I wonder if I come out of habit, or because I know I should be here for myself.

"Motter!" a kid named Brian yells. He's also a Knik town lifer and someone else stuck at the small, private school. "You crashing the Mormon party?"

"Yep!" Elias calls back.

"I call Motter on my team!" Brian yells. "And you know, instead of crashing our party, you should *join* our party." Brian gives Elias two oversized winks.

"You have to know they're going to harass you." I bump him with my hip.

"It's fine." He gives my cheek a quick kiss. "I harass him when he comes to play ball at my church too. No biggie."

We're starting for the building when I hear the distinct whine of a small plane flying far too low.

I feel my body slump as I squint into the sky and see the yellow and blue stripes that mark the side of my dad's plane. "Not now. Seriously."

"What?" Elias asks just as Dad lands his Cessna in the open field next to the church. Dad loves landing his four-seater plane in fields. It's just weird.

"This is one thing I hate about summer," I say as I start for the small fence that stands between the church parking lot and the hay field.

Elias laughs. "I'll be inside playing ball. Good luck with your dad."

I give Elias a smile and a wave, thankful he doesn't feel the need to stick close to me when he comes here.

Dad hops out of the plane with a grin. "Great that we have enough light to fly even after dinner, isn't it, sweetie?"

He ducks under the wing as he walks my way.

"Dad!" I protest. "The Clellans' field isn't a runway."

He waves me away with a snort. "Rhodes has never been in a small plane. Can you believe that?"

So Rhodes is with him.

I should probably tell Rhodes not to encourage my dad. He'll drag him out of New York and shove him right into small-town Alaska, just like he did with Mom. Not that she minded.

Rhodes is wearing a headset and gives me a wave from the copilot's seat in the small plane. The backseat is empty—at least it looks that way from here.

Dad folds his arms with a smile. "I know tonight is dodgeball, which means that you'll be sitting on the sidelines with a book."

I hold my book between us because there's really no escaping how well he knows me.

"We're just going to take a quick trip over the glacier. I promise to have you back before closing prayer," Dad says.

I open my mouth to protest, but there's no point. I haven't seen Dad smile this wide in a long time. "Fine," I say.

He swings his arm over my shoulder and gives me a squeeze as we walk back toward the plane. "And we both know the Clellans don't mind when I use their field."

I stay silent. Of course they don't mind, but normal people use *the runway*.

Dad opens the small back door of his plane, and I step on the small step above the wheel before sliding inside.

"Do you ever get used to this?" Rhodes asks the second I scoot onto the small backseat.

"Yep," I answer. "Did you ask my dad why he didn't use the runway like a normal person?"

"It's too far away from the church," Dad says. "And I did take *off* from the runway." He chuckles as he slides his thumb over the sheet with his preflight checklist. He could recite the thing in his sleep, but he still goes through every item. "I just know how you like to fly over the river, so I thought we'd come pick you up."

I look Rhodes over. He's wearing a too-new North Face shell, pressed hiking pants, and unscuffed hiking boots. He screams tourist, which helps temper my reaction to him much better than the snug plaid shirts, which Jell-O my knees.

I slip on my headset just as Dad yells, "Clear!" and starts the small engine.

He loves flying in and out of this small field so much that he flew us to church a few times when I was small. We bounce up the field as the small plane picks up speed, and I feel the familiar lurch in my stomach as we leave the ground.

Rhodes turns sideways in his seat to face me and presses the microphone closer to his lips. His eyes are as excited as a five-year-old's in a toy store, and I find myself smiling back.

"You really get used to this?" Rhodes asks.

"Yep," I answer. Rhodes turns back around and rests his forehead against the window. I do the same in the backseat.

The river's wide here, channeling paths over the expanse of gravel, winding between three and ten different paths underneath us. Dad banks hard to the left, and I know this is where the canyon narrows and the river will become one solid, churning mass for a while.

"What's that?" Rhodes points.

Dad peers over, but he's on the wrong side of the plane. I can look out either side from my place in the back, so I lean over. "Moose," I tell him. About eight or so brown spots jog along the riverside.

"This is just like *National Geographic*," Rhodes says, and Dad laughs. "Do you two fly a lot?"

"The plane smells," I say, wondering why I'm even trying to counter Rhodes's excitement.

"Smells like *adventure*," Rhodes teases, throwing me another kid-like grin from the front seat.

We continue up the canyon, and finally Dad has to gain some altitude because our airspace is narrowing as the mountains come closer together.

"If Clara was up front, I'd have her take the controls," Dad brags. "She's pretty good."

"Is that legal?" Rhodes asks.

Dad laughs. "Nope."

"All I do is hold the yoke," I say. "I've landed us a handful of times, but always with Dad's help. It's not that big a deal." Half the people I know have small planes—and only half of those are always flown by their licensed pilot owners.

"I think it's a big deal." Rhodes's face is once again resting against the glass as he takes in the world below us.

The two-lane highway follows the same windy path as the river does, like two small ribbons cutting through the evergreens and brown trees waiting for leaves. The plane banks, and I've taken this route often enough to know we're close to the glacier.

The river widens and flattens out again, leaving the highway to follow the curve of the mountain instead of the curve of the water. A few large chunks of ice sit in the water, too big for the river to carry them any farther. The glacier blends into the gravel and glacial silt for a while until it gives way to blue ice and snow.

Dad lowers the plane again, like I knew he would. He loves flying right over the top of the ice. When I was a kid, we'd make up stories about pretend people who lived in all the cracks and crevices of the massive expanse. The glacier is about two-thirds the size it was when I was little, but it's still enormous, growing from the canyon floor nearly to the mountaintops.

"You can come up here every day?" Rhodes asks. "Because this is amazing."

"Plane fuel costs a bit much," Dad says. "But yep, if I wasn't such a penny-pincher, we for sure would. We could fly up here every day that the weather allows it."

"This is why I love to travel," Rhodes says.

"Why?" I ask.

"I love that idea that someone else's normal is an adventure for me. I love it when I can live somewhere long enough that the adventurous part of a new place begins to feel like every day."

I can't imagine anything but my life feeling normal. Can't imagine college feeling normal. New York feeling normal. I can, however, imagine what it would feel like to have my face back.

"I think that's pretty dang admirable," Dad says.

"Keeps life interesting," Rhodes answers.

I want to say something witty or clever. Something that shows Rhodes a piece of the person I hope I am when I make it to college, but I come up blank. Instead I find myself jealous of a guy who isn't afraid to keep moving forward.

When Dad finally lands back in the field, I slip out of the backseat with a wave. I stumble twice after being in the air but find my legs again quickly. The church parking lot is almost all cleared out—so much for making it back in time for the end.

Elias leans on the bed of his truck and smiles, cocking an eyebrow as I get closer. "So, your dad stole you away from your own church activity. I figured you'd be gone max thirty minutes."

"Yeah." I stop next to Elias and then squint when someone's headlights hit my eyes. It is seriously not dark enough for headlights. "Dad's taken it upon himself to be Rhodes's welcoming committee."

I wince as Dad's airplane hits that high whine it does when it takes off.

Elias leans back a bit. "Mr. Kennedy was with you?"

"Next to *Dad*." I widen my eyes as I tease him. Elias normally isn't weird about me being around guys. I'm not sure why Rhodes is different.

I slide my hands around Elias's sides, and every feeling I had this afternoon in my house comes back in a rush. My lips find his. Elias's mouth opens and his hands thread through my hair, holding our faces together as one kiss blends into the next.

I'm pressing against Elias as hard as I can—hips, stomach, chests. I never want us to stop. Ever.

Elias pulls back, gasping for air. "Okay. Wow. Church parking lot. Wow…" He pushes out a couple short breaths.

"You okay?" I ask.

Elias lets out a little chuckle. "I'm okay."

He swallows and his eyes find mine in the dimming light—all soft and serious.

"What?" I ask.

"Do you…" He brushes the hair off my face but doesn't continue.

I tug my bangs back down.

"Will you do…" He clears his throat before glancing at the ground and then back up at me. "Will you do something with me tomorrow after rehearsal?"

Something about his tone starts a new kind of nervous fluttering in my stomach. I can't tell if it's a good kind or a bad kind because my body's so upside down right now.

"Yeah. Of course. Yeah."

He kisses the corner of my mouth. "Okay. Until tomorrow."

I let my hands slide off his waist and then let them slide over his hips before they fall to my sides. I'm not ready to let him go. To let his body go.

Things between us are shifting, and I want them shifted. Changed. Moved forward.

He opens my driver's side door for me and waits until my truck starts before going to his. He always does that—makes sure that I'm okay before he makes a move. That's Elias. I still can't believe how lucky I am.

* * *

"Whoa, what?" Cecily shrieks over the phone.

I wince because I really do see the importance of being careful with my body and all that, but when Elias and I are together, it just doesn't seem as crucial as it does in Sunday school. And now that I'm hours past from lying on the floor with him, guilt at how I felt is starting to squirm its way through me.

"It's not that big a deal." I lie back in bed, the phone pressed against my ear like Dad will somehow not hear my end of the conversation. There are seriously a bajillion things to worry about if you're having sex with someone. Now that I'm not in the situation from earlier, I'm wondering why I wanted to do it so bad. Maybe I forgot how crappy I feel after I do something I know I shouldn't. So, obviously my beliefs play in, but I have a pretty strong practical side too, and…Yes. Lots to worry about. Mechanics. Birth control. STDs. Getting caught…

"But you guys almost…*you know*."

"No! We didn't!" And then I remember that I shouldn't talk so loud. "We weren't even under clothes," I whisper. "Not much."

She sighs. "I actually can't imagine what that's like because the thought of a guy touching my waist under my shirt is terrifying. What if I don't feel right or feel fat, and I can't…just…No."

"I can…*now*."

"Clara." She giggles. "And here I thought I'd for sure be the first one to go all the way, and now it looks like it'll be you."

"No." I sigh. Because between what I believe I should and shouldn't be doing and the practicalities, I can't imagine actually going all the way. And then I think about Elias's fingers at the edge of my jeans and think maybe I can…

"Maay-be," she sings. "What do you think he wants tomorrow?"

"I have no idea." I tap my toes on the ceiling-wall again.

"Well. I'm sure it'll be late here. Again," she adds for emphasis because it's like 1:00 a.m. there. "But text me anyway, okay?"

"Will do. Promise."

"Okay. I'm going *back* to sleep, and now you need to try to get your beauty sleep so you're ready for whatever that man of yours has planned."

I swear I can feel her smirk over the phone in that hilarious, teasing way of hers.

"Night, Cee."

9

Elias meets me onstage after school with that same odd smile as last night in the church parking lot.

"So, where are you taking me?" I ask as I step close.

"It's a surprise." And there's this crazy, earnest expression on his face. I'm not sure what to do with it because his smile says he's excited, but the look in his eyes is more emotional or deeper or…

"Okay." I shrug like it's no biggie, but then he takes my hand and threads our fingers together, and my stomach gets all crazy. I step toward him and our chests touch before he jumps back.

Jumps.

Like stepping back wouldn't be enough of a signal to me that I've maybe suddenly turned into a crazed, horny teenager, which I haven't. I don't think. There shouldn't be anything wrong with getting comfort from being *close* to someone.

"Ready to get started?" Rhodes—no, *Mr. Kennedy*—steps in, scowling at us. "Are you being appropriate for school?"

Elias flushes eighteen shades of scarlet, drops my hand, and moves even farther away.

Thank you very much.

Elias does his homework as we stumble through Act III of *Arsenic and Old Lace*. Rhodes steps in and laughs with the cast and directs in such a better way than Ms. Bellings, probably because he knows better what he's talking about. Hello…MFA program at freaking Columbia.

I stand on the edge of the stage, hands clasped around the cord for the curtain so tightly that my fingernails dig into my palms. All I can do is try not to feel desperate about how Rhodes looks in his skinny jeans or how Elias's body felt on top of me.

After about twenty minutes of very purposefully trying to keep my gaze off the two guys and colossally failing, I close my eyes, lean my forehead against the curtain rope, and just try to get through the hour of rehearsal.

Footsteps stop too close. I open my eyes and startle backward when Mr. Kennedy's smirk comes into view. "Enjoying your nap?" he teases.

I shrug. "Sorry," I mumble, glancing toward Elias whose brow is pulled low

"It's okay." Mr. Kennedy's smirk turns to a smile and the fluttery feeling in my gut is back, mixed with something heavy that feels suspiciously like guilt.

"I'm not—"

"You leave for Seattle in a couple weeks, right?" he asks, stepping so close I can smell his minty breath. "Or is my timeline off?"

Abby and Esther's eyes are wide and staring—I swear I can feel the holes they're drilling with their eyes from across the stage. Whatever. We're just *talking*.

I release a breath, trying not to smell the lickable mint, and nod slightly. "Yeah."

He does the chin tilt that normally makes guys look like jerks, but it just shows off his jaw, and then he squeezes my arm before turning away. "Well, good luck."

I fall back against the wall, release the rope, and stretch out my stiff fingers.

Instead of watching Rhodes walk away, I pry my eyes off his back and stare at the floor.

"How does he know about Seattle?" Elias asks. Each word is carefully placed and deliberate, which means Elias is way overthinking Rhodes's words.

"My dad." The cast is yakking on stage and picking up packs, and they're all blending together under the stage lights. Well…now that Abby and Esther have found somewhere else to look. Esther's hair swishes around her shoulder as she glances back at me again, our eyes meeting and her blushing. The blush is probably because I caught her staring. Or because she feels bad for thinking something along the lines of *why is the hot new teacher paying attention to the ugly girl?*

Elias's hand slides across my back and clasps my side. "It's not just the Seattle thing. It's the way he touched you. How he asked for you after class the other day…I don't know…What's up with him?"

I have absolutely no idea. And for that matter, I'm not sure what's up with me and my reaction to him. My heart is still slamming into my ribs.

I lean down, grab my pack, and move for the back door before anyone else steps into our conversation. My mind is spinning, my fingers are shaking, and I swear my lips are getting numb from nerves. "Nothing. I don't know. Nothing."

"Maybe I should ask what's up with you."

"Just a lot happening," I say as I push through the door. "But I'm good. I promise."

"Okay." His okay sounds a lot like he should have said, "If you say so."

I hope he's done asking questions because I don't have any good answers.

"So. Now are you going to tell me where we're going?" I ask as Elias follows me to his truck.

"One of my dad's construction sites," he says.

I slide into the passenger's seat. One of the construction sites? *Why?*

Elias slips in his side and fumbles with his keys for a minute before starting the truck.

"You're being weird," I say.

"Am I?" He smiles again. "Sorry. We don't have far to go."

I clutch my hands together in my lap because the mood is just... strange. Elias fiddles with his iPod for a minute and then turns the music on so quietly that I can't hear. All I have to talk about are Columbia (which I can't talk to Elias about), my doctor's appointment (which I don't really want to talk about), or Rhodes (which I definitely don't want to discuss with Elias). When did we end up with nothing to say?

We drive through a small street of five homes with Motter Construction signs hung at the end of the driveways. "So these are your dad's, huh?" I ask even though it's obvious.

"Not just Dad's. Mine too. I'm almost done with school, and I've been helping to run the company for a while now." He licks his lips, grasps the steering wheel, and stretches his neck to one side and then to the other.

"Right." I shake my head and squint into the sun, hoping Elias isn't trying to steer us into another too important conversation about where we'll be for the next couple of years.

Avoiding talking about our future during the school day is one thing. It's quite another to avoid it when we're the only two people around. Whenever I think about telling Elias about Columbia, my throat fills with too much saliva and my brain blanks out. He has no idea I even applied. As far as he knows, I'll head to the University of Alaska, and... that's it.

"The place I want to show you is past the neighborhood we're working in, on a bigger piece of property."

"Doesn't that cost more money? Are you guys doing a custom home or something?" I ask.

His head bobs from side to side. "Yeah...sorta..."

I'm not sure what to make of Elias right now. He's not one for surprises or being coy or whatever this is.

We drive up a driveway that winds through the thick forest, and I chuckle at the two-story house filled with interesting angles that probably doubled the framing costs. "This is exactly the kind of thing your dad rolls his eyes at."

"I know." He scoffs. "I've been told many times."

"So...what is this, exactly?"

We stop and there are two tiny stories of house in the process of being built. Just the skeleton walls are up now. This is my favorite part of seeing the building process, and the thing I understand most about Elias. Right now the house is nothing but possibility. This one is going to be smallish but wicked interesting, and I'm sure Elias will do the woodwork inside he loves so much.

The trees are only cleared a short way around the house on all sides, leaving it in the center of a carved circle in the forest.

I close my eyes for a moment and think about how his fingers felt running along my skin, and I can't hide the shiver that courses through me.

"You cold?"

"Thinking about you," I answer before I try to convince myself that Elias is right and it is just the cold.

His dark, wild eyes are back, and I feel my body screaming—*yes, please!*

Instead of leaning in for a kiss or a nice make-out session like I want, he pushes open his door.

"Come on." He slides out of his side of the truck and walks around to get my door.

I take his hand as he helps me down, and instead of him hugging me or at least giving me a smile like he normally would, we're treading over the uneven ground and around small piles of scrap wood to the front of the house. I'm stumbling to keep up as his fingers tighten around mine. This is weirdly nervous and unusual for Elias.

"Okay." He stops in front of where the front door will be.

"Why are we here?" I smile, thinking of a few things I'd like to do while alone with him, and maybe the cold will keep us from going too far. That should make me feel better. Or him feel better. Or something.

"I wanted to show you my house. I designed this one for…for, um…for me."

Air becomes unbreathable as everything around me freezes. "Your *what?*"

"My house." His smile is a mix of pride and sheepishness.

My jaw drops, and even though I knew Elias was sticking around here after school and working construction with his dad, the reality of that hits me. Who would want to be tied down to a house at *eighteen?*

"You look like you're gonna pass out, Clara." He rests his hand gently on my waist. "You okay?"

"Just…surprised," I squeak.

"How can you be surprised? You've known I was going to keep working at the construction company with my dad. I've even shown you like fifteen houses I've designed for myself."

"Right."

What does this mean? Anything? Nothing? Cecily's words echo in my head about how Elias would probably marry me a month out of high school, sooner if we have more "incidents" like on my living-room floor the other day. I firmly believe Elias would be a virgin at thirty if it took him that long to find the right girl. But as close as we are, and as much as I care about him, I'm just not ready to think about forever.

"I wanna show you. Come on." He wraps his arm around me, which is good because it grounds me enough to keep me in the moment instead of allowing me to run screaming.

"And this'll be the kitchen…" He lets me go long enough to wave his arms around countertop spaces and sink placement and fridge and oven, and it's all so final and domestic and…*foreign.*

His brows are up and I know he's looking for me to show excitement that I've got to find. Got to.

"Show me upstairs?" I ask after swallowing something that feels like a basketball.

"We're not done down here." He pecks my cheek before leading me out of the kitchen and into the dining room, which looks like every other corner in the house that's still just two-by-fours and two-by-sixes and a few wires running through walls that barely exist.

"Right." *Silly* me, whose brain is on total overload right now.

By the time Elias is done raving about what he's going to do downstairs, he takes my hand and leads me up the wooden steps to the top story.

My stomach's turning over at the adultness of it all and how comfortable he is with that, and how he's barely let go of me, and how I should be jumping up and down with him. Instead I want to go home and bury myself in TV or crawl into a corner of the barn for a while so I don't have to think about Elias and houses and school.

I'm pretty sure I make a few witty, Clara-like comments as he shows me bedrooms for *future family*, which kicks my heart rate up, and then he stops in the middle of a very cool but slightly odd-shaped room— one side protrudes from the house a bit, the walls surrounding us in a semi-circle.

"This is the master bedroom."

"Nice." I nod a few times as I look around. "Cozy," I tease as my heart continues its sprint.

He's giving me that "Elias" look. The one that says a million things right behind his eyes. All the ways he loves me and wants to take care of me, and wants and needs me to know how special I am to him. I suck in a few gulps of air, but it's not enough, and the room starts to spin.

"Clara?" His voice is so far away that I'm not even sure if it's him.

I reach out to grab a wall, but nothing's there, and I reach again and stumble. Elias grasps my waist, steadying me.

My stomach turns over again. *House. Family. Master bedroom.* And he hasn't asked me to marry him. Hasn't asked me to be with him. But what is this, if not that? This is not part of my plan. I can't do this. Way too close to permanence. But maybe I shouldn't be suffocating. Not with a guy I've known since forever, but…

"Are you okay?" he asks.

"Feel sick. Hit me fast." At least it's all truth. Hopefully he won't ask me what made me feel sick because there would be no good way to deal with that one—at least not without some very creative lying. I have to buy myself some time.

"We should get you home."

"Yeah." I gasp for good effect, even though, once again, it makes me a little horrible. "Thanks."

I'm pretty sure I'm going to be sick tomorrow. And maybe the day after. And maybe again the day after that.

10

I lean my head against the wall in my tiny, narrow stairway and take another sip of hot chocolate. The rain spatters and pounds on the metal roof and slams into the panes. Spring storm, which suits my mood perfectly. I push my feet back and forth on the wooden steps in my fuzzy socks and let my eyes fall closed. There has to be a poem in this hollowed-out feeling in my chest. I just haven't found it yet.

Because I'm "sick," Dad ordered pizza for our dinner night with Mr. Kennedy so I won't have to cook. I hear him in the kitchen though, wandering probably. He's at loose ends because it's raining and his outdoor projects can't happen right now.

We leave for Seattle in just over a week. My life is going to change—or at least be on the path to changing. I should be dancing with excitement, but instead my stomach is tighter every day. The tension strings in my body have turned into wires—and not the good kind of tension wires I get from kissing Elias.

In about four weeks, I'm supposed to tell Columbia if I'm attending next year or not. Which I'm not. I know the deadline is a Tuesday and I know I should write my explanation for asking for a deferment until next year. I just haven't brought myself to do it yet.

"Rhodes!" Dad's voice carries through the entry and dining room, through the kitchen, and to where I sit on my tiny stairwell. "Great to see you again!"

"Sorry I'm late," Rhodes apologizes. "I got a call from a friend who's heading to Nome this summer to help with an old native-site dig."

I groan because I know exactly what Dad's going to say next.

"I helped on a dig once. Totally unexpected. I had to land my Cessna on the road north of Fairbanks and was flagged down…"

I tune out, stand up, and slide my hands over my soft, gray-striped pajama pants. No point in getting dressed when you're for-real sick, so I'm not going to bother even though I'm just pretend sick. My socks slip as I slide my foot across each step before allowing myself to step down. Being social isn't really in the realm of what I'd like to do with my evening.

"Just amazing that you can have experienced so much at your young age," Dad says. "I'm proud of you for it, even if your parents don't quite understand."

What did I just miss?

"Well, thank you," Rhodes says. "I guess they thought with all the traveling we did when I was growing up, I'd be ready to settle when they were, and…" His voice has gotten quieter and slower. "And I wasn't."

"Well, that's too bad. But I'm sure glad it brought you to our neck of the woods. If you're at all interested in getting your pilot's license, we should definitely go up as much as we can before your time here is over."

"That would be…really great. Thank you so much." Rhodes chuckles, but it sounds heavier than normal. "It's on my list for sure."

I clutch my mug in both hands as if it could somehow protect me from whatever I might think and feel around Rhodes tonight—especially with how uncertain I feel about finding a forever with Elias when it means starting that timeline now.

"Clara." Rhodes's brows shoot up. "Your dad said you've been sick."

"She's a toughie." Dad winks at me as he flips open the top of a pizza box.

"I'm a little better." I take another sip of hot chocolate.

Dad and Rhodes continue to chat about airplanes through dinner, but Rhodes is slow to answer and, unlike most nights, doesn't offer any stories of his own.

I cut up my pizza and then push the bites around on my plate. Elias isn't going to just *not ask* if he was about to ask what I think he was about to ask at his house, and I have no idea what to do about him wanting so much with me. I should be thrilled that anyone as stable, sweet, and good-looking as him would even give me a second glance, but there's something off. Like when I finish a poem but don't turn it in because something in the rhythm just isn't…right. I so wish I could stop thinking about this.

"Rhodes should be able to handle the horses on his own if you're not up to it," Dad offers.

I stand, grateful for the distraction. "I'm up to it."

Rhodes stands with me. "I can help, at the very least."

"Muddy out there today." I point to the water flowing over the windowpane.

"I got Toughies to fit in." Rhodes smiles and I nod. The XTRATUF brown rubber boots seem to be almost a uniform in Alaska on crap weather days like this.

He grabs his boots from the front entry and meets me at the back door. I figure he thinks I'm sick, so I don't worry trying to make conversation or anything. I zip up my raincoat and tug my hood forward before stepping into the downpour. The noise outside takes over every thought. Being too sick to bother with politeness is something I could get used to.

Rhodes pulls open the barn door, and the warmth of the animals is a stark contrast to the deluge outside. We work in silence to feed and water the horses. He's familiar with the routine now. My heart feels weirdly heavy, and I can't place why.

When we finish with the last bucket of water, my eyes connect with his. I'm holding my breath, waiting to see if he'll say something or start walking out of the barn, but he's so still. His eyes look almost sad, so instead of walking back into the rain, I sit in front of Snoopy's stall. Rhodes pauses for a moment longer in the middle of the open area before sitting next to me. I'm not sure how being around him turned into something less frantic feeling. Maybe I'm just exhausted with all the thinking I've done over the past few days.

Neither of us speaks. Maybe he gets that I'm in a weird place. I stare at our brown boots with the scuffed mustard-yellow edges. Well, mine are scuffed, his are new. Mine are also about half the size of his.

"You have boat-like feet," I say.

Rhodes chuckles and taps his toes together a few times. "So I've been told. Twelves, in case you were curious."

The rain continues its frantic slap-tapping on the roof and walls.

"I forget that you're younger." He turns to face me, and his light blue eyes feel more...gray. Definitely sad. "That you're a student. Maybe I'm here too much to make the distinction the way I should."

I fold my arms, trying to stay warm in the damp air. "You're younger even than you let on."

"Twenty-one, almost twenty-two." He taps his toes a couple more times, the rubber-on-rubber noise barely carrying over the sound of the rain. "I graduated from high school early. And then did some traveling through college. But I also signed up for courses during the summers from different schools, depending on where I was living at the time. I took extra credits every semester, and I've been burning through school at a frantic pace."

It's on the tip of my tongue to ask about New York, but the idea of the move still feels fragile. There are things that I need to get done before I think about moving.

"Why did you graduate from high school early?"

His feet stop tapping, and he pulls his knees up in an almost defensive posture. He suddenly looks sixteen instead of twenty-one. Small, maybe sad, a little afraid...

I'm holding my breath when he answers.

"Homeschooled."

But something in his face says there's a whole lot more to the story. "Gonna give me the real story?" I ask.

"My brother died of leukemia. I was fifteen. He was thirteen. My dad was stationed in Italy when my brother was diagnosed, and we were transferred to San Diego so we'd have access to better specialists. I know it happens all the time, but he was my brother, you know?" He picks apart a piece of straw with his fingers, peeling down the sides until there's nothing left.

I stare at his features—his eyes cast down to the straw-covered floor, his slight frown. "I'm so sorry." I can't imagine having a sibling, much less one who died.

"The pain runs so deep that I sometimes think I won't be able to breathe or wake up the next day, but then I do and I'm still healthy, and my brother's still gone and that's it." He finally looks at me, and this is the real guy. The one that's not smirky or annoying or older or younger. He's just a guy.

"Wow." I know this part of him. "Losing someone you love steals parts of you that you'll never get back."

"My parents are sort of okay. They have these staunch beliefs where they say *he's in a better place*, but all I can think is that he should be here. He shouldn't have gotten sick. He should be *here*." Pain and anger infuse his voice. "I'm sorry. It's my brother's birthday today. Every year I think it'll be better, and every year it's not. I'm not as okay as I want to be."

He tells me this like I'm old enough or worthy enough to hear it. And maybe I am. I have things to say. To share. His legs slide back down, and he rubs his hands up and down his thighs a few times.

The rain clatters on the roof and makes plopping, plipping noises as it hits the soft dirt outside. I breathe in the sweetness of the hay. "I think that about my mom sometimes."

"I bet."

"Losing family affects us in ways other people can't understand."

He nods slightly as he strips apart another piece of hay with his fingers.

Most people I know have lost someone, but very few people have lost someone from their immediate family. It's not the same. "When a person..." I'm not sure if I can say this right, but I feel the need to try. "When a person is unquestionably a part of your every day, and then they're gone...My house is still hollowed out and emptier without Mom. So is my heart. Always will be. Without believing she's somewhere better, I'm not sure how I would have survived the loss."

"Hmm."

I chew on the end of a piece of hay, still just looking for a way to keep busy. "My dad, you know. I mean, we've always gone to church, but after we lost Mom it became everything to him."

He leans back against the stall and faces me. "And do you push back?"

"No." I shake my head. "It works for me. I like our church. I like what we believe, but..." *But everyone doubts sometimes.* Maybe I'll always doubt a little, but it's definitely not something I'd share with Rhodes. Or Elias. Or even my dad. I'm a firm believer in faith being personal, and that's gotten me out of a lot of awkward conversations.

"Your scars—" he starts but pauses. "I look at you and I'm reminded of how very lucky I am. Your internal scars are probably related to your external scars, and it's not like you can hide those. Mine are easily hid."

"No," I agree. "I can't hide." And for the first time I think someone understands a part of why I hate my scars. It's something I've never been able to put into words in such a simple way.

"I'm glad we're friends," he says as his eyes float over my face, spending a few extra seconds on my scars.

I snort like the very attractive person that I am. "Is that what we are? Because I'm pretty sure you're my teacher."

He leans toward me until our shoulders bump before moving away, but just slightly. "In six months, we could end up in the same college class, Clara. I feel much more connected to that idea than the fact that I'm student teaching. I'd love to be a teacher, but I have more school I'd like to finish first. I'm student teaching now because it felt like a good opportunity to spend time in Alaska, and I've never been. I think I'd like to be a teacher later because I love learning and I love the school schedule. I'd have a lot of freedom for travel. Well...if I ever stop going to summer school."

"Oh." The divide between us shrank with the story of his brother and shrank with him slumping next to me, and he's right anyway. When I start college in the fall, it *is* possible that we could end up in the same class. Not likely. But possible. I hold my breath as the reality of how close we could be sinks in, and then I want to ask him about all the places he's been. Is that something I'll do? I'm not sure. New York still feels like an insurmountable wall.

Rhodes shreds a few more pieces of hay with his fingertips. "You and Elias have been together a while."

I nod but don't speak. Talking about Elias with Rhodes feels like another kind of unfinished poem—awkward in a way that makes me unsure of how to move forward.

"It's just…" He frowns a bit and shakes his head.

What Rhodes thinks shouldn't affect me. It shouldn't matter. But the weight of his obvious disapproval rests on my mind.

"You think it's silly or something? I've known him since I was little. He's one of my best friends. Having that close friendship turn into dating is a pretty awesome place to start a relationship."

He leans closer to me, just enough that I notice, but not enough that I pull away. "Don't you want to experience more?"

"Yes." *I want Columbia. Maybe a little bit of you…* Guilt hits my stomach like a brick. I shouldn't have even let the *thought* of Rhodes formulate. I shouldn't have answered yes to his question. Elias deserves better.

He jerks his head my way, his eyes widened in surprise. "Then why…?"

"I got into Columbia," I blurt out and then slap my hand over my mouth.

"What?" His whole face lightens. He pushes off the stall and scoots until he's cross-legged and facing me. "You got in to Columbia? From *here*?"

I nod again. The reality of me having a chance to go to *that* school is just…

Rhodes laughs. "We *could* be in the same classes!"

I shake my head before closing my eyes.

"What's that, Clara?" he asks. "How are you not jumping up and down? Is it a money thing?"

I shake my head. "I know it would be tight, but Mom and Dad have always saved for me. I think, with some student loans, it could be doable."

"Clara. I mean…*wow.*"

I finally open my eyes. "I can't go. Not this year."

Rhodes snorts. "Uh…why not? Why would you jeopardize your chances? Not all deferments are accepted, you know. You have to have a really good reason."

"I'm..." I swallow. I don't know how to tell Rhodes that there's no way I can go there looking the way I do. "I just have things to do first."

"Does this have to do with Elias?" he asks with so much disdain and contempt that I push to standing.

"No!" I press my hands to my heated cheeks. "No. You wouldn't understand."

Rhodes is in front of me, bent forward to look in my eyes. I want him to look smug or annoyed, but instead his brow is all wrinkled with worry. "Clara?"

I blink because I'm once again standing in front of Rhodes in the barn and now I'm almost *crying*. "I have homework."

He frowns. "I wish you'd tell me what the hang-up is so I can help. Columbia might not be for everybody, but Clara...I think I know you well enough to know how much you'd absolutely *love* it. Think about what it would be like to go to school with people who do the required reading for fun."

Amazing.

"I have to go." I step around him and start for the barn door, heart pounding.

"It's a big deal to get in, Clara. Someone saw something in you. Don't let them down."

It's too much. I have Elias. I love him. I have a dad to prepare for my departure. I have a face to fix...

Someone saw something in you...Don't let them down...

My stomach tightens as if it's trying to squeeze me in half. I should have never applied a year early. I turn and face him. "I'll figure it out."

He cocks a brow like he's not sure what to do with me. "If you say so."

At least he says "if you say so" when that's what he means.

"I do."

Rhodes shrugs. "Okay then."

Okay.

Only something tells me this is going to come up again, and I may need a better answer.

11

The rows of wooden pews at my church have started to blend together as my blinks get slower. I've been playing sick for enough days that I'm not about to ask Dad if I can skip. Elias has been so busy at work that we've barely spoken since my near pass-out at his house. I'm afraid to think of what it might mean if he's avoiding me, even though I'm "sick" to avoid him—at least while I try to sort out what I'm feeling.

I stare at the second hand of the clock that sits high on the wall, achingly traveling from one number to the next. The speaker today is one of the old, white-haired guys. He's nice enough and I'm pretty sure their family is loaded, but he always looks like he took a trip through the washing machine in his suit before coming to church.

I've flipped through the hymn book, slid through the pages in my scriptures, tried counting the number of people sitting in the pews but got bored at fifty, and anyway, there are a lot of little kids moving around.

How is Dad even focusing? Better question. Why didn't I pull the girl-problem card and stay home today?

I glance at Dad to see if we can give a mutual eye roll at a talk I feel like I've heard a million times, but Dad's blotting tears from the corners of his eyes.

What am I missing?

Don't get me wrong, Dad tearing up in church isn't all that unusual. In fact, it's a near-weekly occurrence, but for this? All I know is that I'm pretty sure Jesus's name was mentioned and I think there was a story about a hunting trip the guy took. The rest sort of went over my head.

I'm dying.

Seriously *dying* of boredom. I lean my head down to cover my face with my hair better and try to scan the room to see if anyone else is as bored as me. Sadly, the only company in my boredom is very small children. I wish Cecily were here. This is when I should pull out my scriptures and read, or try to think deeply about my life and the decisions I have to make, but it seems like all I'm doing is making decisions, or at least being faced with them. This meeting is normally my break and reset time, but today it's just not working for me.

I stare at my feet and tap the toes of my ballet flats together. Then twist my hair with a finger. Suddenly I hear the words that signify the end of his talk.

"Amen."

Whew. Survived. Still awake.

Sunday school is Old Testament studies, and instead of following along in the lesson, I read in Psalms. The rhythms of the words and the interesting thoughts bounce in my brain, settle my heart, and help me remember why I come to church in the first place.

* * *

"You seem distracted," Dad says. He holds the passenger door open for me after church. He's done this since I was a kid, and I went through a phase where I thought his overt politeness was stupid. But Suki pointed out that Dad lost his wife, and I'm his little girl, and sometimes we let people do nice things because it makes them feel better. It isn't always about the person on the receiving end. I guess she has a point.

"Maybe a little distracted." I give him a noncommittal shrug.

"A lot distracted since you and Elias went out the other night."
Dad walks around the front of the car, and I notice his graying hair and
growing belly in a little different light. My dad looks...older. Noticeably.
Like I can remember a time when he barely had any gray, and it doesn't
feel like that long ago.

A fluttering panic beats in my chest as Dad slides in the driver's
seat. "Well?"

"Senior year. Just busy. Getting over being sick." *Fake sick.* I blink a
few times, wishing for his age to fade.

It doesn't.

Dad looks at me sideways as he turns on the car. "Don't think for a
minute I don't know you use 'just busy' as an excuse."

Well, crap. "I'm good, Dad."

He gives my knee a quick squeeze. "Well, okay. I wanna stop by your
mom's grave today. You up for that?"

No, I'm not up for that. She's gone. She's gone and I don't get to talk
to her or get her help or..."Yeah, of course."

Dad slides the car into reverse and we move out of the parking lot.
"I wanted to ask you..."

I wait. And wait. And tap my fingers against my skirt and then stare
out the window...

"Two things, I guess." Dad's hands tighten on the steering wheel.
"Mr. Kennedy is..."

The car clunks over the uneven pavement as we wind through the
trees, and Dad doesn't speak.

"Get it out, Dad. You can do it," I tease, wondering if I should have kept
my mouth shut or had a pretend coughing fit to avoid the conversation.

"I want to know if you and Elias are being careful." The words blur
together in Dad's nervousness.

I can totally feel my brows rising, and I'm once again holding my breath—sort of counterintuitive when I'm trying to make myself sound relaxed. "Um…shoulders to knees and everything in between, Dad. Elias and I are okay."

And I'm still not sure how I feel about that.

Dad shrinks about three inches as he relaxes. "I also want to know if it's awkward for you to have your teacher over at our house so much. I just remember being that young and on my own, and he's in a town he's never been to before so I thought it would help if he felt like he had people."

"I know why you've invited him over." It's so like my dad to take in the new stranger in town.

Tapping my fingers on the window, I watch the trees blur by as we wind our way up the road to the cemetery.

"So…Kennedy?" Dad asks. "Is it okay, or should we slow down the dinners?"

My heart does a fantastic *ka-thump*. "Why do you ask?"

"When you leave for the barn, he stands up so fast that he nearly knocks his chair over. Don't get me wrong. I really like Rhodes. I just want to make sure that nothing is awkward. I also might be seeing things that aren't there."

"Oh." Huh. "No, um. No weirdness. I mean…like you said, he's my teacher, and he's hanging at our house a lot, but it's fine. I mean…" Why must my brain be farting out now? How many times have we tossed out the fact that he's my teacher? "I mean it's totally fine. He lost his brother and likes to talk, so he follows me. That's all." *Is it?*

"Relax, honey." Dad flicks on the stereo. "I was just curious. I'm glad you've found a friend in him because it might be good for you to know some people who aren't from here. I'm just giving you a hard time."

And there's no way to hide the rush of my relief breath, which earns me a sideways smile from Dad. He sees way too much.

"You and Cecily decide on Anchorage or Fairbanks for school in the fall?" he asks.

Oh. Right. "Cecily's going to New York." *This fall. Like a traitor to our plan.*

"Sorry, hon." Dad pats my knee. "I wrote out a few checks for out-of-state college applications. You heard back from any of those places yet?"

I hold my breath. I could tell him about Columbia. I totally could. He'd be proud. We're about to go visit Mom. Timing is good. "Nope."

Dad nods in this odd, distracted way. I'm not sure what he'd say to my acceptance. He'd probably panic.

We pull into the small, empty parking lot of the cemetery. The grass is still yellowed from winter, and the leaves have tinged the branches slightly green, but the drab brown covers the landscape. At least the headstones aren't buried in four feet of snow and drifts like they are for most of the winter.

We move slightly uphill until we pass the third bench, then we take a right onto the grass. Dad grasps my hand and gives me a squeeze. "You have to miss her," he says.

I swallow, my palms sweaty. I take back my hand. "Of course." *I also wish I could tell her that I got into her school. In person.*

"Especially now."

Folding my arms, I ask, "Why especially?"

He chuckles. "Because I'm not a good sounding board for clothes and boys and all that."

"I have Cecily." But I'm swallowing the familiar lump of emptiness, sadness, and that horrid pit of *loss*. "And I don't care about clothes." There's no point in dressing nice when what I wear can't change my face.

We stop. Her simple stone stands about waist high, and seeing the words of her name, her birth, her *death*…it's as if someone's etched them into my skin. Like every time I'm faced with this place.

I. Hate. It. Here. My heart is once again stuffed into that too-small box.

Dad closes his eyes and touches the cold stone, like he does every time we come. I'm pretty sure I should feel something more than the gut-wrenching, heart-squeezing I do. Some sort of peace or closeness, but I don't. Never have. She's not here.

I wait for Dad to finish, for him to blot his eyes and take my hand again. "You're unusually quiet."

"Am I?" I ask.

We walk back toward the car in silence. The blue sky stretches to the mountaintops, and the faint rush of the river reverberates through the trees. When the inevitable breeze blows, it hits the back of my neck, making me shiver. The glacier air is biting, even in summer.

Dad unlocks the car and I slide in, letting out a breath I didn't know I held. I've been doing that a lot lately, which probably says something about my stress level.

"Do you ever…" But I stop. What if Dad's answer is yes? If it works for him and not me?

"Ever what?"

"Ever hear her. Mom. Like…feel like you can talk to her."

"No. Maybe sort of."

I press my hand to my chest as the relief leaves a numbness in my body. "Oh."

"I remember the feel of her. Of being around her." He makes a frowning sort of smile. "So sometimes I probably pretend I can talk to her without realizing it. I talk to her out loud when I'm working on the plane sometimes. It helps."

"I remember the feeling of her too." I wish I could close my eyes and feel that, but it doesn't happen often. Maybe because I don't take the time to. Maybe because it hurts too badly when I'm done. I'm not sure.

He pulls me into a sideways hug. "I don't know what I'd do without you, Clara."

And he won't have to worry about doing without me—at least not for a while. I glance at the face that seems to be aging even as I watch. No, it was good I didn't tell Dad about Columbia. I need to figure out what I'm doing first, *then* we can talk.

Dad doesn't say anything else as we follow the windy road back home, and I close my eyes in the passenger's seat. I'm battling on too many sides right now to try to talk through anything else.

12

I'm cataloging all the props, checking off lists for each character.

I slide all of "Teddy's" props to the right side of the backstage table and start matching objects with my list. My phone beeps with another text from Elias. I'm grinning like an idiot before I think to stop it because he rarely texts me when he's working.

Elias: We still on for later?

Clara: Come on over. Dad will be home. All okay.

"All okay" for both of us—for Elias because we won't be alone, and for me because he won't ask me anything crazy about houses or forevers in front of my dad.

When I set down my phone, Rhodes is watching me. The intensity of his gaze starts to warm and pool in my stomach. Abby stops next to me, and I snap back to reality.

"Is this my stuff?" Abby asks as she peers over my shoulder. Left side. This girl has never, ever approached me on my right.

"Yep."

"I'm an old lady, remember?"

"I know the play." I keep my voice even, despite the fact that I knew her lines before she did. Of course I know which character she is.

"I just mentioned that because I think I need a shawl, and—"

"Mrs. Craddle's nearly finished with one for you." I check off two more boxes. My job of collecting props is nearly over.

Abby glances toward Rhodes and then back toward me, but I continue scrolling down my list, unwilling to follow her gaze and add fuel to whatever delusion she has running through her head.

"Seriously?" Abby frowns. "It'll smell like dog. She has, like, eight of them, and Esther said she makes her own yarn out of dog hair."

Gross. But I'm not about to let on. "I gave her money for yarn, so I doubt that's the case." *Lie.* "But if you'd rather, you could go to the Salvation Army and pick up one that smells like old urine."

Rhodes snorts, Abby frowns, and then her eyes shift from me to him like three times before she moves away. As if I didn't already see her sideways glances.

It's not that I don't get along with Abby, but I have Elias when I'm at school and people to talk to when I'm at church. Cecily is almost home. I'm not about to open myself up to more scrutiny from Abby and Esther who can dish out more crap judgment than anyone else I know.

"Okay!" Mr. Kennedy calls. "You better have those lines memorized starting tomorrow. Go enjoy the sun!"

I want to drop everything and run outside, but I only have one more small section of prop table to cross off as finished and organized. The sounds of backpack zippers and clomping feet fill the small auditorium for about three minutes before I'm met with silence. So much better.

"Need any help?" Rhodes's kind, deep voice sets my nerves on edge because now we're alone. I really wish the aloneness didn't send my stomach into a flurry. But we were together in the barn and could talk…This should be fine. Maybe even nice.

"I'm good." I keep my eyes on the table and put down a few more small labels.

Teddy. Shovel.

"Your last paper was really good…It's college-level work. Easy. You're so ready for school."

I don't look up. "You said on the paper." I might sound like a brat right now, but I'm just not sure how to act around a teacher whose lips I watch too much.

"Did I do something to offend?" he asks.

I so wish he sounded condescending instead of genuine. Having him be worried isn't supposed to pool warmth in my stomach.

"I'm sorry." I finally look up at him and instead of seeing my teacher, I see the guy who sat next to me in the barn and told me about his little brother. I step closer before forcing my feet to stop.

The corners of his mouth are slightly turned down. "I'm about to sound like a cheesy commercial or something, but you seem… really distracted, and I just didn't know if it was something I could help with."

As a teacher? A friend? I have zero idea how to begin to decipher what he might want from me. "I'm good. Just a lot of decisions to be made, and that's sometimes hard to deal with." I move back to the table and check off another box on my prop list.

I know I sound like every other high-school senior stressing about what to do with my life, but maybe that's better. Rhodes is way too easy to be around for someone who has a boyfriend and is also *his student.*

"I can totally understand that." He folds his arms and leans against the table. "It's going to be a matter of figuring out what you want outside of what everyone else wants."

"No." I shake my head. "That's not it at all. Because when you love the people around you, your decisions and your future are not just about you, they're about them too."

"Maybe."

Pressing the pen against the paper, I mark off another box, ripping the paper. I take in a deep breath and my finger finds the scar that tugs on the corner of my mouth.

"Your scars…" His head cocks to the side as he unashamedly studies my face. "*They're* not slowing you down, are they?"

Heat rushes up my neck and I spin away from him, hating how quickly he understood this about me. I set my clipboard down and snatch my backpack from the floor, already moving for the back door. The idea of my scars making me afraid is something that cuts far too deep to discuss. A knife is lodged in the center of my chest, and we're just *talking*.

"Wait. Clara." He gently grabs my arm, and instead of shrugging away, I let the feeling of his energy soak through me as I turn to face him. His hand drops, and the loss of warmth is startling.

"If you don't know what you want for *you*, the people you love won't either. And if they're worthy of that love, of what you have to give, they'll want for you what you want for yourself. And the scars…"

"My face…I…I'll make some decisions after we see the plastic surgeon." That's the most honest answer I've given anyone. Maybe we *are* friends. Maybe I'm stupid for continuing to think of him as my teacher. I'm once again breathing in like it'll bring us closer, which is something I shouldn't be wanting or doing or thinking about.

"I know I'm a guy, so my opinion might not matter as much, but stand tall and own the scars, Clara. They're a part of your past, a part of your life experience, and part of who you are now." He leans against the doorframe, his blue eyes locked on mine. "Use them as ways of opening conversations. Use them to write. Or get them fixed. I mean, I'd totally get that. But let go of the idea you have in your head of…" He trails off, which maybe means that I'm shaking my head or frowning or crying and not even realizing it. "Let go of the idea that you should be without the marks that are part of you. I think for me, it adds to how interesting you are, so maybe my perception is warped."

I grit my teeth, but I'm determined to get out the words. "They're not *part* of me. They were *dug into me*." My eyes flutter a few times before the tears stop pressing into my eyes. I say nothing else. I have no more words.

He reaches for me again but stops and scratches his forehead. "I'm sure you think I'm a weirdo. I'm really usually better with people than this..." He waves his hand between us. "Than I am with you."

I know exactly what you mean. "It's fine. I'm probably going to go home and head out for a horse ride."

"Enjoy your ride. I'm on my own for dinner tonight, which means I'll probably hit McDonald's."

"Have fun with your heart attack." I wave as I try not to run for the door.

"Don't fall off the horse," he says back with a laugh.

Right. Because what would happen if I had more serious damage than I already do?

13

I step into the barn to see that Elias has saddled both Tori and Snoopy. The two horses stand in the middle tied to posts, while Elias runs his hand under the edge of the saddle blanket to make sure it lies right. Even with the horses he's careful.

Snoopy jerks his head my direction, probably wondering why I stopped in the doorway, and Elias turns. Guess we will be alone this afternoon, which is not at all what I planned.

"Oh. Shoot." He chuckles. "You're earlier than I expected."

"What…?" I'm not sure how I feel about Elias intruding on my quiet time until his arms come around me. The tension drains from my body.

"You've been distracted lately, and I know you're worried about your trip to Seattle. I thought this was a good way to fix both of those things."

I hold Elias. He knows me well enough that he's exactly right. A horse ride *is* the perfect thing. I need this. To sort of reconnect with him and myself. We've been…off…working on different rhythms.

My eyes fall closed, and I rest my face on his shoulder, feeling like maybe he'll be able to fill some of the hollowness in my heart.

His arms pull even tighter, crushing our bodies together. "Ready?" he whispers.

I don't move. "In a minute."

And that's when he really relaxes against me—our bodies, our hearts, our breathing. This is why Elias and I work.

* * *

Trees climb around us on every side, and the horses' hooves pad on the clay trail. The tiny buds of green have turned into full leaves almost overnight, adding a greenish tinge to the sunlight that reflects off the white bark of the birch trees. Days like today I'm so glad I don't remember walking with Mom when the bears came. Right now this trail is the exact kind of peace I've needed.

Elias nudges Tori next to Snoopy, and we ride in silence. Side by side. Like we've done a million times since we were kids. We round a corner, and the thick spruce trees block out even more light.

"It's so quiet," I whisper.

"Why we both love it here," he says.

He's right, but some days my head is so loud that I wish I could drown out the noise with something other than silence. It hits me then. Elias is quiet—the whole feel of him. Quiet in manner and spirit and thought. Rhodes screams. That's why I react to him. He's loud even when he isn't speaking. That's the rhythm of him. The meter.

An hour into our ride, a house begins to appear through the trees. "What is that?"

"That's my house." He grins over his shoulder.

"It's so much closer than I thought." He's a horse ride away from my dad's house, which means by four-wheeler, it would take no time at all. By road the trip is much longer. If I stayed here next year, it would be perfect. An hour horse ride, but probably only a few minutes on my four-wheeler.

"That's sorta perfect, huh?" I ask.

"I hoped you'd think so." Elias smiles again.

We stop the horses next to the house and tie reins to the trees.

Elias takes my hand and leads me into his house. The idea of him living in and owning a house is still so…permanent. And I want permanent. Eventually.

"Sheetrock's up. Paint will be next, but I'm slammed helping Dad frame in a few smaller places." Elias's excitement touches every word. He's proud of this place, and he should be. The angles and interesting cut of the stairs are very cool, and it's coming together fast.

He stops us in the living room, taking both my hands in his. "I love you. You know that, right?"

"I know that." My heart's thumping because the feeling between us is suddenly so…serious.

He breaks away and begins gesturing around the room. "So, picture wood floors and a wood stove in that corner, and—"

"So, really, we're right in front of the wood stove?" I ask, wondering what the weird serious moment was about and why his chatter feels so full of nerves.

"Yep."

"Sounds warm." I step closer to him and let his arms slide around me like I knew they would. Being alone with Elias is like heaven when he's not being weird about us being alone.

He lets out a long, slow breath. "I need to ask you something."

"Okay." I pull back and look over all the parts of his familiar face. Dark eyes, smooth lips.

"I love you. I can't imagine my life with someone else, Clara. And I've been saving and making money forever, and I'll be doing my own contracts as soon as I graduate, and…" He takes a few breaths in and out as his smile wavers. "I didn't think I'd be so nervous."

My chest seizes up. And in this split second I get what our afternoon is about. I'm thinking about too much. Dealing with too much to take on something else. He doesn't even know I got in to Columbia. He can't do this now. Not yet. Not…He's going to—

"Marry me, Clara. Please. I love you. I know we're so young, but I know you. I promise to take care of you. Marry me." He shuffles in his chest pocket and pulls out a diamond ring, holding it between us.

A ring. Final. Real. Permanent.

My head is so full that words keep coming.

Forever.

Change.

Same.

Stay.

Go.

Fight.

Relent.

Safe.

"This is big, Elias." I hold the ring between my fingers. A simple square diamond—perfect. And something he probably used up most of his savings for.

"I love you. I don't want to spend my life with anyone else, and I know we're young, but that doesn't change how I feel." His rough hands lightly grasp my shoulders, and the gravity of his words hang between us. "I've watched my parents be so happy, and my brother, and…I've known you for so long. I want that. With you."

"I just…college and…my stuff…" And all the difficult decisions I rambled on about to Rhodes earlier. Dad likes Elias, but I'm not sure how he'd feel about him as a son-in-law—at least not right now.

Elias rubs up and down my arms because he knows me well enough to know I'm freaking out a little. I'm sure my silence and the way I'm staring at this ring are sort of a dead giveaway.

"I know you have things you want to do, but we can do it all together. I'll help you do whatever you want, Clara. *Anything* you want. But I want you. Always."

The problem is I don't know what I want yet—at least not completely. My face needs to get fixed first, then I'll be able to think.

My mouth opens a few times, but no words come out. What could I possibly say to make this not happen? For us to be what we were before he pulled this ring from his pocket?

"Look." He folds the diamond back into his palm.

I swear I can hear how hard his heart is beating. Or maybe that's me. I have to say something. "I'm..."

"I've been thinking about this for a while, but you haven't. It's okay." His words tumble out. "You can think about it. I mean...you don't have to answer now."

I'm staring at the floor because I'm so confused. Completely... confused.

Elias lets out a defeated sigh, which feels like a knife driven into my heart. I don't want to hurt him. Without having the guts to look up, I pull him toward me. As my head rests against his hard chest I think about what it would be like to not have to be careful with Elias anymore. What it would be like to go to sleep with him at night and wake up with him in the morning and maybe be naked with him for some of that time in between, and my body shudders in anticipation at the thought of it.

"You'll think about it?" he asks.

"I'm thinking about it right now." I'm just not sure if I can give him an answer yet.

His arms tighten around me. "You know me, Clara. I know you. We can work through everything together. Live our lives together."

Elias would be everything. My life here would be everything. I *could* be okay with that. It's not like I *have* to go to Columbia to be a writer or

anything…and it's not like I couldn't do *some* of my adventures later…
But I think about the ring and Elias and the forever-ness of it, and my
face, and I need to make sure.

* * *

Dad's at the table with Suki when I step in the door. There are two
Subway bags in front of him. The laughter at the table feels jarring and
unsettles my already-scattered insides.

Elias and I rode back to the house in quiet and unsaddled the horses
in silence. The way he stared at the ground and the way his shoulders
stooped almost made me tell him yes before he drove away.

But I didn't. We hugged, which turned into him clutching me for a
moment before driving off.

I'm pretty sure I can't feel my limbs because I'm still in shock.

"Dinner?" I ask as I tap a Subway bag.

Dad nods once as his laughter dies down. "Hope that's okay. I was
down in Palmer today and picked up sandwiches."

"How are things, Clara?" Suki's smile is still so wide that I'm not
sure she'd hear me even if I answered. Her eyes are on Dad.

I clutch the bag in one hand and rest the other on the back of the
chair next to Dad. I could tell him what Elias wants. I could tell him
about Columbia. I could ask him for some kind of shield that would
enable me to not have to decide on anything until I'm ready. Suki
might have some kind of fantastic insights too.

"I have homework," I say before heading for the narrow stairs to
my room.

"Good to see you, Clara!" Suki calls behind me, laughter still raising
her voice.

I turn back just in time to see her rest her nose on Dad's cheek.

Laughter has died.

My heart flips over again at how close they're sitting. Best head upstairs.

I open my Subway bag, but food doesn't...I can't really feel my stomach so I have no idea if I'm hungry or not.

I'm still in shock. I guess that's what this weird, panicky feeling is. Writing will help me sort it all out. I snatch my notebook and flip it open to the next empty page.

My pencil makes little scratches in the margins, and I start to write a few times, but everything in me is too tight to let loose on paper. Two hours later I have a few stick figures and a wilty sandwich.

This has never happened before.

14

Not knowing what else to do with myself, I start on a walk from my house to the river. Five days ago Elias proposed, and for five days, I've joked around instead of answering or kissed him instead of answering or hugged him instead of answering...

All Cecily said was, *Yep, I figured he would*, which was completely unhelpful.

The muddy river is beginning to clear, and the rushing sound is as much a part of my childhood as my parents. Timson's large green warehouse and junkyard comes into view, the sun reflecting off the edges of the metal roof. As I get closer, I can see large, unnatural shadows cast through the trees, made by the old fairground rides left to die. The paint on the ancient Ferris wheel is faded reds, greens, and blues, the lightbulbs long since broken out. I wander between a few rows of rusted-out classic cars before stopping next to the ancient Tilt-A-Whirl. The apple-shaped cocoons are tipped at odd angles and frozen on a ride that won't move again.

This is a favorite spot of mine in the summer. The old rides lose something when buried in snow instead of warming with the sun, but today is perfect.

I sit in one of the large apples and give the wheel in the center a jerk, but the ride doesn't move.

Why don't I know what to do? Most people make goals. They work toward those goals. I had a plan, and…and my stupid idea to apply to Columbia threw everything off. And Elias threw everything off again by asking me to marry him while we're *still in high school!*

It's not like I'd be the first girl to get married right out of high school. I'm just not sure I'm *the right kind* of girl to get married right out of high school. Why did he have to ask *now?*

I rub my face, my left hand meeting smooth skin, my right hand traveling over hideous lumps and lines.

Mom would know what to say. What to tell me. Dad's advice would be so tainted with what he wants for me that I wouldn't know what to do with his words, and I'd just feel guiltier if I didn't choose what he suggested. But Mom? She was always one to jump in and move forward. She'd get it. Get *me.*

"I don't want to scare you, but—" Male voice. Close.

My heart flies into my throat. "Crap!"

Rhodes's laughter doesn't carry far. It's dimmed by the surrounding dead grass and the small field of broken toys. He's leaning against the rails of the ride.

I quickly pull my hair back over my face, and my chest weighs down. "What are you doing out here?" I snap.

He holds up a camera half the size of my head. "And you?"

"Thinking." I pause, narrowing my eyes. "Alone."

"And now you don't have to think alone." He grins, steps onto the ride, and swings his legs over the railing.

In this moment I should stand up and walk away. There's no reason Rhodes and I should be sitting here and talking. At the same time, I find my body relaxing further into the old seat as he sits opposite me. The energy around him changes a little each time we're together. Or maybe it's my energy that's changing, making us on a much closer path than we should be.

I can't let that happen. I have too much confusion already.

"Rumor mill says your boyfriend proposed." A corner of Rhodes's mouth pulls into a partial smile.

I shiver as the morning chill weaves through my light coat.

"Rumor mill?" I cock a brow. "Does anyone use that expression anymore?"

"Just me, I guess." He smirks. "Was he serious?"

"Elias is always serious, but I'm a little curious about where you got your information. You should probably say something like you were having breakfast at the diner, and the owner of the diner goes shooting with the guy who was getting his watch fixed at the jewelry store, and you heard someone talking…"

Oh, crap. I have to tell Dad before he hears it from somewhere else.

"Nope, but you're close. Abby and Esther were whispering about it after school because Esther's dad owns the jewelry store."

"Oh. Normally they're chatting about how Elias deals with my hideous face. I'm sure they'll be *thrilled* to know you were listening in."

He rolls his eyes. "You never answered my question. And I've never heard them whisper about your face, on top of which, I can't fathom how you could use the word 'hideous' in association with how you look. You're scarred, but not hideous."

I ignore his comment about my face. "Does this answer your question?" I hold my bare hand up between us.

He shrugs. "Not really."

"I should get home." I let out a sigh. My life would be so much easier if he'd never come.

"How does Elias feel about you going to Columbia? You're running out of time to give them your answer. Is your dad excited?"

"I…I haven't told them." I've told Rhodes and Cecily. That's it.

"Why haven't you told anyone?" He leans toward me. "You got into an *Ivy League school* from Knik, Alaska."

Rhodes can't understand a tenth of what I'm facing. I'd feel a million miles out of my league at Columbia, but going to that school, or any big school, with my horrid face and small-town Alaska-girl writing? Who would bother trying to look past my face?

"I did tell Cecily. And there was no point in even telling her because if I go, I'm going to go a year later when my face is fixed!" My breath comes hard and fast, echoing in the small space.

He shakes his head and frowns like *he's* frustrated with *me*. "Excuses. Maybe you don't deserve to go there." He stands and starts walking for the railing.

Rage breaks through every feeling I've been dealing with, and the heat of it takes over. "Stop being an asshole to me, okay?"

Rhodes faces me and smiles like I didn't just yell at him. "I like you, Clara. You're a cool person. And I think that right now, someone has to be an asshole so you don't dig yourself into a situation you can't get out of."

Likes me? Being an ass to help? "Don't think that by saying you like me, it'll make me listen. I can make my own decisions about my *own* life."

He chuckles, wags his brows, and then just turns and walks away.

Rhodes might be the most irritating person who ever existed.

15

Elias kisses me again as I push on his chest so he'll leave. But my back is against the side of the house, Elias's front is against my front, and the familiar ache of tightened *want* pulses through me, clutching my fingers more tightly around the fabric of his shirt. Why does Elias have to think beyond this? Why does he have to want more than what we have?

"I gotta finish dinner," I plead but can't stop smiling.

"And I can't stay?"

"Suki's coming over tonight." And Rhodes, who I don't mention. And who I don't really want to see after what he said to me yesterday.

"Then it would be perfect." Elias nips at my lower lip.

"Maybe next time." I kiss him again, loving that we're in the playful moment instead of the pressure of the decision…But I feel his mood change as his movements slow.

"You're still thinking, right?" he whispers. "Because I'm trying not to be terrified it's taking you so long."

I stare at our feet on the porch, the playful mood twisting into the fear of forevers. "I'm still thinking."

"I love you."

"You know…you know that I want to go to college." *Maybe in New York. And maybe the idea of getting married starts that whole permanent thing so soon, which has me freaked out…*

His grip tightens on my sides. "Of course I know," he whispers. "I know you. I love you. We can do anything."

Elias bends forward, and his lips touch my lips only briefly before his tongue slides against mine. This kiss isn't hesitant or careful. It's full of the need and want that have held my body captive for a very long time. His arms wrap around me, pressing us as tightly together as we were when he lay on top of me.

And then the next second, his mouth is gone. "Good." And then his body is gone.

And his warmth. And presence. But not the thickness of desire that comes from kissing him.

He spins away and jogs toward his truck, leaving me with rubber legs, leaning against my house.

I suck in a deep breath to try to recover from all the swoony kissing as Elias pulls out of the driveway.

Okay. Dinner.

My fingers still feel weak as I slip open the front door, and I freeze at the sight of Dad and Suki embracing in the dining room. His lips on hers.

My hands shake as I slowly close the door again and just stare at it. I'm not sure what to think. I like Suki. I want Dad happy. I just...

"Hey," Rhodes hollers from somewhere behind me, and I jump.

I spin around to see him walking from the direction of the barn.

"How did you get here?" I ask when what I'm really wondering is *when* he got here.

"Four-wheeler. Very rugged of me, right?" He continues walking my way. "I'm conforming to your small-town ways already. You and Elias were making out when I pulled in, so you didn't notice, and I was nice enough to give you some privacy."

"Since when is staring from across the yard giving someone privacy instead of stalking them?" I turn for the door. Getting into an argument with Rhodes is not a routine I want established—especially with nearly four weeks left in the school year.

And then I stop. Dad and Suki are in there. *Kissing.*

"How long you gonna keep that boy waiting?"

"I don't know what you're talking about." I rest against the door and cross my arms.

"Don't think I don't know what's going on here." He looks so freaking smug with an eyebrow cocked up slightly and that ridiculous partial smile on his face.

"Mind reader, are you?" I snap.

"Just a good observer, that's all," he says as he steps up next to me. "We going in?"

Right. They can't *still* be kissing. I push open the door to see...no one. Maybe they moved into the living room. I kick off my shoes and head for the kitchen.

I can't hold Elias off forever, I'm sick of Rhodes's form of honesty, and Dad, and...Too much.

I ignore Rhodes and start pulling out the lunch meat and special cheese Dad got for baked sandwiches. A simple dinner tonight since we're leaving for Seattle in a couple days and I want to use up our groceries.

"Wanna know what I observe?" he asks.

"I just want to throw out there that you're way too comfortable in my house, and no, I do not want to know what you *observe*." I grab the hoagie rolls from the cabinet and start to fold them open so I can add ingredients, trying to ignore him. "Besides, I think you made yourself pretty clear the other day. And I thought I made it pretty clear that you're being an...an...an..."

"Asshole. Yes, I remember that." Rhodes doesn't even pause before continuing. "I think he's comfortable for you. I think you love him, or you like him a lot. There's no doubt he's in love with you. And I think part of you wants to say yes because it means you'll be safe. That everything about your life will be safe." He pauses for a moment, and then his tone turns serious. "That world out there seems too scary right now, but—"

Anger builds to bursting at how patronizing he is. I spin to face Rhodes, shutting him up. "Nothing in life is safe, Rhodes. *Nothing!*"

His eyes widen a bit as he takes a step back, but I don't stop.

"Look at my face." I tilt my face and pull up my hair so he can get a full view of my scars. Then turn farther and tug the back of my shirt down just far enough for him to see they continue down my back. "My mom and I went for a walk behind the house like we'd done a million times before. On foot, on a four-wheeler, on a snow machine, on horse-back, and this time there happened to be a bear out there.

"I survived. Mom didn't. So don't you *dare* lecture me about how staying here is safe. And don't you dare lecture me like I'm a kid when everything else you've said around me says you don't see me that way."

Nothing but my angry breathing echoes in the kitchen for a moment as Rhodes's face softens.

"I'm sorry."

"Whatever." I spin back to the stove just as Dad steps into the kitchen.

"All okay?" he asks.

My cheeks flush and my stomach seizes up. Every time I have to talk about Mom in the past tense I also have to remember that I used to have a mom and don't anymore. Dad kissing Suki is like screaming at me that Mom's gone. Tears begin to burn at the edges of my eyes, but I can't cry right now. Not in front of Rhodes.

"You okay?" Rhodes rests his hand on my shoulder.

"I have no idea."

His other hand rests on my other shoulder, and he gives me a light squeeze that I feel shoot through my body to my toes.

"I didn't mean to upset you. Crap, Clara. I'm sorry. I'm really—"

"It's not that." I drop the cheese and glance up at Dad.

"You okay?" Dad asks.

"I'm gonna do homework." And I charge out of the kitchen and run up the steep steps to my small room and shut the door.

The image of Dad and Suki is imprinted. I thought I was okay with this. The feeling of Rhodes's hands on my shoulders is imprinted. The way Elias felt pushing his hips against me is imprinted.

I have to sort this all out. Have to.

My stomach growls as I sit on my bed, and even though I feel a little sick at having too many things running through me, I really should have at least brought up a piece of bread. There's no way I can go back down after that exit.

16

I zip my small suitcase for Seattle closed with trembling fingers. Everything changes for me. So soon. Two days ago Elias begged for an answer, Rhodes got in my face, and I watched Dad take another big step forward with Suki. And for two days I've once again just gone through the motions.

I walk down the stairs, slide on my boots, and head for the barn.

The short walk slows my heart, and the moment the dusty smell of hay and horses hits my nose, everything in me shifts and I draw in a deep breath. Hand over hand, I climb up the ladder into the loft and dial Cecily. Dad was worried about my outburst in the kitchen, so it took me forever to convince him that I'm just tired.

Rhodes can't keep his opinions to himself. Elias won't be put off much longer. I'm about to meet the doctor who will change my life.

Every day I feel like I'm walking the edge of a cliff, and I don't know if I'm supposed to run from the edge or jump off.

We leave for Seattle tomorrow. Maybe that's my jump. Or maybe I'll just feel like the edge is even closer and I'm running even faster.

"Hey!" Cecily screeches into the phone. "How are you? One more week and I'll be there!!"

Finally. "That's it?" I ask.

"That's it."

I flop onto the floor of the loft and release a breath.

"What's up? Sounds like a lot."

"A way lot." We rehash Elias's proposal, and how I love him but it's so permanent. And Rhodes, and how confused I am when he's around, making him…whatever he is to me, but that I can't get him out of my head. And Dad kissing Suki, which I knew was coming but is still weird. And I still haven't figured out Columbia. Or told Elias any one of a lot of things I should be talking to him about.

"I'm just…" I close my eyes. "I feel like my life will restart after Seattle, and then I'll be able to make decisions. But before that…"

"Head is too loud. Isn't that what you say?" she teases.

"Definitely too loud," I agree.

"Mom's telling me to get off the phone, but I'll be there soon!"

"See ya."

Only neither of us hangs up. Nothing feels resolved, I guess.

"Hang in, Clara. It'll all sort itself out."

"Yeah, maybe." I don't really see how. I hit End wishing she was here *now* instead of "soon."

I slide my phone back into my pocket without getting up and push the hair off my face. There's too much in my heart at the moment for me to know what's right for me.

"You must miss your friend." Rhodes's voice echoes in the barn, and I sit up in the loft, heart thumping.

"How long have you been here?" *Did you hear what I said about you?*

He slides his hands in his pockets and glances down guiltily. "Long enough."

"For…?" I start down the ladder, even though I sort of want to hide in the corner. "Do you know that it's once again sort of creepy super-stalking to be listening in?"

He sighs. "I *should* have left. For sure. I'm sorry. I know none of this is my business, but I was here long enough to know how the Elias thing is going to play out."

This is none of his business. *Zero*. He always seems to be around at just the wrong times saying just the wrong things.

I'm suddenly so infuriated that I step toward him, shoulders tight, hands in fists. "Don't act like you're watching from the sidelines, knowing what'll happen!"

Rhodes holds his hands up between us. "Hey. I'm just here. Not my fault if you're reading too much into it."

"Bullshit." I push him. "If you wanna come in here and play predictions, you can go to hell."

He lets himself take a step backward, still holding his hands in the air between us. "Big words coming from the Mormon girl."

"Why are you being such an ass about this?" I ask, breathing hard. "*Why?*"

He freezes and stares.

I don't freeze. I keep on ranting. "Because I cannot fathom how *anything* I do with my life could be *any* part of your business."

His jaw tightens as he steps close enough that he has to look down at me. Close enough that I feel his breath on my forehead. The warmth of his body. His nearness sends a tingle low in my stomach.

"Because it'll be my turn to call 'bullshit' if you don't feel something here. This is not something I expected to happen. But Clara… you're stubborn and amazing. Nobody's made me stumble over my words. Ever. And you do."

I blink. "What?"

"You're terrifying, Clara. You're uncertain but certain. You're so… amazingly strong…I can't tell you how intimidating you are, and that doesn't happen to me often."

"I'm not following." At all. He's describing someone else. My heart slams into my ribs at how close we are. At how our breath mixes between us.

He's so still and quiet and serious. "I wish I were here every night. And you shouldn't be thinking about wearing Elias's ring if you're conflicted. Even if you're not conflicted, you have so much life to live before you settle down like that. I heard you on the phone with your friend. I'm not in this alone."

He touches the center of my chest, and I bat his hand away, not wanting to let the idea sink in that he feels the same as me.

He feels the same as me.

He likes me. For real. Not in my imagination, or not me thinking, *Is he flirting with me?* but actually. For real. Older. Cooler. *Columbia.* All the beat poetry and quirky rhythms, and everything I want to be.

I step closer, rest my hands on the chest I'm still staring at, and feel his heart thumping as fast as mine.

"I should go," he whispers but doesn't move. "I shouldn't have listened in. I shouldn't *care* so much."

He should go. So should I. I should be running out of this barn and away from this guy who is so much older and more experienced and... *frustrating.* But instead I lift my eyes to his, and this time when I breathe in, I don't stop my body from leaning closer.

He tips his head down and his lips lightly brush mine, sending a wave of tingles from my lips into my chest that spread through my body and warm me from core to limbs.

We hover just inches apart until I close the distance again.

He rests his hand behind my neck. His kiss slides its way through my body and curls my toes and turns my legs to rubber. My hands find their way to his shaggy hair, and I thread my fingers through it, holding us together. Am I a masochist? An idiot? Do I want something from my boyfriend he won't give me, even though it's definitely not something I should want?

Want, want, want is all that runs through my head.

We stumble twice until my back is against the stall door, and I need him to push harder, kiss me harder, but I don't know if it's possible. His chest is on mine and our stomachs are together, and his hips keep us pinned tightly, sending a rush of perfect heat up my body. Rhodes pauses long enough to slide his mouth down my neck and reality hits. My body freezes.

This is not my boyfriend. I love my boyfriend.

Rhodes pulls away first, his forehead wrinkled in confusion. "I–I'm sor-sorry." He stumbles over his words. "I shouldn't have…Not with who I am…The school…your dad…I'm sorry."

He backs away from me still staring, and I'm left with my arms at my sides, knowing I just broke about a million rules. Rules that have to do with what I believe and what the school would think and what Elias deserves.

"I should go," he says just before disappearing out the door.

How did I let this happen?

My fingers come to my lips, rubbing lightly where Rhodes's mouth touched mine. When did I turn into the kind of person who would do this?

A simple phrase runs through my head again and again as I stare at the open door.

Torn between two
when loving just one.
My heart lies in pieces
before life's begun…

Now what do I do?

17

Dad shoves his hands in his jeans' pockets as we walk up the crowded sidewalk. The one-way streets in this part of Seattle are a bit maze-like, but Siri seems to know where we need to be.

"We should have said a prayer when we parked the car," Dad says quietly.

I tug my bangs down. Try not to make eye contact with anyone we pass. I can't handle stares this morning. New York would be a million times worse—at least until my scars are gone. I really need to work on what to tell Columbia. Soon.

"Clara?" he asks.

"I'm fine," I say.

"You're not fine." We walk a few steps in silence. "You've been quiet and detached and…I keep hoping it's just this upcoming trip, but…"

"Elias proposed." I'm not sure how those words escaped my mouth, but he knows now.

Dad stumbles once. "Elias—"

"And I got into Columbia."

"Wait, *what*?"

"And I saw you and Sukiniq. Kiss." I don't slow. Don't speed. Just keep putting one foot in front of the other.

"Clara," Dad says slowly. "Stop."

The moment I stop, someone bumps into my shoulder. Dad tugs my arm so we're both standing next to a red brick building. He leans toward me, his eyes flooding with worry. "I don't know where to start. Why didn't you tell me any of these things?"

I fold my arms. "I dunno," I mumble.

And then he smiles. "I'm so proud of you. Your mom's school, huh?"

Mom's school. I can't think about Mom now. Cannot. I just shake my head as my throat swells. "You and Suki, huh?"

A corner of Dad's mouth twitches. "Took me long enough, but yeah."

"We're going to be late," I say and turn to keep walking.

"I'm...What do you want?" Dad asks. "What are you going to do? What did you tell Elias?"

"Nothing. I can't...I can't talk about this yet."

"When you're ready."

I nod.

We pause at a set of double doors. Dad checks the address, and I follow him inside. I barely breathe as he checks me in and we're led down a hallway into a massive office. Dad casts too many glances my way as we go. The nurse leaves us alone with a practiced smile.

"You can go to Columbia," Dad says. "I'll miss you terribly and it won't be easy, but we can make it happen."

Not yet. "Was just curious, Dad. And I really, really don't want to talk about any of this right now."

Dad and I sit in leather chairs in an office that's at least five times the size of my bedroom. Diplomas cover one wall, books another. Nerves dance so forcefully through my body that I'm concentrating just to breathe. *In...out...in...out...*

My fingers find the familiar lines on my face. I can feel Dad's eyes on me. Feel his concern wafting around him. I drop my hand and stare at my lap. I should be excited. Bouncing in my seat. Instead my stomach's turning over all the things I wish I wasn't dealing with on top of this appointment.

Dad swallows again. Hard. Doesn't speak. He blinks a few times. His arm comes around me, and his fingers squeeze a little too tight on my shoulder.

"That day...I'm so sorry, Clara. I'm so sorry I didn't get there sooner. Didn't know...I could have stopped the bear. I could have..." He tightens his arm again, his breath shaky and his eyes fixed on the wall in front of us. Maybe I should have asked to come alone.

Mom.

I need my mom here. I needed her when I woke up bandaged in the hospital, I wanted her when Elias gave me my first kiss, and I need her now when I'm about to talk to a doctor who can maybe change some of my life back to how it was before.

I swipe a tear off my cheek.

Mom is not what I want to think about. I need to focus on me and my scars, and how we're going to fix them. My fingers trace the outside edge of the notebook tucked into my back pocket.

"We have a lot to talk about," Dad whispers.

"Maybe," I whisper back. *Just not now.*

"Sorry to keep you waiting." A quiet voice penetrates the near silence in the room. A small man, probably mid-thirties, closes the door behind him and takes a seat in another chair facing us. Even with the furniture arranged like a living room, there's no disguising that this is a doctor's office.

"I'm Thomas." Dad reaches out his hand and Dr. Breckman shakes it.

Mine are so tucked into my sides that I don't think to put my hand out until Dr. Breckman is already facing me, waiting.

"And you're Clara."

"Hi," I mumble.

He studies my face, tilting his head to the side and scooting his chair closer.

"May I?" He reaches forward and I sit still, letting his too-soft fingers touch my face. Elias's calluses are familiar; this is…foreign. As foreign as the office and the city and the situation.

Dr. Breckman lets out a breath, sits back, and starts to look more like a person than the doctor whose website I've stared at too much.

"So?" I ask.

"So, I'm glad you came."

I sit silently.

"What do you envision happening?" He gives me a relaxed smile. "I'm assuming you came here to see what I can possibly do for you. So in your dream scenario, what would you like to see happen?"

"I want you to fix my face."

"And what does 'fix' mean to you?" he asks.

Dad shifts in his seat. Lets out another shaky breath.

"Fix." That should be obvious enough. "Make me look like I'm supposed to. Like I *should*."

"Scoot forward," he asks.

I do. He slips on glasses, and his soft fingers smooth over my scars again. My heart starts beating in my throat.

His mouth twitches, turning into a slight frown before he leans back. "You have hypertrophic scarring. Do you know what that means?" His soothing voice scratches on me like fingernails on a chalkboard.

"It means my scars are raised." My voice sounds pinched and foreign.

He nods. "And that very often comes with the darker color."

"Like mine." Like all the things he's supposed to make go away.

My lower lip trembles and I suck it into my mouth, biting down to hold it still.

"I'm going to be very honest here because the last thing I want is for you to have expectations that we simply cannot meet." His hands clasp together. "But I can help. I promise."

My skin pricks with heat. I stay silent. If acid wasn't rolling in my stomach, I'd feel detached from my body.

"I reviewed the pictures you sent. You don't seem as concerned about the scars on your side and back."

I shake my head.

"Breathe." His smile widens as he leans forward, resting his elbows on his knees. There's an odd, watchful quality to the way he's looking at me. "I said I can help."

"How?" Dad asks. "Wh…what can you do?"

Dr. Breckman clears his throat. "We can do skin grafts, but they're not perfect. And I for sure wouldn't recommend doing everything at once. We'll want to see how one set of scars heals before we attempt the others—at least that's how I've found the most success."

He pauses and glances back and forth between us a few times. "Are we okay?"

No. I've been waiting. *i*'ve been waiting for years for this, and now he's talking about doing one small part—and then how long will I have to wait?

"If you decide to go the grafting route, several surgeries will be involved, and we'll be trying to make that skin blend into your facial skin, which will have scars of its own."

He pauses again.

"Just spit it all out, please," I choke. *More scars?*

"Clara." He clasps his hands together.

Dad rests an arm over me.

"I'm sorry," Dr. Breckman says. "I know I'm not telling you what you want to hear. But I wouldn't be doing you a service if I lied and said I could make your scarring disappear. I can't. You'll have new scars instead of your old ones. They'll be smaller, less noticeable, but that's all we can do."

My lower lip starts to shake.

"For the grafts…" he starts and then continues when neither Dad nor I stop him. "We'd cut out scar tissue, possibly filling in some, adding tissue." He pauses again. "With all of that work, there is no way to make skin appear as if it had never been touched. We can make a difference, but you cannot expect perfection. And this isn't something that's going to happen with just one surgery. Maybe not with just two. We'll have to see how well your body accepts what we're trying to do."

Every sentence is saying the same thing over and over, nailing the same words into my brain.

He. Can't. Fix. Me.

"So." Dad sits up a little straighter, his arm still resting around me.

The doctor uses a flashlight pen to highlight my face as he talks. "I'd suggest we start the skin graft with that outer corner of your eye. After the first attempt, we can take a break and decide what you'd like to work on next, or"—he frowns, but maybe realizes he can't just stop mid-sentence—"if you'd rather stop at that point, we can see what happens with some upscale microdermabrasion and bleaching creams."

Microdermabrasion? Like stuff you get at the drugstore? Seriously? That's a half step up from doing *absolutely nothing*. How can that be his recommendation?

Dad scoots forward in his chair. "How…um…You'd take skin from somewhere else?"

The doctor nods. "Very common. We usually take a small piece from the thigh." He points to my eye. "There's so little needed here between your eye and your hairline that you'll barely notice that small graft. And even the corner of your mouth wouldn't be—"

"This is *nothing*," I say. "You're talking about this one little spot. We're talking about maybe *months* and several surgeries or…"

The doctor nods and sits back again. "I don't believe in giving false hope to people, Clara. I also think that some minor bleaching by a good dermatologist could help with the discoloration. We can do a lot. I just…I don't want you to think it'll happen fast, and I don't want you to think that I won't try everything I can. But the reality is that without some kind of new technology, I can't make your scars disappear to the point where your skin looks as if nothing touched it. I'm very good at what I do, but I'm not a magician."

"I was told…" My chin quivers, my lip quivers, and my fingertips rub against each other as if the movement will keep me grounded. "I was told after it happened that I should wait until I was eighteen, or close to eighteen. Until I was done growing and my scars had taken time to heal. That someone would be able to fix them."

He watches me with the same relaxed intensity he has had since walking in the room. "I can minimize your scars. But we need to ask— is the minimization of your scars worth what we'll do to your body in the process? That's going to be up to you. I say we should plan on the lip, maybe the outer corner of your eye, and I can get you in touch with Dr. Mickelson in Anchorage who could help smooth over the scarring from the surgeries and maybe lighten some of the redness. Once we spend a year on that route, you can decide how much more you'd like to do."

No. No. No. This is not how this was supposed to go. *At. All. A year? I can't walk around like this for another year.* This appointment was supposed to be the beginning of the end of this horrific thing, and instead…instead…I feel like I'm starting over.

My legs tense. My eyes close. My hands clutch the arms of the chair so hard my fingers ache. Dad's hand rubs up and down my back a few times, but it feels like sandpaper instead of comfort.

Dad and the doctor exchange a few words about scheduling and timing and possibilities. Dad mentions the cream I already sometimes use, and they talk about other options, which I tune out. It's all too calm and quiet compared in the screaming in my head. "I saw the pictures."

"The pictures?" the doctor asks.

"Of the…" I'm blinking again. And again. "…of the people on your website."

"Every situation is different. Of course the pictures show the scarring in the worst possible light and the aftereffect in the best one." He holds my gaze for a moment, his face still relaxed and far too calm for the situation. "I will readily admit that. But even in the photos, Clara, you can see that the lines don't completely disappear. And only a few people I've worked on have hypertrophic scarring as severe as yours on facial tissue."

Dad asks another question, and now they're talking about a treatment that's been done with some kind of shots, but I can't focus. Their voices fade together and the walls fade together and my thoughts fade together into a black hole threatening to collapse around me.

I don't hold back when my legs tense up, and I'm standing. I'm floating just outside my body as I move for the door, shake the doctor's hand. The walls blur, Dad's arm around me blurs, I blur. The black hole is winning. We move up the hallway, out the door, back onto the busy sidewalk.

"I want to go home," I whisper.

"Our plane leaves in the morning."

That's a whole afternoon, evening, and night from now. We were going to hit Pike Place and celebrate by eating everything in sight. And then hit the mall to get me some pretty clothes to go with the new face I was going to get. Instead I need to get up the sidewalk to our car and into the hotel room before I shatter into pieces I can't pick up.

18

Tears roll in a continuous stream down my face. The hotel bathroom tiles cool my legs. Nobody knows how much I've lost today. Maybe Cecily. Maybe.

Dad knocks to ask if I'm okay. Normally I have words for everything, but I don't have words for this. The only smart thing I've been able to do is to not look at myself in the mirror.

"Clara, please?" he asks quietly.

Guilt pushes me off the tile because I can't sit here with Dad breaking on the other side of the door.

When I step out of the bathroom, the worry lines have etched so deeply that Dad's aged another ten years. I step toward him for a hug, but his warmth rushes another wave of tears down my face. I push back, staring at the floor. No hugs. Not now.

The cheap hotel comforter scratches me when I lie on the bed, and I wish I'd begged Dad for two rooms because I need to be alone.

My phone buzzes. It'll be Elias or Cecily, and I'm not sure how to talk to either of them. Some car race is on the TV, and the droning of the engines helps to dull the screaming in my head. How stupid am I? Did I really, really think I'd be able to be fixed?

"Why don't you give it a try?" Dad tosses the remote over to my bed. "Watch whatever you like."

"No thanks." I tuck my knees closer to my chest, grasping my shins.

"Clara…" he starts, but I can tell by the tone of his voice that I'm not going to like what comes next. "We can do as much of the surgeries or as little as you want. I promise. We can talk to someone else if you like."

I chew on my thumbnail. "I thought it was a mistake."

"What was a mistake?" Dad asks, but I can't answer him.

No.

I could answer.

I won't.

All this time I thought being out there in the woods was a big mistake. That my scars didn't belong on me. That they were also a mistake. I was wrong. They were for me. I'm just not sure what I did to deserve them.

I pull out my notebook to write but still can't get words down. I need words. I need to write. My fingers shake with my desire to put something on the page.

I finally start to write.

How many times can I break till I shatter…

How many times can I break till I shatter

How many times can I break till I shatter

How many times can I break till I shatter

How many times can I break till I shatter

And then I stop when I realize my hand has followed the same rhythm over and over.

19

I will always be the scarred-face girl. Not the writer girl or the cool girl from Alaska. I'm stuck. Who would bother looking past this? I'm not sure I would.

All the next morning at the hotel I cough. A sore throat means I can't talk. An illness could keep me from school. I'm planning ahead.

I'm numb as we move through the airport and climb on the plane. I watch some ridiculous family movie on the flight with a dog and a crazy brother, but I'm still numb.

And then we're driving in the dim light of midnight, and my life isn't different. I was supposed to come home hopeful, knowing *different* was on its way.

My future crumpled in front of me in a way that no one could possibly understand. I close my eyes as Dad drives and try to talk to Mom.

I need you here. Don't you see that? Dad isn't a girl. He won't understand. I can't believe so much was taken from me.

Where are you?

Some people say that they can hear the voices of people they know who died. Why can't I hear you?

WHY?

Mom?

My body shakes. My heart is crammed inside a box a million times too small. I hold my breath to stop the tears. My body shakes again. I'm being pushed apart from the inside. I can't go to New York like this. I can't. Columbia is out. University of Alaska is fine. It's *fine.*

Why did we pick that day for a walk? Why weren't we warned? Why didn't we feel something telling us to go inside? People at church talk about being led out of dangerous situations all the time. Why weren't we? What did I do that was so horrible?

Dad's shushing pulls me out of my internal pleading but doesn't slow the crying.

Even the guilt over how I'm sure I'm tearing Dad up isn't enough for me to want to overcome the cracking and splintering.

The moment we're home, I run for my room and lean against the door as it shuts behind me. I'm so done. I'm done with everything. My heart feels as if it's been burned and shriveled from the inside, on fire and melted or crushed. I curl up in my bed and wish the world to disappear. I can't do this. Everything was supposed to change after Seattle. My life was supposed to get better. I was supposed to get a face that I could stand to look at in the mirror. A face that would take me places. A face that had the chance of blending in.

I don't want a lesser version of the face that was carved into me.

I want *my* face.

I want people to know me for me. I want to speak for myself. Use my own words, instead of my scars screaming about experiences I wish I could hide.

My phone rings for the millionth time, and I check the ID to see the only person I might want to talk to right now.

"Hi."

"There you are!" Cecily.

My throat is too thick for talking. "I'm not...He can't..." And I don't say anything else.

"Oh."

We sit in silence for a few minutes, but I know she's there. "Wish you were here."

"Set your phone down. Let's listen to Ed Sheeran and drown in sorrows, okay?"

A sobby, quiet laugh escapes, bringing more tears down my face. "Okay."

The music starts almost immediately, tinny and faraway sounding. Cecily's on the other end of this, being with me in the only way she can.

* * *

I let my wool socks slide on the stairs until my foot drops to the next step. The two days we've been home have felt like an eternity. An eternity where I sit in my room and don't answer anyone's calls or texts. I'm past caring how juvenile I'm being.

"Which spatula do you use for pancakes?" Dad calls from the kitchen.

"The black one with the silver handle," I call back as I slowly slip down another step.

Dad's been whispering to Rhodes in the kitchen, and I can only assume he's talking about me. So strange that Dad and Rhodes have struck up this odd sort of friendship. I take a few silent steps closer and strain to listen.

Dad's voice. "I don't know what to say to her about Elias..." His voice fades with the sizzling bacon. "...She blurted it out, but I haven't said anything...Like your idea...a weekend..."

So.

They're talking about me. How totally unoriginal. Part of me wants to call them on it, but if I do, they might just drag me into their conversation. I'm so not up for that.

The sweet smell of pancakes and the salty smell of bacon hit my nose as I slip into the kitchen. Breakfast is the only thing Dad can cook unless the barbecue is lit. So, pancakes for dinner.

"I can ask a friend of mine," Rhodes says. "Cool girl. Might be fun for—" He stops the second our eyes meet.

"Glad to see you," Dad says with a too-wide smile.

Yeah. Because I just caught him talking to Rhodes about me.

My phone beeps again.

Elias: **Clara? I'm seriously worried. I wanna talk.**

I lean against the counter. **After dinner, ok?**

Elias: **Perfect.**

No one but him would put up with the silence I've given him— especially since I'm not sure I'll be able to talk to him after dinner. I glance back and forth between Dad and Rhodes for just a moment, wondering if I'll get any more clues about what they were discussing.

"Wow." Rhodes is staring. "You look like hel—"

But he cuts off when Dad frowns.

"Tired." Rhodes nods. "You look tired."

This is the guy who I *kissed*. What do we do now? He licks his lips once and then again, and I should maybe stop staring at his lips.

"Yeah. Travel," I say.

I'm waiting for him to say something else, but he steps toward Dad without a trace of tension on his face or his body.

"When do you need to give Columbia their deposit?" Dad asks.

I just stare. He can't be serious. "I don't remember," I lie.

Rhodes glances back and forth between Dad and me a few times. I'm sure neither of them has any idea what to say right now.

"I can help with dinner," Rhodes offers.

"Great." Dad scoots over and I back out of the kitchen into the dining room, knowing that tonight I'm just going to count minutes until I can be alone again.

I clutch my phone and look over the texts from Elias over the past few days.

Been thinking about you...want to talk...miss you...thinking about you...hope everything is okay...I love you...Can't wait to see you again...

Why? Why am I afraid of this? Of him? Elias is offering the kind of solidarity and constancy I can't get anywhere else. I glance up at Rhodes. Think about our kiss and what it might mean or not mean. There is nothing certain about Rhodes. Nothing. And he's going to be all over the world. I can't do that.

The idea of being with Elias. Of creating something permanent and something lasting...something I can count on when everything else is in the air...My shoulders fall a little, my chest loosens a little, and I finally relax into the chair.

No, Elias is definitely someone I shouldn't be afraid of. For the first time, I make myself really think about all the good things that might come if I can say yes to the boy who loves me. And Elias is right—whatever I want, we can do together. I know him. He knows me. My scars won't seem so horrible with someone as good as him. The permanence and foreverness of Elias is a lot less terrifying than the foreverness of my face.

20

It's nearly midnight when Dad finally goes to sleep, but the yard is still lit up in near daylight—another sign of summer. Anxiety zips through me. I just want to move forward. I'm ready. I'm settled. The ripped-insides feeling has finally subsided. I've come to a decision, and it feels like the reprieve I've needed.

Rhodes didn't follow me to the barn when I went to feed the horses. Another sign that he knows our kiss was as much of a mistake as I do.

I jump on my bike and start pedaling up the road. After a few miles, I'm in front of the wooden beams and rock facade that make up the front of the home Elias and his dad designed together. It's so very Alaskan in its massive ruggedness.

I sit in his driveway and lean my bike on its side.

This is it. Why does seeing him now feel so *different*?

Maybe I had hope before that my life would be something bigger than what it's going to be. I'm just going to need some time to settle into my decision. That's all.

I walk around the manicured yard and head for the back of the house.

When I knock on Elias's window, I wait maybe two seconds that feel *way* longer than only two seconds, so I knock again. And then again.

Today I realized I've been too afraid to choose. I wasn't choosing

Elias or choosing school…Now I'm making the choice that will keep me close to Dad and Elias and close to home. To Mom.

Why is Elias taking so freaking long to get here?

I use my fist this time and his window finally jerks up. "Impatient?"

"Yes." I scowl.

Elias's features soften. "I'm so glad you're home. That you're here."

This is it. Him. *The* him. "Me too."

"I wasn't sure if we were going to talk. I fell asleep with my phone in my hand." He tilts his head. "Come to the front and I'll let you in."

"But your parents…"

"My parents own this house. They're allowed to know when I have people over, even when it's in the middle of the night. It's fine." His voice is kind, but the words…Can anyone be as precise a rule-follower as him? That trait should not set me on edge.

Elias backs away. "Meet you in the front."

I walk around the house, and he lets me into the front hall. He's wearing an old T-shirt and basketball shorts.

Right. It's the middle of the night. This now seems like something I could have talked to him about tomorrow. The clock on the mantel starts chiming, and I realize it is now tomorrow, so maybe it's less weird that I'm here? Or more weird since no matter what, it's the middle of the night.

"Your dad said that I shouldn't feel bad if you didn't return my calls after your appointment…which you didn't." His brows go up slightly. "So, I'm hoping I did the right thing by giving you space."

Space. Doctor. Dad. The whole experience keeps crashing over me and shattering my insides.

"He…the doctor…" I sniff as emotion wells up behind my eyes again. "I can't be fixed. Not really. It'll take forever, and he's not even sure…" I hiccup over the words. "He's not sure…"

Elias's smile doesn't falter as he steps closer, his fingers lightly touching mine. "I wasn't aware you were broken."

"I meant my face."

"Clara." His lips slowly graze my cheek. "You have to believe that your scars aren't an issue for me. I get why you hate them. It's not like they're something you can hide. I get it, but...they don't change who you are. Not to me."

Of course I don't believe that, but I can't keep this binding sadness pressed inside my chest either. I need to try and believe him.

I slide my fingers through his. Elias's hands are so familiar that it's almost like holding my own. This is good, I think. It means I'm comfortable with him and feel safe with him, and that's super important. I hear married people at church talking about that all the time. *Super* important. I stare at where our hands come together and rub my fingers over his, sort of taking them in again like he was new. This is what I should focus on—all the things I love about home.

Even his palms are calloused from working hard, but not scratchy calloused. Smooth. Nails so short it looks like he bites them, but he'd never do that. Strong. Super strong hands. But then Elias has a super strong body from all the hauling of wood he does. I close my eyes and try to picture him naked. The weighted feeling that's been making it hard to breathe turns into a dancing-in-my-stomach feeling that's decidedly better.

"Clara?"

"Thinking about you," I say.

"I'm right here."

"Kiss?" I ask as I turn to face him.

His nose touches my cheek.

I tug on Elias's waist, bringing our hips together and making that butterfly feeling overshadow everything else.

His lips touch mine far too briefly, and then again. And then I part my lips and our kiss deepens. His hands cup my face, and I feel the rhythm of him—all soft sonnets and lullabies. I can do this. Just as fast as his calming energy comes in, my nerves take over. I'm doing it. Now.

I pull away and stare at the guy I know better than maybe anyone else. "My trip made me think about me and you, and what I want and where I want to be, and I love you and I want to be here, and I want the house you're building for us, and I do. I want you. Everything. A life together. So, yes. My answer is yes."

I'm panting when I'm done because the words just sort of flew out of my mouth. But I do feel how much I love him. It's desperate and has a tight hold on my chest, and I miss him even though we're in the same room. Has to be love.

"Just…" He bends down for a soft kiss. "Stay. Right there."

Elias backs up and sprints down the hall. He emerges seconds later, not stopping until he's inches from me. "I love you, Clara. I know we're young. I know this is sort of crazy, but I promise you won't be sorry."

He takes my hand in his shaking one. The sincerity of it all nearly sends me into hysterics, which would definitely not be the right way to react in this situation. It's just too real to feel real.

As he slides the ring on, I do feel settled. I close my eyes, feel his hand on mine, and let myself take in a breath that loosens the tension in my chest.

Decision made.

Now I know how to move forward. From here on out, I'll move forward in all the ways that brought me to this decision. The one that's done. Something can be cleared out of the cluttered mess that's my brain.

"Thank you," I say. "I love you. Really."

Elias stares at my hand, the ring resting on my finger. He touches the ring, smiling, before softly pressing his lips to mine.

"Is that how you're going to kiss your new fiancé?" I tease.

He takes my face in his hands again. "Yes. Because I love her that much."

I'm not sure what he means, but the whole thing feels incredibly genuine and sweet and sort of perfect, so I decide not to ruin it with my rambled thoughts.

"I should get home. I'm pretty sure Dad isn't going to let me miss school."

"Wait. I want to hold you for a minute." Elias wraps his arms around me and pulls me to his broad chest, which feels like the perfect place to celebrate this moment. Because this is one of those big moments you should be celebrating.

And I totally am.

* * *

I'm way too restless when I get home, so I slide out my small notebook and start writing.

Settled

In a way that calms and breathes

Wants

Peaceful in a way that pushes and holds

Off

Directed in a way that's chosen and safe

Done

Lost in a way that's not expected

Lonely

I watch as the words scrawl across the page and then I stop. That's not my point. My point is that the decision has made me feel *better* about everything. I have a direction. I have a purpose. I have that feeling of *safety* in a boy who knows me. I crumple up the paper and throw it in the direction of my trash. But just like every time I try to throw something away I've written, I can't do it. Sliding out of bed, I pick up the crumpled paper and smooth it out on my desk.

21

I sigh as Elias leans against me backstage. Performance night, and I should be feeling more excitement before the show starts, but it's just another show and just another cast that I only sort of know. I stand by the curtain, my script in hand, watching for my cues.

When the show's over and the final curtain is drawn, I'm dragged into a group hug and I should be feeling elated and excited. I've helped with the plays since I started here freshman year, and this was the last one I'll be a part of, but the experience is…It's just one more thing that's signaling the end of something and the beginning of something else that I don't quite understand yet.

A wedding?

A new kind of life?

Or just a small tweak of an old one? I hope the tweak is more than a small one. I need to feel the change. The difference. The excitement and energy and everything people feel when they step into a new part of their life.

Elias stands off to the side of the stage, letting me have time with the people I should care more about, only I'm standing on the edge of the circle and just nodding when people talk. Rhodes steps next to Elias, and I stare at them from the group of actors still chattering about the show and after-party.

"I keep meaning to tell you congratulations on your engagement."
Rhodes grabs Elias's hand and shakes it, only I have this feeling they're
doing one of those typical man things and squeezing as hard as they can.
Both smiles seem a little forced, and Elias's knuckles are white—even in
the dim backstage light.

"Thank you." Elias's smile gets wider as Rhodes is the first to let go.

I'm watching, frozen, from a few feet away. It's like when you see animals running across the road and you're sure they'll get hit. You know
it's too late to do anything, so you're still and stop breathing, as if that'll
somehow help.

"Has Clara decided if she's going to Columbia this fall or is going to
defer until next year?" Rhodes asks.

My stomach drops from my body, and I step closer.

"Excuse me?" Elias asks.

I slip my hand through Elias's arm. "We should go."

"You applied to a school in New York?" Elias's brow furrows.

"I…" I glare at Rhodes, whose face is completely relaxed and un-
bothered, making me wish I were a more violent person so I could
smack that smug look off his face. "I just was curious, that's all," I say.

Elias glances toward Rhodes as I drag him away. "He made it
sound like—"

"Rhodes doesn't know what he's talking about." I let out a nervous
laugh. "It's fine. We'll do whatever together, right?" I ask with a too-
forced smile. "Just like you said."

Elias pauses, and I'm forced to stop.

"Hey." I step closer to him again. "I love you. I just—"

"Why didn't you *tell* me?" Elias's eyes widen again. "Even…I don't
understand why you wouldn't share this with me."

I throw Rhodes another glare over my shoulder, but he's now *leaning*
against the wall like this is no big deal.

There is no way Rhodes didn't bring this up on purpose. In his warped mind, he probably thinks he's being helpful by pulling another asshole move.

"Why don't we get out of here and talk?" I suggest. And hopefully I'll be able to think of what I could tell Elias to make him feel okay about me not telling him.

He nods once, slowly. "Yeah. Okay."

"Don't forget that we strike set tomorrow," Rhodes says, suddenly all teacher-like, but when our eyes meet I feel like a million questions are being shot at me.

Are you sure?

Why?

How can this be the right thing?

Are you going to let Columbia go?

Do you remember our kiss?

"Of course I won't forget." I loop my arm through Elias's as we head for the side door.

Ten days. I have ten days to give Columbia my deferment request or deposit. Ten. Days.

"Help me understand, Clara." Elias stops beside his truck. "Why would you apply to a school across the country without telling me? Do I think we're closer than we actually are?"

I take his hand. "We're close." I shrug. "It's where my mom went. I was just curious. I never thought I'd get in."

"And you did."

"I did."

"And now Cecily's going to New York this fall instead of being here with you. Do you..." He swallows. "Do you want to go?"

I snort and roll my eyes. "I just wanna be with you."

He tilts his head to the side. "Clara."

I step closer to him, let my body rest against his. "I chose you. I choose you. I love you."

His eyes fall closed as he bends forward until our foreheads are together. "I love you too."

"My house?" I ask.

Elias's lips find mine briefly. "Sure."

* * *

Elias is nestled behind me on the couch at my house, and it's not exactly perfect, but at least our bodies are lined up and his warmth is pressing into me and his arms are around me. Dad's asleep, and the world is still and quiet.

"This is nice." I sigh.

His arms squeeze tighter as he kisses the side of my head. "I love you so much. This feels incredible."

The weight of the ring on my finger still feels foreign, but with Elias holding me and seeing what every night could be like, the weight is okay. Doable. And I'm sure it's totally normal.

"I love you too." And I do mean it. I'm definitely sure I love him more than some married couples I see. I know he'd take good care of me, and he'd help me get through school, and he gets along with my horses and my dad and my best friend. And I won't have to leave any of them. He wants me. He wants me all broken and frustrating and ugly and moody.

He moves an arm to scratch the side of his head, and as he moves his hand back around my waist, it rubs against the bottom side of my breast. Elias stops, and I don't want him to stop. I want to know what it would feel like if he moved his hand over my chest, maybe felt me. Squeezed a little.

"It's okay," I whisper, wondering if wearing his ring will be enough.

His thumb grazes over me more purposefully this time, but just once and then again, and I swallow a moan that's really trying to push its way out.

Elias's lips find the small spot under my ear and press against my neck. Now his hand is on my chest fully, and when he squeezes, I can't stop a whimpering noise from escaping as the want tightens the strings in my body.

He slowly sits up without a word. His arms untangle from mine and from my body, and his legs find their way away from mine until there's suddenly enough space between us for a whole other person.

Elias's breathing in these weird, slow, regulated breaths, and I'm curled on the couch and wondering why we had to stop there.

"Elias, I…" I reach toward him, but he shakes his head. Just once. What is *wrong* with me that I can't stop pushing him? Maybe we aren't at the same level of closeness.

I glance down at the ring. Maybe Elias is pushing me in a totally different way, only I'm letting him.

"Do you understand how much I love you?" he asks as he slowly looks toward me.

No, I don't. Not even a little bit. I don't get it. I feel the rewards of it in the way he looks at me and treats me and takes care of me, but I don't understand it.

"I can't touch you like that. Not now. Not until later. I want that for me. I want that for you." He finally reaches toward me and takes my hand, sliding his fingers over my ring.

I almost open my mouth to ask him if that's why he's marrying me, but it would be the stupidest thing to say because I know it's not. *But is it part of the reason I'm marrying him?*

Now I'm sort of frustrated and angry that I'm in this position.

Elias stands, but I stand too, not ready to let him go.

"Please, Clara." His voice is low and almost gravelly sounding, which hits me in good places and makes me want more kissing. "I can only take so much. My body can only take so much. I want to do the right thing—to stick by how I promised myself I'd act."

Tears well behind my eyes as I stare at the carpet between us. How could I do this to him? To *me*?

"You have to understand," he whispers.

"I do," I say, still staring at the floor.

"Clara." He clasps his hands over mine and I finally look at him.

Elias frowns when he sees my tears.

"I don't know why I feel this need to touch you, to have you…" I set his hands on my sides, just at the edge of my bra. Almost on my chest, but not quite. He grasps my sides, spreading relief through me so fast and hard that my body goes weak. "To have you touch me, and I know I should be happy when you don't push, but part of me…" *Part of me feels rejected.* I'm just not sure if I can tell him that.

He leans into me, resting his forehead against mine, keeping his hands hovering just under my chest. His thumbs resting on the bottom edge of my bra.

"I wish I could explain better how I feel when you touch me." How I crave more. Need it almost. How what I feel in my heart and my head doesn't always match what my body wants, and how I seem to always want more, more, more…more of Elias, more of Rhodes, more feeling wanted. Desired. Elias kissing me takes some of the sting out of my hideous face. "I want more."

His hands slide up slightly, just resting on the bottom side of my chest.

And of course this is the moment my dad picks to walk into the room, hair sticking out, bathrobe tied around his waist.

So many things happen at once that it's hard to know which is the most important. Me laughing is probably the worst reaction, which is exactly why my body feels it's the thing to do.

Elias turns eighty colors of red as he jumps away, and my dad is many shades of confused and angry.

I'm snorting in my failed attempt to hold in my laughter, while both Dad and Elias try to talk.

Contrite Elias: "I'm so sorry, sir. If you just let me explain…"

Angry father: "I'm not even sure where to *start* asking questions here…"

And instead of letting them sort it out, I jump in. Like an idiot. "Don't stress, Dad. I told you that Elias asked me to marry him. I said yes. And it wasn't his idea to put his hands…*there.*"

Seems like my brain is working because I said "there" instead of boobs or breasts or anything else that might give my dad an aneurysm. "So, this really is absolutely not as bad as it looks because we're getting married." Which is something I wasn't going to tell Dad until I had another day or two to get used to the idea.

Dad rests a thumb and a finger over his eyes.

Elias has his wide-eyed panic face on, and I'm smiling like maybe the bigger my smile is, the less chance there is of this ending in worse disaster.

Dad points at Elias. "You. Go home."

"But, Dad," I protest.

"Don't take it personally, Elias. I just want to chat with my daughter." Dad actually pats Elias's shoulder on his way out, which is obviously way more touching than I'm going to get from Elias because he won't even make eye contact. What does he think Dad'll do? Laser us with his anger vision?

"I totally understand, sir." And Elias is gone. Just like that.

Isn't there some sort of code or something? Like when you're about to get married, you stick together. Or…help out with angry fathers or something. I sort of get that Elias is trying to respect my father's wishes, but I'd really like to come before my dad.

I slump on the couch, well aware that Dad won't let me out of this room until he's said what he needs to say. Only he's not saying anything. And my eyes float to the TV, which is off, and to the clock on the wall, which is still ticking away at a few minutes past 1:00 a.m., and still Dad isn't speaking. I think at this point I'd prefer yelling, and when he opens his mouth to talk, I brace myself but he doesn't yell.

"Were you serious?" Dad asks. "You told him yes?"

I give him a brief flash of my ring, wondering if there's a way to make my dad understand my decision when I'm still processing it myself.

Dad rounds the couch and sits facing me, but on the opposite end. This is good. He's not so angry he's pacing or anything. And I still have breathing room and a possible escape route over the back of the couch.

Dad takes in a few deep breaths, probably as he processes all the parts of what I said and what he saw.

I open my mouth to speak like five times, but nothing comes.

He scratches his forehead and stares at the carpet for a moment. "I think I've done you a disservice."

"What?" That was not anywhere near the realm of what I was expecting to hear from him.

Dad's worried eyes find mine. "Instead of just sitting down and talking to you, I keep wondering how *best* to sit down and talk to you. I should feel relieved you'll be staying in town and will be well taken care of." Dad rubs his forehead again. "I'm actually sad for the experiences you might not have."

I open my mouth to speak, but again there are no words. This is so weird. And so not like me.

Dad's eyes rest on mine—tired and anxious. "Do you love him?"

I think about seeing Elias the other night silhouetted in the hallway, and about how kind he is, and how he loves me. "Yes."

"Do you love him *enough*?" Dad's brows go up a little.

"Dad." I sigh. "Does anyone know that? Ever?"

"Yes." He nods. "They do."

I don't have anything to say to that.

"Is this in reaction to…to…to…" Dad swallows. "Is this a reaction to Seattle?"

"No," I say quickly. Not *totally*, anyway.

"How have you two reconciled your beliefs?" Dad asks. "For your forever marriage…You and I both get a lot of comfort knowing we'll be a family with your mom after this life. If Elias never joins our church, you will never get that forever wedding. The temple wedding. You won't get that *eternal* marriage. Don't you still want that?"

My church will recognize our wedding, but a temple wedding is forever and can only happen if Elias is Mormon.

"You might want to bring him to church one Sunday with us, and then you go with him one Sunday."

"Wait." I hold my hands up between us. "You'd let me go to a different church?"

"Clara." Dad scoots closer to me and takes my hand. "I don't think you can understand how much I love you until you have kids of your own. And maybe not even then. Losing your mother…It just…It changed me, and you've been more precious to me, knowing how fast things *can* change. If you want something. *Really* want something. And you know it'll make you happy, that's what I want for you too. Okay?"

Tears run down my face because even though I said yes to Elias, I don't know *what* I want. It's all messy in my head and in my heart. "Okay."

Dad brushes my tears away. "You know I'm going to tell you what I always do…"

"To give it a lot of quiet thought."

"Right. And I'm going to ask something else of you," Dad says.

I hold in a sigh because I can't imagine doing anything else right now.

"Don't get mad. This was my idea. I talked to Rhodes who has a friend that's a girl in New York."

"Oh-kay…" That's not at all what I expected him to say.

"If you want me behind this wedding, I want you to understand what you're giving up by saying no to Columbia. And it's not even about Columbia—it's about you needing to see that there's a whole world out there."

Oh no.

"I think it would be smart for you to spend a weekend in New York. I can put it together in a day or two, and…" Dad frowns and blinks, and I'm terrified he's going to cry. "And I think it would be good for you."

I blink a few times. I open my mouth to tell Dad that I don't want to go to New York with my face, but he looks so hopeful.

"You're okay with me going to New York alone?" I ask, wondering how okay *I* am with going to New York alone. People don't just…People don't just decide to go to New York for a weekend and then leave.

Do they?

Dad squeezes my knee. "Yep. I want you to see the city. The campus. Might be nice to finally see a place your mom…" He swallows. "Your mom loved."

"Uh…thanks?" I smile but it feels all weird and probably looks strange. This isn't real.

"Want me to light a fire and you can sleep down here?" Dad asks with his frowny apologetic face.

I'm afraid to say no to anything right now. Is this seriously happening? New York? "Thanks."

Dad ruffles my hair before standing up and moving out of the room to get firewood.

This means I'm left by myself. With a ring on my finger and wondering how I didn't realize the whole world was opened up to me if I wanted it.

22

I can't believe Dad told Rhodes he could come over tonight. And Elias is here because it's the night before I'm *gone*. To New York City. I'm packed and it still doesn't feel real.

So now we're sitting around the table, each with fried chicken and mashed potatoes on our plates, and Rhodes can't shut up about New York. There's no *way* he doesn't know how uncomfortable this whole trip is for Elias.

And all I can think about, as Rhodes eats and talks with Dad like they seem to do, is how we kissed. And how I haven't mentioned that little event to Elias.

Cecily gets in tonight, which is a night too late, because I could really use another girl at the dinner table right now.

"My friend Lachelle is so stoked," Rhodes says. "Her apartment has been empty for a week because spring semester is finishing finals. Her roommates have been absent, and she's bored and lonely." He glances at my dad. "At least you don't have to worry about Clara getting into trouble with her. I'm sure they'll have a blast. Lachelle has the energy of four people and loves everyone."

Elias shifts in his seat next to me. He seems baffled by the whole thing, so I have to explain that my dad just wants me to make sure I understand my options, and this seems like a good way to get him onboard with the wedding.

But this is only half the truth. The other half is that as scary as getting on a plane by myself sounds, it also sounds awesome. Walking around the Columbia campus? Amazing. I'm about to get married. These opportunities might not come again.

Rhodes grins at something he shared, and I stare at his mouth for a moment before jerking my gaze back to the table and then slowly toward Elias's face. No girl should have to sit in the same room with two guys she's kissed. Ever. Especially when she's horrible enough to have done it the way I did.

"Don't you think?" Elias asks.

I stare at him with what must be a totally blank look because I have zero idea what he just asked. He tenses next to me again, making me feel worse because I'm being a really bad girlfriend tonight. Or fiancé. Or whatever.

"I'm sorry. Zoned out." I rest my hand on his leg under the table, and Elias relaxes into a soft smile—the one that tingles in my stomach.

"I was just saying how generous it is of your dad to give you such a nice break before school gets out and before we start wedding planning and all that."

Dad drops his fork. I stare at my plate. Elias's jaw sets.

Rhodes coughs a few times before slapping his chest. "You're not getting married *soon*, are you?"

"I don't see any reason to wait." Elias takes my hand under the table. "We love each other. We know we want to get married. The house will be done in a little over a month."

"What about Columbia? You don't turn down something like that," Rhodes says.

"Stop," I say quietly, glancing at Rhodes for just long enough to see his face fall and for my heart to squeeze because of it.

I pat Elias's leg under the table and kiss his cheek.

Rhodes coughs again, and I feel Elias's leg muscles tense under my hand. I really, really hope this is the most awkward situation I'll ever encounter, because I'm wishing to burst into flames. It would get me out of this situation and be infinitely more comfortable. I close my eyes and make a silent wish to disappear from the table, and then I start to bargain.

Dear Heavenly Father,

I know I'm not perfect, but if I could be excused from this situation, I would much appreciate it. And I promise to be better about reading my scriptures and saying my prayers and not wishing so hard that Elias didn't feel the need to be so good around me.

Thank you, Clara

But I open my eyes to see Rhodes poking at his food with too much force, Dad leaning back in his chair staring at the wall, and Elias a little red from frustration or embarrassment, or both.

"I'll get more chicken." I stand and grab the serving dish, even though there are still three more pieces, and head for the kitchen.

Does running from the table count as an answer to my bargain-prayer? I'm not sure. But I grab the iron skillet and a furious pain shoots up my arm because the burner is still on.

"Ouch! Shit! *Shoot!*" I slam on the faucet and shove my hand into the cool stream of water. Three sets of worried eyes are on me within ten seconds. The water has soaked my sleeve up past my elbow, but I'm not ready to take my hand out of the stream.

"You okay?" Rhodes appears first, but Elias pushes his way around him and gently turns my hand under the faucet to investigate. Dad's on the end of the kitchen rubbing his forehead at the two boys' hovering concern.

Well, this is some crappy way to answer my bargain-prayer. Is a burnt hand my way out? Now I guess I know to be careful what I bargain for.

"I'm gonna get some aloe," I say quickly. The best way to win back some points with Elias is saying, "Can you help?"

He follows me up the stairs without a word.

Once we're in my small bathroom, I strip down to my camisole, drop my wet shirt on the floor, and stick my hand back under the water.

"You okay?" he whispers as he steps close behind me.

"Just needs to stay underwater for a bit." I relax as the burning fades into the stream of water.

"Okay."

Elias's fingers start tracing patterns across my back and shoulders. He follows the lines of my scars where they disappear into my tank top. His warmth presses against my back as his fingers slide across my collarbone. Chills run through me, and I look up in the mirror to see Elias's eyes closed and shiver when his breath hits my neck.

When his lips meet the top of my shoulder, I'm still staring at us in the mirror. My marred face. His perfect one. Elias, who is so familiar and who I should be swooning over right now. This is what I wanted. Only I still feel empty. Elias is right here, and my chest is hollow. I have no idea how to fill it back up. I don't know why this isn't enough.

"Can you just hold me?" I whisper.

And without question, he does.

* * *

"Clara." Dad's gruff voice carries through my door and I roll over to see the clock. One a.m. What the...

"It's me!" Cecily leaps through the door around Dad, and I grin.

"I'll leave you two." Dad backs up a step. "Just don't keep an old guy awake."

Cecily slides in my bed and giggles as she tugs the blankets up to her chin.

I relax under the covers. "I can't tell you how glad I am that you're here."

"Tell me everything," she says. "Because getting half stories over the phone *isn't* cutting it." Her large brown eyes widen. Her face is so familiar. It's what I imagine a sibling's would feel like. Her dark-toned skin makes my white sheets glow and makes her smile feel even bigger. I've missed her so much.

My brain's chaos settles, my chest relaxes, and I know we'll barely sleep for the rest of the night. I tell her about how weird it feels to be engaged, and then about my burned hand at dinner and how Elias came upstairs with me. How my thoughts are jumbled over guys and school, and how I wish they weren't. I wish I knew what to do.

And the silence fills my room.

"I'm glad I'm back," she says, tucking her short hair off her face.

I'm not ready for advice. I haven't even sorted out all my thoughts.

"I'm *so* glad you're back." I laugh a little and scoot lower in my bed.

"And now as you try to fall asleep I'm going to whisper all the millions of reasons I think you should come to New York with me in the fall…"

And she does.

At some point I fall asleep wondering if I'll ever go to New York again after my weekend. I really need to make this trip count.

23

I'm doing it alone. I'm at freaking LaGuardia Airport. I'm half-terrified and half-empowered. The noise of the terminal slams into my ears, and the only thing I'm sure I got right is that I'm on a curb that Lachelle *can* come pick me up from.

It's just so *much*. I tilt my head forward as I get yet another sideways look from a passerby. Whispers on the plane, at the airports...*wonder what happened...She's almost pretty...A gang? A knife? An animal?*

I grasp my phone more tightly and send Cecily a text. I'm telling you she's not coming.

I tug my hair down again and keep my face tilted toward the ground while also watching for Lachelle.

Chill. She'll be there.

And I'm sure Cecily is right, but she was crazy excited when I brought up the trip to New York so she'll do anything to put my mind at ease.

My stomach's rolling again. What do I do if I hate Lachelle? If she hates me? If she forgets to pick me up? I've never sat in a cab. I don't even know where to tell the driver to go. Would the driver speak English? They rarely do in the movies.

A small, white VW pulls up at the curb, and a girl I only sort of recognize from Rhodes's phone waves from the driver's seat. She reaches over to push open the passenger door before I realize I should maybe get in the car.

"Clara?" she asks. Her small blouse is collared and she's in a fantastic snug skirt, even for just coming to the airport. Her short, wavy hair sticks around her face like a girl from the twenties. I already feel a little unworthy in worn jeans, running shoes, and T-shirt—her being so put together only makes it worse.

"That's me."

"I guessed." She smirks, her eyes scanning the right side of my face and her smile faltering, but just slightly.

Right. I told her about being the scarred-up girl. I'm pretty easy to pick out.

I sit down in the passenger's seat, and she slips back inside the car.

"Wow." She leans forward and gets a good look at my face. I'm never sure what to do when people do this, though I prefer it to the weird half-glances when people try not to stare. "They didn't look so dramatic from the pic Rhodes sent. But…wow. I can't believe you're *alive*. Intense, Clara."

Instead of trying to figure out how I feel about her reaction, all I can think is, *Rhodes has a picture of me?* I'm not sure how I feel about that. Mostly warm and sort of flushed all over, which in turn makes me feel mostly bad. But not *all* bad. The wave of heat is a kind of high in itself.

Lachelle snorts as she pulls into the lanes of airport traffic. "You didn't know he took a picture?"

I shake my head.

"Awesome. This is even better. He now gains stalker status. Everyone's already given him crap because he's talked about you. The pic he sent is one where you're in your desk next to some hot guy, and I couldn't see your scars as well as I can see them now. But you were very obviously a student, and he's obviously crushing on you a little, so you can *imagine* we've been giving him a hard time."

"Oh." And the hot guy is Elias. The guy whose ring I took off before my flight. It felt weird to keep it on and weird to take it off. In the end I took it off because I knew I'd already feel like the small-town girl, and being engaged before high school is over sorta pushes that to the forefront. At least that's what I keep telling myself to ease some of the guilt over being relieved that it's in my jewelry box at home.

"Anyway. I've been curious to meet the girl who has our Rhodes's panties in a bunch." Lachelle laughs lightly as she hits the gas, jerking us into traffic.

"I'm…um…dating the hot guy next to me." *Engaged, actually…*another part of my life that feels foreign.

"Oh." She lays on the horn and our car jerks to a stop. "Watch it, asshole!"

I grab my chest as my heart races. Lachelle pats my knee. "Don't stress. New York is always like this. But be warned. I haven't driven in ages. Borrowed my cousin's car for the weekend, though it might be more trouble than it's worth. He lives in Jersey."

"Oh." There's too much to take in.

"Bridge or tunnel?" she asks.

"What?"

"Shit. Never mind. It's too late." She hits the gas.

The buildings along the expressway suddenly give way to bridge supports, and I hold my breath at how *incredible* everything is. Across the river, Manhattan looks like a forest of buildings—a forest of ingenuity and design and function.

Lachelle chatters about needing to hit the library and that there's some party for literature students, and I just stare out the window of the small car. The bridge gives way to more city streets. People. Everywhere there are people—more beats and rhythms and meters than I could ever hope to count. I'm already a little in love.

"A parking space!" She points as she turns the car down a side street. "Holy shit, a *space!*"

I cringe into the seat as she once again hits the gas, slams on her blinker, and in two seconds has us next to the curb.

"I've never parked this close." She slips off the seat belt. "At least the few times I've borrowed the car. What were we talking about?"

I clear my throat, determined to at least *try* to be the cool version of myself. "I don't remember."

My body's stiff from the flight, but my suitcase is out of the back of her car and in her hands. She's on the sidewalk with dozens of other people. She just stands there waiting for my stiff body to unfold itself from the car.

"Okay." I get out, slide my hair forward, and shut the car door, determined *not* to be afraid. "I'm ready."

"My apartment's up this way. So. First, library and my boyfriend. Second, we can walk campus. Third, party. Is that cool?"

"Yeah," I say as I carefully follow the path she's paving through people on the sidewalk. "Thanks for showing me around."

Lachelle grins over her shoulder. "I love this place. I want everyone to love it. Pleasure is all mine."

Another block and she holds open a scratched metal door for me, and I step into a narrow hallway.

"Up those stairs. It's a squeeze. Good thing your bag's small." She laughs.

I'm trying to figure out how anyone would even get a bed up these stairs, or a couch, or even a big load of groceries.

"Stop!" she hollers when there are doors on my right and on my left. She slips her key into the door on my right and shoves it open.

Lachelle's apartment is almost comical in its smallness. The kitchen is just a tiny counter, hot plate, and microwave over the top of a mini-fridge.

Her hand is on mine as I stumble around the tiny futon into an even smaller room than we were in before. "How many people usually live here?" I ask.

"Three." She points to bunk beds. "Two of us in here and one in the living room."

She flops my suitcase onto her futon. "Let's see if you brought something fun to wear. If not, I have a wretched addiction to my sewing machine and to Modcloth."

I'm still admiring her skirt. "You...you look like a fashion student, not a...writer." I clamp my mouth shut because it's probably a rude thing to say or an insensitive thing or something.

"No judging, Clara," she chides with a smile. After a quick scan of the very few things in my suitcase, she surveys an assortment of hooks on the wall.

"To hang out with my people, I think..." She shifts her weight a few times in front of her wall of clothes. "This." She tosses down a simple black dress with antiqued ivory lace. I grab it and stare, wondering if I'll look cool or like someone's grandma.

"With this." She tosses a jacket. "And this." A wide belt hits me in the head before I can duck. "And this." A small, soft cardigan lands on me next. "Which means you don't need this." She snatches back the jacket.

"Um..."

"Just change." She flits her hand between us as she smiles. "I'll be right back."

She closes the door to her room, which might even be smaller than our entry closet—clothes hanging on pegs on the walls, books stacked above my knees in other places. Music filters in on one side, there's the constant noise of the cars and the streets, and every time the upstairs neighbors move, it sounds like elephants are roaming the roof. This is amazing.

I clutch the dress and belt and cardigan.

The feeling here is so different. A place I've never been with people I've never met…I resist the urge to dial Elias for a piece of home about four times before finally undressing and putting on clothes that belong to a girl I just met.

I slide on the dress, and it's a couple inches above my knees, which my dad would give me raised eyebrows over, but he's not here, so it seems fine. The thin sweater is trickier, but I adjust it over the dress and get the collar laid down and the belt on, and I'm feeling…like me, but better. In someone else's clothes. A tornado of a girl I just met, who I'm pretty sure would never fit into the confines of any kind of poem.

"You done?" Lachelle hollers.

"Coming out," I call back. Maybe my outfit is cute enough that no one will notice my face.

"Holy fantastic body!" she squeals. "You comfortable in that?"

"I think so." I glance down again. It's just more put together than I ever bother to be.

"And it even matches those little flats you brought." She kicks them toward me. "Also, I have people for you to meet, so let's play with makeup so we can get out of here. Cool?"

"Cool." Because I don't know what else to say. Everything since I left home for this trip has felt like a whirlwind, and Lachelle is just helping my spinning thoughts pick up speed.

* * *

"You have an insane amount of energy. You know that?" I say as Lachelle smudges more eyeliner on my lids.

I'm sitting on her toilet, and I'm sure her back is pressed against the wall opposite me as she straddles my lap with a makeup brush in hand.

"Life is so incredibly short!" She shifts her weight and bites her lip as she concentrates. "I just don't wanna miss anything, you know? I mean, I've seen almost none of the world, which is totally not okay. I'm a city girl though, so I've already realized that if I'm going to be a happy traveler, I need to be a city traveler. I really wanna go to the Sorbonne. The second they accept me, I'm dropping everything to go."

I laugh as she moves around the eyelid that leads into one of my scars. "I'm about as opposite of city as you can get."

"But look at you, all fitting in and wearing my clothes like you own them," she teases as she pinches my shoulder. "I'm so glad we get along. I mean, I get along with most people, but still. So glad."

"Me too." I release a breath. "I know my scars are—"

"A good challenge to work around. You'll have to tell me if something I do feels weird." She pops her lips a couple times and sets down a brush on the worn white counter only to pick up another one that looks exactly like it. "Don't apologize for having scars. They're here. We'll deal."

Since we started, I've tried not to think about how she's going to know my scars probably as well as I do after this. She's gone over them with concealer and foundation and who knows what else.

"So this party tonight..." I start, needing to not think about how she sees my scars.

"Just lit students. It's our end-of-the-year bash." She starts smoothing shadow over my other eyelid. "You know, once you get mascara on, you have such long lashes that it sort of masks how that one big scar touches your eye."

My stomach tightens. Masking a few missing lashes is very different from being one of the pretty girls. "Huh."

I wait for Lachelle to ask me something else, but her hands have stopped pressing on my face and she's leaning over me with her cat-eye makeup and glossy lips. "I think...Yep. I think I'm done. The scars aren't easy...you know...to work with, but..."

She backs up to the doorway and gestures toward the mirror.

I stand slowly and turn. The second I catch my reflection, I freeze. My scars are there, but they're less...No. They're the same but lighter. Maybe this is sort of what they'll look like after I do some more serious bleaching. But the rest of my face...My eyes look bigger and my lips fuller and my cheekbones higher and my skin smoother. Aside from my scars, I actually look like the kind of girl who could belong here. "You're...amazing."

"A bit. Yep." She rocks back on her heels. "Now slip on your flats. I'm pretty sure the night will end with a scavenger hunt for those of us who aren't sloppy drunk, and neither of us will want heels for that."

"I don't drink," I blurt.

"Then don't drink." She snorts and shoves me toward the living room. "Now go get what you need so we can get out of here!"

When I'm in the living room, I flatten my hand over my heart and feel it pressing into my palm. I look so...not pretty but so much better than I thought possible. I always thought that drawing attention to myself would just draw attention to my scars, but...but what if I was wrong?

24

I follow Lachelle out the door as she chatters about modern poets, and the archaeology trip she went on with Rhodes, and I see why they're friends. They're both into everything. It further makes me wonder if they were ever a thing. An unease traces over my nerves, which is stupid. Rhodes can be with whomever he likes.

I check my phone again for any word from Elias, but there's nothing new. He's probably at work. No, wait. Four hours earlier. He's at *school* right now. By the time he's out of school, we'll probably be at the party. And then when I'm crashing, he'll hopefully be off work so we can talk. Well…he *might* be. How awkward.

The streets here are busier and more frenetic than Seattle. Fuller. So many rhythms and beats and thoughts and ideas clash, but I find the chaos calming. Like I don't matter as much. My freaky face won't be noticed as much. There's too much to take in.

"This is such a fantastic school. Seriously, aside from a few pretentious assholes, you'll totally love it," Lachelle gushes as we move up the sidewalk toward the school. "Ya know, if you decide to come."

Columbia.

For a moment I forget I'm so far from home because we've stepped off a busy street and I'm on a gorgeous campus with old brick buildings and sidewalks and grass lawns with big trees. All the while the noise of the cars and the city buzz through me. New York stretches above the campus buildings, making it feel almost like a sanctuary in a city so massive it doesn't feel real.

When I breathe in, the smell of city and heat and exhaust mixes with grass and trees and the warm smell of the coffee shop we pass.

A small group walks by and the guy on the end glances at us, gives Lachelle a quick wave, and glances at me again before frowning and turning away. My gut rolls, and I pull my hair down, figuring I'm not doing well at shading myself. Maybe I *will* be noticed in the crowd.

"This is…gorgeous," I say as the grass spreads out in front of us and the old school buildings become the backdrop rather than the sprawling city.

"Yeah." She slips her hands into her skirt pockets. "This is the greenest part of campus, so it's in all the brochures and all the online pictures. What they don't show you are all the odd buildings on the fringes of campus with classrooms that are impossible to find."

I'm still twisting my head back and forth, trying to see everything. "Huh."

"I love the library," Lachelle whispers as we move through the wooden doors. "This is the undergrad services one."

I open my mouth to say okay, but the ceiling stretches above me, study carrels stretch in front of me, marble walls and wood paneling and…every kind of perfect stereotype of an amazing campus library.

"Renee!" Lachelle whisper-yells to a gray-haired woman sitting at a desk stacked high with books. "This is Clara. From *Alaska*. You chat with her for a minute while I look for Trey."

I feel my jaw hang as I keep staring at my surroundings.

Renee points toward a corner. "He's that way," she whispers.

Lachelle taps my arm. "Be right back."

Renee peers at me over thin glasses, her gray hair cut short and framing a long, thin face. "So, you're from Alaska?" she asks in a practiced whisper.

Her light blue eyes scan my face, and I feel myself shrink under her gaze.

This sucks. One day. *Any* day I wish to meet someone without this. "Yep. I want to write." I want her to see that part of me, not the scars.

There's no way for me to meet someone and for them to not see my scars. Without them being blind, it won't happen.

There is. No way. For that to happen.

I stare at where Renee sits, her studying eyes and long face. I'm not sure how to feel okay about people staring. And they always will. At least a lot of them always will.

"And I'm guessing you're thinking of coming to Columbia? That's what Lachelle said, I believe?" Renee asks.

"Or University of Alaska," I say quietly. Where being attacked by a bear would be a big deal, but maybe not as big a deal. Maybe I can't escape it anywhere—I'd just have the comfort of home *or* I'd have the comfort in knowing I'm tough enough to be in New York.

"But you were accepted here? Why wouldn't you take advantage of that?" She slides a few library books across her desk, scanning them as she does.

"UAA is more what felt available to me."

"Why would you be tied to your local school?" she asks.

"I'm…" *Not sure.*

"You a criminal?" she asks with a smirk.

"No," I sputter. "I'm not quite eighteen. About to graduate from high school," I say more quietly.

"Then come. You're eighteen, my dear. With no major criminal history. *Everything's* available to you." She grins as she leans forward and rests her elbows on the desk between us. "So the question is…what do you want to do with all that freedom?"

Those words are terrifying. *Everything*? That's so many choices. So many unknowns. So many people and places I've never seen or even thought of. My hand comes to my face, and I find the scar just off my mouth, touching the familiar welt and tracing the same section over and over. But maybe…maybe if I allow a bit of hope at how much could be open to me, I might find more hope and then more until I'm not afraid to move forward. *That* would be amazing.

"I don't know what I want to do. Not exactly." Honesty seems like the only safe thing right now. "I have to tell the school if I'm coming this fall so soon, and…" In four days they need to know, and it'll come so fast.

Renee chuckles. "At your age, you also have to remember that as you move forward you may open doors, but you also shut others. As you're making decisions on where you want to go to school and what you want to do with your degree, keep that in mind. And then make sure that the doors that are most important stay open."

She gives me the same raised-eyebrow look my dad does when he wants me to seriously consider something he's just said.

"I'm…I'm thinking about it."

"If you're even thinking of coming here, you might want to read some books by the staff." She reaches to a shelf behind her and pauses for a moment. There's a sign just above her that reads, "Staff Publications," and then she turns and places five books in front of me. "Our modern staff, I should say."

I've read books by graduates of Columbia, but how had I never thought to read the books the professors here were writing?

She taps the top of the books with pale fingers. "It would be smart for you to read a little *outside* of the standard reading lists—especially before classes start."

I run my hands over books written by people who I might get to learn from. These aren't books from small Alaskan presses. These books have stamps on them from awards and more awards listed on the back.

"Take pictures of them or whatever you kids are doing to keep track of your reading piles." Renee slides the books she scanned onto a cart. "It was nice meeting you, Clara. I need to find a lackey to put these away. Just leave the books on my desk, and I'll slip them back onto the shelf after you leave."

I flip over another book. "Thanks."

I want to write Rhodes and tell him I'm in "his" library. I want to FaceTime Elias so I can show him the inside of this incredible building. Instead I breathe in again. I close my eyes and listen to the sounds of people moving past me. Books being removed from shelves, slid across desks…

The whole *feel* of this place is exactly what I pictured. I picture Mom standing where I'm standing. I picture what it would be like to be able to call her and tell her how excited I am.

"There you are!" Lachelle tosses her arm over my shoulder, making me jump. "Let's blow this joint and find some grub," she teases.

"Okay."

I follow her, running my feet across the worn floors and breathing in the book smell. A new kind of wanting ache takes over. This time it has nothing to do with Elias or Rhodes or scars or doctors and everything to do with me.

25

As I move up the sidewalk with Lachelle, I realize it doesn't get dark here for a totally different reason than in Alaska. Too many cars, streetlights, stoplights, store lights…

Lachelle's hair is up in one of those messy updos that makes her look like she tossed her hair together, when in reality it took her like twenty minutes. Mine hangs straight around my face, and I tug my bangs forward again. Smooth my lips together. They're used to ChapStick, and the gloss feels thick and sticky.

"They're up here." We push through a door into another narrow hallway.

Nerves dance through me. Will I stand out as the high-school kid? The scarred girl? Will I manage to fit in? *Please let me blend enough so I don't feel like an imposter.*

After what feels like seconds while my feet just keep moving forward, Lachelle's dragging me through a door and into a room that's filled, but not packed with people. Cigarette smoke burns my nose, but it's not so thick it's hard to breathe.

"I'm Edgar and your host." A guy yells over the pounding music. His shoulder-length brown hair falls forward as he does a mock bow. He holds out his hand and I take it, grateful for the dim light in his apartment.

"Clara."

"Dude. She flew down from *Alaska*." Lachelle grins like it's something interesting.

"Oh wow. Nice." His brows go up. "Holy *scars*, girl. I'd love to hear that story."

Someone's hand is on his arm, and he's being dragged backward with a smile on his round face. A group in the corner of the small living room erupts in laughter, and a guy jumps on another guy's shoulders and then snaps a picture of me and Lachelle in the doorway.

"Seriously!" She smacks his leg. "Knock it off!"

Some girl jumps between Lachelle and me, swinging an arm over each of us. "Can I get you two a drink?"

"Um…" I start but my phone vibrates in my pocket. And then again. I slide it out and slip out from under the girl's arm.

Elias.

"Hey!" I say, but the music drums into my ears too loudly to hear his response.

"I can barely hear you!" I call into the phone.

Lachelle steps next to me and points to an open window.

"Just a sec!" I yell again, wondering how these people live in an apartment building that lets them play music so loud.

"Step onto the fire escape," Lachelle says.

Right. I ease down until I'm sitting on the windowsill and then slip my legs through the open window. All I can see from here are the building next door and several other fire-escape platforms with people sitting outside. The buildings are only a few car widths apart, and window after window shows life after life of people living in the city I've wanted to see and feel and breathe for as long as I wanted to be a writer.

The night breeze sends goose bumps across my skin.

"Clara!" Elias yells. "Can't you go somewhere quieter?"

I jump at the sound of his voice.

"Um…I'm already outside on the deck." Which is really a fire escape, but whatever.

"Where *are* you?"

"It's just a little…." *Party.* "A few literature students."

"I…still…why…Clara…love…"

"Elias. I can't hear you," I yell again, my heart sinking a bit. "I wish I could share this with you." But how could I? Even if he were here, would quiet, calm Elias understand what I love? I'd be surprised if he did.

"Never mind!" he hollers into the phone, obviously annoyed, which pinches at my chest. "Call me when it's quiet!"

"Okay!" *Crap.* I send him a quick text.

Sorry so loud. Love you. Miss you. Wish you could have come. Even though I can't imagine Elias in this place.

I get a response almost immediately.

Love you. At work. Talk soon.

At work? Oh, right. Four-hour time difference. Four hours and a different universe.

I look back into the party. Think back on my afternoon. Scan the building next to this one and the masses of people in every direction. My cheeks hurt from smiling. Elias said we'd work it out, but how… How could we live in two worlds that are so incredibly different, both love those respective worlds, and still be two people who should be together?

I can't answer that question now, so I tuck the phone in my pocket. Lachelle reaches through the window, grabs my hand, and announces that we've decided to run through the city on a scavenger hunt. "Groups of four, and I've picked our other two, so we're good."

I pause for a half second before remembering it was Dad's idea to send me and I've already talked to Elias, so there's no reason to even pause and wonder if it's okay that I do this or not. "You sure they want me along?" I ask.

Lachelle gives me a sideways squeeze. "Why not?"

"I'm so in."

"She's in!" Lachelle yells as she drags me back inside.

"Grab your phones, ladies," a guy I sort of met at the party says. "The list this time is pretty craaazy."

And three minutes later, we're running up the streets of New York looking for a diner in hopes of snatching a picture of someone eating fries for Item 8.

I'm just here. Walking up the streets and listening to everyone vent about professors and how glad they are to have survived another semester and what they want to do with their summers...It's all so much more normal. Being here should feel like a different world with how much has felt off lately, but it doesn't—at least not in a bad way. My chest is tightened in excitement, and I'm smiling like an idiot as I listen to everyone talk, but yeah...belonging here doesn't seem like the impossible task it used to.

"You should totally be a zombie for Halloween," one of the guys says, pointing at my face. "Pale you up a little bit and darken up those scars. Killer."

"I'll keep that in mind." I try to suck my smile back in because I know it doesn't look quite right, but maybe we're past that now.

"You're a friend of Rhodes?" the other guy asks. His eyes skim over my face before he looks away, which is much more what I'm used to from new people.

The memory of the kiss flashes in my mind before anything else. "I guess. Yeah."

He snorts. "*I guess*, as in yes, or *I guess*, as in more than friends but I won't tell you?"

"*I guess* as in he's my teacher right now, only my dad insists on him coming to dinner at my house, and I have a boyfriend who is not him." All true and much safer.

The two guys laugh and high-five.

I didn't realize I could be so far away and still be me, *and* be enough for this experience. The longer looks are going to happen no matter where I am. And maybe no matter how much surgical work I put into getting my scars removed, I'll get looks. I hate it, but I at least feel like I know what I'm fighting now. I'm fighting how I react to the way people see me.

Lachelle loops her arm through mine and drags me faster across the street. Laughter bubbles up as excitement pushes me forward. Middle of the night. Students who are smart enough for the Ivy League but still know how to have fun, and a city that I don't think I'll ever get enough of.

I'm going to be making another hard decision sometime very soon.

* * *

I write and write as I sit at the airport to go home. If I'd hated New York, so many things would be so much simpler. The poem tears at me a little as I get it down, but it feels good.

Before giving myself too much time to think about what I'm doing, I send it to Rhodes. I'm Clara. A writer. I can send my poems to people who go to Columbia.

It's an odd thing to be broken
Inside. A place where most can't see.
But the cracked bits inside of me seem to be my token.
And trapped in my body, a silent plea
For wakeful hours less filled with messes,
And thoughts unhindered and laid bare.
The touch of the familiar somehow lessens

The thrill of finding my heart there.
Minutes, days, hours planned.
Wishing for guidance to overtake,
To know the place my soul should land
Before my heart finds need to break.
The mess in me and mess in him,
My soul, transparent, unfilled, and dim.

I can't be torn. I can't live half in one place and half in another. I blink and a few tears slide down my cheeks. How is it possible for me to feel even more undecided and torn apart now than before I came?

Rhodes sends back a message right away: **You knew I'd love this one. I hope you found what you were looking for in New York.**

I did, I tell him.

And I'm now in the biggest mess of my life.

26

Jet lag and New York lag have me stumbling over my feet by the time Dad and I make it home. My throat is sore from dry airplane air, staying up all night with Lachelle, and trying to recount every detail for Dad on the way home.

The house feels the same. But different. I look at our wooden walls and rustic dining table and…Why does it look different? I know this place. I know the chairs. The dents. The scratches…

"I'm so glad you had fun, honey," Dad says as he hangs up his coat. "You must be wiped."

I am wiped, but I'm also amped.

"Sounds like you love the city every bit as much as your mom." He gives me a small smile.

"Did she miss it?" I ask as I stare at the inside of the house—still feeling like I'm looking at it from the outside in for the first time.

Dad wanders into the kitchen. "I asked her all the time if she was sorry for marrying me instead of finishing her degree."

"And?" I prompt as I follow.

Dad grabs me in a sideways hug. "I was always sorry for her, but she wasn't. We were happy. We were in love. And we had you."

My heart is feeling hollowed out and unsure.

"Do you know what you want to do yet?" Dad asks. "For school?"

I shake my head, and his brow gets all wrinkled with worry.

"Okay."

"I'm…" What am I going to do with myself? "No Rhodes for dinner?" I ask.

Dad chuckles and the worry on his face relaxes. "I figured you'd be exhausted."

I nod once. Of course I am, but Rhodes knows New York and Lachelle and Columbia. We could talk about the chaos of the city and how it feels to wander the streets in the middle of the night…The campus library. Maybe he'd have some ideas of books I could start with. I'm tired but bursting at the seams.

"I'm gonna unpack and get stuff ready for school tomorrow." Where I'll see Elias. Who I don't know what to do with after my weekend away.

I hoist my bag and head upstairs. My stairway isn't too different from the one in Lachelle's apartment building, but it's…I notice the scuffs on the walls and the dings in the wooden steps that I don't see when I'm here every day.

Will I end up with my own apartment in New York? One with its own dings and quirks and imperfections? I'm sure there's no way I'd get into student housing at this point—I'd have had to put my name on that list ages ago.

Am I *ready* for my own apartment? Utility bills and roommates and contracts…this fall? It feels so soon. So grown up. So faraway. Even though I was just there.

I flip open my jewelry box and stare at the ring Elias gave me. Sliding the gold band between my fingers, I wonder why he had to do this now. I can't conceive of Elias understanding any part of what I loved about my trip. I can't imagine Elias understanding why Columbia is a big deal. He'd understand the part about my mom, but would he understand why I want it for *me*?

He won't understand if I go. Not really. I'm not sure if I will even. My mind is still stuck on the idea of spending a year at home first. The truth is that I still don't know what I want. I don't know how to tell if my decisions are my own or if I'm being influenced. Is that normal?

I flip the ring over in my hands again.

This is too permanent.

Lachelle talked about dropping everything to go to the Sorbonne.

Rhodes talks about traveling and being somewhere new for long enough that the newness wears off.

I want to write. I want to write everything. Read everything. And for that, I need experiences.

I want to find a way not to feel sick when people stare at my scars. I want to find a way for people to see me as something more than the scarred girl.

I flip the ring over again. It's the finality that this ring signifies… That's what's weird about this ring. Dad said that I need to feel like our love could get us through anything, and I don't feel that. I'm so uncertain. I'm so afraid that what I feel for Elias will taint everything else. If I were actually ready to get married, I'm not sure I'd care how tainted my decisions were.

Why now? Why did he have to do this now?

But now that I'm home, maybe I'm looking at Elias and me in a different light too. He is everything good and sweet that belongs in a small town like the one we're in.

I'm…

My heart twists and I set the ring down.

I don't totally know what I want yet, but I don't think I can be tied like this.

Not now.

Not yet.

Leaving for school and being long distance with Elias seems like the obvious solution, but just the thought of it doesn't fit somehow. The idea of being split like that makes me feel completely off my path and totally out of balance. Unfinished. In limbo. Like a life stuck in rough draft.

If I go to New York, I don't want to be split between here and there. I want to *go*. If I stay here, I don't want to look down at my hand and wonder if that's what's keeping me here. I want it to be about *me*. No matter what I decide right now, I need it to be for *me*. Maybe that's just me being stubborn... selfish... or maybe I'm finally realizing that saying yes to Elias was putting myself on a much simpler path than the one I want to be on.

I send Cecily a text, the words still not seeming real.

I told Elias yes, but I think it was a mistake. What do I do?

She writes back almost immediately and says pretty much exactly what I knew she would. **You know what to do. I'm sorry.**

Sorry... sorry... There are not enough sorrys in the universe right now. I don't want to hurt anyone. I don't want to hurt. But with the way I feel, there's no way around it.

* * *

It's so surreal. The whole situation. The ring is clenched in my fist and I'm about to give it back to Elias. "I can't marry you. I'm so sorry."

We stand in the parking lot of my school because I'm horrible and it took me all day to work up the courage. I'm fully aware of how I'm destroying him, and I feel like I'm being ripped apart for it.

"You're not making sense, Clara." His voice breaks twice, which just splits my heart further.

"We can't get married," I say. "I might be leaving for school."

His head shakes quickly. "People who are married are separated all the time."

I knew he'd fight this. I just wasn't totally prepared for what I'd say. I wanted our split to be quiet. Something I didn't *have* to fight. If I have to argue my way out of marrying him, I'm bound to say something horrible that will hurt him even worse. I don't want to hurt him at all. It's just that every time I think about not getting married, I feel lighter. Mom would have understood. Would have known what to tell me to say. Instead I'm…I'm fumbling.

Tears start down my face as I struggle to find the words I rehearsed last night. "I just can't…I'm so sorry." Where's all the strength I got on my trip? The idea that I really have to look out for me?

"Military. Even the people who work on the oil slopes. We know so many. They're gone half the time." His fingers don't stop tracing patterns on my arm. "We can last through that."

"I'll be gone for two semesters a year." *I can't be torn like that. Not with you. I can't wonder how many of my decisions are tainted by wearing a ring on my finger.* "I don't want to hate you for wondering what if…"

"What does that mean?" he asks.

"I…" But I don't know how to explain. I'm supposed to know what to say. What words to put together. I'm coming up with nothing.

He cocks his head to the side, his brown eyes pleading, and my heart breaking. "And you'll be home for holidays, and I'd fly you home for long weekends if you want. Maybe come hang with you for a week once in a while."

"And stay where?" I ask.

"I don't know. With you."

This is so weird. I realize in this moment that I'm breaking up with him. I, Clara Fielding, am breaking up with Elias Motter—the boy who is far too good for me and far too good-looking. And me with a face that will never really be fixed. How did this happen?

The ring is beginning to turn into a chain—holding me far too tightly to let me breathe.

I don't want safe anymore.

"Elias, I just can't. I'm not ready to commit to forever."

He pulls in a breath. "I get that. I don't need you to right now. We can see each other over the summer and Christmas, and I can still come visit. We'll just—"

"We'll just have to be careful until we get married?" I offer, feeling like I'm negotiating the sale of a car instead of my relationship with Elias.

"Exactly." He takes my hands, but my left hand is curled into a fist around the ring he gave me.

He steps back as he stares at my hand. "You took it off. Clara. Why? I don't understand *why*."

"This is what I need. I'm so sorry." And just like that, with the look of utter devastation on his face, I hand him the ring.

And like somebody who is a complete and total coward, I turn and walk away, my body both stretching from the relief and caving in from the pain.

I pull open the door of my truck and am openly sobbing by the time I get it started. I don't look at Elias. I don't even do a double check in my rearview mirror before pulling out. I just drive away because I can't handle the aching hammering in my heart—especially knowing it's my fault.

27

I now have this big, black cloud following me because I know how I devastated Elias. I know giving back the ring was the right thing, and *I'm* devastated. He, I'm sure, does not believe it's the right thing, which has to make him feel even worse. The second I pull into our driveway, I run for the loft of the barn.

Every time I close my eyes I see the pain on Elias's face when I said I couldn't marry him, and bile slides up my throat, even though I know in the deepest parts of me, *down into my soul* as Dad would say, my decision was smart.

I tried to talk to Rhodes today about Columbia, but all he said was that he was glad I had a nice trip.

That's it.

How can that be it?

I'll be back at school tomorrow. And so will Elias. And I know it's going to be awful.

The barn door opens, and I can't deal with Elias or Rhodes or any kind of advice Dad might have for me. I just can't.

"I am absolutely, completely, and totally not in the mood," I say in a flat voice.

"Just me," Cecily says, and the ladder creaks as she makes her way up. Without a word, she lies down next to me in the hay. I turn to face her, knowing I'm a mess and beyond happy that she made it home before this.

"How'd he take it?" she asks, reading the expression on my face.

An odd cough-laugh comes up my throat. "How do you think?"

"Bad?"

"Actually, I sort of shoved the ring at him and ran away." I run my hands through my hair again, and it's already half covered in hay. "But not well."

She gives me a weird frowny face. "So, even now, you can't be totally honest with him? This has to be a sign you did the right thing."

"Maybe. You're judging me. I can see it on your face."

"Sorry." She rubs her hand over her face a few times like she's roughing it up and then smiles. "Better?"

It's now my turn to frown. "Only a little."

"So?"

"So I tried. I tried to tell him I was seriously thinking of leaving. That there are so many things open to us right now and that I want to experience some of them. I know I didn't say anything the way I should have. I just can't have my decisions tainted right now. I can't."

"And he tried to talk you out of it?"

"He tried to say he and I could be together while I went away to college." All the feelings of being torn between two places and never actually leaving home help me remember why I had to split with him. Doing the right thing shouldn't make my chest feel like it's cracking apart. It's that I said yes to Elias for selfish reasons. I pushed him further for selfish reasons. I kissed Rhodes for selfish reasons. I have to move past that, and I'm going to have to find a way to talk to Elias for real to explain.

"*Married* together while you go to school?"

"*Any* kind of together." Tears start flowing again as I think about how much Elias was willing to give up for me, and how little I was willing to give back. "Am I just a horrible person?"

"No. You're doing what's right for you. And he needs someone who's ready to turn their life upside down to be with him, the way he was for you."

I don't have an answer to that. Why don't I love Elias enough to be what he needs?

"It'll be okay. And maybe we'll be in New York together this fall."

That's another huge thing I don't know if I can think about or tackle, but if I didn't split with Elias to go to New York, why did I split with him?

"And maybe if you have a ten-year reunion, you and Elias will be friends again and you'll meet each other's spouses, and it'll all be fine." She smiles.

I roll onto my side, and the pain of being separated from him hits me again. Elias with someone else?

But then when I think about me with someone else, stupid Rhodes's face comes in, and then the guys I hung with when I visited Lachelle, and I wonder if *I* could be with someone else. It's kind of exciting thinking about first glances and first touches—there's some hope that maybe someone else wouldn't mind my face…

I could start over and ask them all the things I never asked Elias. Do things Elias wasn't willing to do, though I'm not sure I'm ready for that either. It's just… "I don't have any idea what I want." Splitting with Elias gave me that twinge of relief, but I wasn't prepared for the new weight.

"Why don't you just try to *let go* and have some fun for a while. I think it's been entirely too long since you've just *had fun.*"

"Yeah…" I pull in a deep breath. "Maybe."

I'm just not sure, even after all my own selfish thoughts, if I have it in me.

28

I'm trying to brush my hair, but my stomach keeps flipping over, threatening to relieve me of the half a toaster waffle I barely crammed down this morning. Oh, and my hands are shaking. My eyes are bloodshot and rimmed with dark circles after my sleepless night.

It's a horrible, horrible thing to think, but I should have waited for a Friday to break up with Elias so we'd have a couple days before we'd be forced to face each other again.

"Clara!" Dad calls. "Please don't be late for seminary! Sister McEntyre puts a lot of effort into your lessons!"

I'm so wishing I hadn't already used a fake illness…or two.

I cough twice before the word makes it out of my mouth. "Coming!"

* * *

My fingers slip on my scripture pages in Sister McEntyre's basement, and I'm asked to say the prayer and have no idea what comes out of my mouth. My flipping stomach has turned into a knotted one that twists tighter every time I think about running into Elias at school. My heart breaks a little when I think about seeing him and him not smiling at me. What will it be like?

The drive to school, which normally takes hours, takes seconds.

I stand outside my truck staring at the front doors of the school, still wondering if I have the guts to drive away. Give myself a few more days to figure out how to put my feelings into words for Elias.

My last hope of Elias possibly taking a sick day is dashed when I see his truck parked on the opposite side of the parking lot. Meaning, the opposite of where he used to park it so we could park next to each other on the days we didn't share a car.

Yeah, today is going to be as awful as I figured.

* * *

By the end of first period, whispers are all over the school. It's not totally their fault. Any news in this tiny place is big news. The last rush of news had to do with the ring on my finger, which makes this turn of events that much more interesting. Whispers follow me down our short hallways.

Just stringing him along…so weird…He could do so much better anyway… Wonder if she's leaving for college…wonder if he got sick of kissing a scar…

I'm blinking over and over, staring at the books I have clutched in front of me like a shield and darting between students to get into English. I take a deep breath the moment I sit down—and then panic because the seat next to me is empty. But it's Elias's seat and he'll be here any second. Maybe it'll be okay. Maybe we'll be like the friends we were before we started going out.

I open my binder and start the warm-up assignment on the board. It's just two hundred and fifty words, but these few words are about to occupy my brain and take over enough that I won't notice when Elias sits down, and then when I do look up, it'll be to listen to Mr. Kennedy lecture, and the whole class will be looking because…well…he's Mr. Kennedy and the class is almost all girls, and then I can busy myself with my things while Elias walks out and it will all be fine and perfect and okay.

My pencil is poised over my paper but words won't come. Nothing. I'm blank. Two hundred and fifty words on any poem from our last section. *Any* one. And my mind refuses to cooperate. The bell rings, and Elias still isn't here. I write my name and put yesterday's date on the top right and then wait for inspiration to strike.

I stop breathing when Elias steps in the room. Two minutes after the bell. The smell of sawdust and whatever manly, delicious soap he uses waft by, followed by Elias himself. He doesn't even pause at his chair, just continues to the front of the class stopping at Mr. Kennedy's desk.

Now I'm straining to listen but people are sharpening pencils and whispering to each other like I don't need to hear what's going on.

Elias's voice carries over the noise. "…I was helping in the office, and now…"

Mr. Kennedy's brow pulls down. "A different seat…?"

My eyes widen. Elias can't even stand to sit next to me. The burning in my chest is unexpected. Now it's Elias who's rejecting me. Rhodes's eyes catch mine quickly and whatever I'm feeling must be banner-sized across my face because Rhodes nods and Elias takes a seat at the front. No glance back. No double check to see if I'm in the room.

I start calculating the hours we'll be in school until the end of the year.

Nearly seventy.

I might puke.

Rhodes gives me a sympathetic smile after Elias sits down. At least there's nothing I-told-you-so about it. But I catch the familiar sight of the back of Elias's head and my heart feels weighed down again.

29

"Are things any better?" Dad asks as he walks into the kitchen, freshly showered for his date with Suki.

"Like in the three days I've had to share a school with him since breaking his heart?" My lame attempt at a joke falls flat, and we stare at each other with weird, blank expressions until Dad frowns.

"I'm sorry, Clara. Forever is a long time to be with someone when you're not sure." He blinks a few times as if he's struggling to find more words to maybe help. "Eternal perspective. Remember that."

Instead of rolling my eyes, I close them. Right now the thirty seconds it takes to pass Elias in the hall feels like an eternity.

Dad straightens his tie, and I hop on the kitchen counter to watch.

"Things are changing with you and Suki," I say. It's not a question. I already know. If the kiss wasn't enough, the date he's been getting ready for since four this afternoon is.

"Is that weird for you?" Dad pauses as he turns from the small mirror on the fridge.

"More than I thought it would be." Probably best to be up-front.

Dad stands and his eyes go from the mirror to me. "I can hold off… until you've gone to school or…"

I wave my hand between us. "That's silly, Dad." I try to find some version of a narrow-eyed, teasing face even though I want a serious answer. "Is that why you want me in New York?"

Dad leans against the counter next to me. "No. You being in New York terrifies me, but not as much as you being unhappy. I sent you there because I needed you to know I'm okay with you going wherever you want to go and doing whatever you want to do, as long as—"

"I'm living a good life and doing what I want in my *soul*." Which in Dad's mind is following church guidelines and finding ways to be happy—using my *eternal perspective* instead of the bigger part of me that wants to do whatever's easiest *right now*.

Dad rests his hand on my knee. "Exactly."

"So…" I trail off.

"I made an appointment with the specialist in Anchorage that was recommended by Dr. Breckman. Happens just after you graduate, if you'd like to give her a visit."

Instead of answering I let my eyes fall closed. "And this is just to… um…maybe bleach my scars out a little?"

"That's the idea, but I don't think you need—"

I force my eyes open, even though the darkness behind my lids suits my mood. "I'll think on it."

"We haven't seen Rhodes in a bit so I invited him for dinner tomorrow. If you're not up for it we can reschedule."

Without dinners or play practice, I really haven't had a chance to talk to Rhodes since coming home. "Dinner's fine."

Dad pauses again near the door. "How are you? Really?"

I swallow because for the past three days, every time Cecily asks, I get this huge lump in my throat. Dad asking is the same. "Feeling sort of hollowed out and weird without Elias."

Dad holds the door handle and faces me. "He's a good kid, Clara. I'm not saying he's not. I'm just glad you're at least giving a chance to the idea of other possibilities."

Other possibilities…

Go have fun…

I wonder if Dad and Cecily have any idea what they're pushing me toward. Or even if I know where I want to go.

* * *

Rhodes holds up his hands as he steps into the barn. "I promise I come in peace."

I drop Snoopy's brush and lead him back into his stall. "What does that mean?"

"It means that you're running from class to class with your face practically buried in your books. Elias is being a douche by not even talking to you, but I won't dwell on that because I said I come in peace. I just—"

"Is there a point in your rambling?" I ask as I step back out of Snoopy's stall. I don't know if I'm annoyed or just resigned that Rhodes is in my business. "I figured you'd be over here every night trying to convince me to go to school in New York after my trip."

"That's your decision to make, not mine." He smiles widely. "So I've tried to keep my mouth shut about it, even though that's the last thing I want to do."

"Hmm." I'm not sure what to do with him being here.

"But you had a good time, didn't you? Lachelle said you were a blast."

"She's something else."

Rhodes grins. "She is. I'm glad you got out with her."

I step back out of the stall and flick Snoopy's lock closed.

"Your dad texted to say he ended up with a client late today, and we'd reschedule dinner. So. Come to Palmer with me. An hour away. We can get some Taco Bell or whatever it is that you and Cecily do, and I just…I won't touch you. I won't be a jerk. I just want to talk. We were friends, and I feel like we haven't really talked since…"

The kiss. No one needs to say it out loud.

I'm so totally suspicious. "Talk about what?"

He gives me a dramatic eye roll as he shakes his head. "Geez, Clara. I don't know. Whatever we want. Anything. Nothing. Movies. Music. Colonizing the moon. *Doctor Who…*"

I actually laugh a little, needing something different. Anything different. If I'm being totally honest, wanting Rhodes's life is part of what made me go to New York in the first place. Maybe I'll learn something else. Get another reminder of why I did what I did to Elias and me. I lock Snoopy's stall door and step toward Rhodes. "Okay."

He freezes and stands up with his brows lifted in surprise. "Okay."

He stops at the barn door and gestures for me to continue. Then he closes the doors behind us, and I climb into his car smelling like barn and horses. Just like that.

"So, really, what I'm trying to do is take you on your first post-breakup date." He turns and drives up the road.

"No."

"Hear me out." He laughs. "It's not really a date. I'm your teacher, and we both know there are a million ramifications to anything past friendship here. You have zero problems telling me to shove off, which means you're comfortable around me. We're both into books. This should be fun."

Hmm. He wants to force us to hang together? We'll do it my way instead of his.

"I don't want to talk about me. I want to talk about you."

His jaw drops in an excited and teasing gesture. "I'm so good at this topic! There's just so much to say!"

I snort before holding in my laughter.

"See? Better already." He grins. "Ask me anything."

Ask him anything…He wanted this little venture, so I might as well start big. "Do you believe in God?"

"Oh," he groans. "I'm not doing this."

"You dragged me into your car." I sit sideways to face him. "I wanna do this. Actually get to know you instead of this sidestepping thing we've been doing."

"Is that what we've been doing? Because I feel like I've been pretty direct about how I feel."

My face starts to flush, but I pull in a slow breath and shove it away. "So maybe I've been sidestepping, but it still means I don't know as much about you as I want to. So yes, we're doing this."

"Then let me ask the question first. Why do you?"

"Because when I believe in God, I also believe I'll see my mother again. That gets me through a lot." I don't allow myself to feel more than the familiar twist of missing Mom because I refuse to be a weirded-out mess today. "I also live my life in a way that I feel good about—most of the time. So…so I also believe because of that."

"You don't find that a bit of a tease?" he asks.

"What?"

He stares at the road for a few moments. "Like your mom's out there somewhere, just not with you?"

"Don't you find it horribly depressing your brother just disappeared from existence simply because he died?" The words leave my mouth, and Rhodes sits so still that I think I went too far.

His jaw flexes before he answers. "Yes."

"So, I get the feeling you think I'm stupid for believing in something bigger than me. Like I'm the fool here, but you know what? I don't care if it's not true because I *want* it to be true. I'm going to live my life so much more at ease than you will. So who cares if I'm wrong if it makes me happy while I'm alive?"

He opens his mouth a few times like he's about to talk, but nothing comes out. His smile gets wider, and I notice he has dimples too. Nice ones. "I think you've made the first good argument for religion I've ever heard."

"Good." I slug his shoulder, but not because I'm looking for ways to touch him now that we're in this small space. Alone. Together. "Because as lazy as I can be about what I believe, that's not something that'll ever change about me."

Rhodes's eyes lock on mine for a moment. "Good to know. Now ask me something *else*. Please."

I stare at him for a moment. "You know what you're like?"

"Oh man. Do I wanna hear this?" he asks with a smirk.

"Yep." I grin. "You're like a short-story collection. I feel like you're you, but every day you're also a little different."

"Huh." He nods a few times as if letting my words sink in. "I'm... I'm going to choose to take that as a compliment."

"Good."

"So. Questions?" he asks.

Yes. I nail him with question after question, and it feels fun and like a game and distraction and exactly what I needed.

This is what I learn about Rhodes Kennedy as I drill him on every aspect of his life that I can think of:

First. He lost his virginity when he was seventeen to a girl he took to prom. This is embarrassing simply because it's such a stereotype, but at the time he didn't much care because she was hot and he was a horny teenager. I tell him he hasn't changed much and get an eye roll.

Second. He doesn't talk to his parents often, and a lot of it has to do with losing his brother. (Rhodes doesn't say this. I infer this from all the other family and religious stuff we talk about.)

Three. He'd major in almost everything if he could. Not biology or physics, but almost everything else.

Four. Rhodes has traveled to twenty countries. He's spent a significant amount of time in ten of those countries. He has college credits from California, New York, France, Great Britain, and Italy. He's hoping to rack up some credits in Greece next.

After student teaching, he still wants to teach high school or maybe college, but not right away. He's totally okay with this because he's loved the experience.

Even in all the conversations over dinner and the deep conversations in the barn and *the kiss*, now is when I finally feel like I'm starting to know Rhodes.

While I listen to him talk, I can't imagine traveling so much. So many new faces. New languages. New explanations. I wouldn't know where to start. "I could never just travel around like you have."

Rhodes stares at me for a moment, ignoring the road. "Why...why would you say that?"

I stammer a few times before the thought formulates into something that can leave my mouth. "I just...All that traveling...I don't know. How do you even start?"

He shrugs. "You just do. You learn about a program in Italy, and you look into what paperwork you might need, and where you might get student loans or grants for it, and you apply."

"But that's..." *For other people.* That's seriously how I was going to end that sentence. Why is it for other people? Why can't I be the *other people*?

He smiles wide. "It's finally hit you, hasn't it? That you can do it."

I shake my head a little and sit back. "I don't know."

"It has. It hit you. It just might not have sunk in quite yet."

I'm not ready to say, but I do know my world feels just a little bigger than it did this morning.

30

I breathe in deeply when we step into the bookstore. It's no Columbia University library but it works.

"See?" Rhodes bumps my arm. "You needed this."

I'd never admit this to Dad, but sometimes the bookstore feels as much like church as church—on the non-boring days. "I did need this."

We walk in silence for a few minutes and then head over to the young adult section, because I'm pretty sure the new Ellen Hopkins book is out and she writes whole novels in poems.

I snatch her new one off the shelf even though it's in hardback and is going to wipe out my cash.

Rhodes taps the book. "I knew you'd like her, but young adult? Really, Clara. You're going to Columbia."

I clutch the novel more tightly. "I haven't said if I'm going to Columbia or not. And anyway, I love her." I raise my brows. "*Love*."

"You know, if you want to keep reading fiction for juniors, Sonya Sones writes in prose. Carol Lynch Williams has—"

"*Glimpse*. Read it. Brilliant."

He cocks a brow. "We really need to do something about this."

"About what?"

"Your book selections."

"What would *you* have me read?" I ask.

"Wouldn't hurt to find something by the professors of the school you should go to."

"I thought you weren't going to push me on which school I should go to," I say.

Rhodes shrugs.

That's what Renee from the library said too. "I'm not giving up my Ellen Hopkins, but…where should I start?"

Rhodes cackles and claps his hands. "I'm so putting together a reading list for you. I doubt this tiny store will have what we're looking for, but we can try…"

I follow him back a couple of rows. There's something so different about this place now…like looking at my house after the New York apartment. Now I'm looking at my very pristine, very small bookstore and realizing how limited I am in my choices.

Rhodes taps his chin as he scans titles. "There's this great class I took about Dostoevsky and Tolstoy, and another on American novelists… You could start there. I'm assuming you've read *something* by one of them? I don't think we'll have any luck finding books by any of the profs here, but I can hook you up online. You need to read some of the modern award-winners. Need to."

"Why are you doing this?"

Rhodes pauses after slipping two books off the shelf. "Doing what?"

"Being so nice to me?"

"*Because.*" He leans in close enough that I can smell whatever spicy aftershave he uses. "I like you, even though I shouldn't."

And then he leans back like he didn't just admit something that could change what we are.

I shake my head and stare at the books, that connection I've felt with him striking me again and making it hard to breathe. The fact that he's a teacher doesn't even register when we're outside of school, and being a student teacher and still in school himself doesn't…We just don't feel as separated as I thought we would. I feel more intimidated by the fact that he goes to Columbia, and the fact that he's living a version of the life I think I want to live, than I do about his age or position at my school.

When I step back, I finger author names on the front of books and imagine mine there. But it won't happen, not if I stay here. At least it would take me a lot longer to learn enough. My breaths get short as I think about leaving. Really.

"Shakespeare!" He shouts loud enough that I spin around and shove my hands over his mouth. "They actually have something here that's not SparkNotes," he says through my hand. "That's cool."

"Shhh…" I laugh, thrilled for the distraction. "This is the only bookstore near me. I can't afford to get kicked out."

He takes my hand off his face but doesn't let it go. Our fingers weave together, and now my breathing is shallow for a totally different reason. He feels so *good*. He shouldn't feel so good this soon after I've broken Elias's heart. I stare at his eyes, wishing I could read his mind.

Rhodes seems to know he's pushed some kind of boundary because his face changes again and lightens with a smile. "I want to see your name up there." He taps a book. "You should be an author. That would be so cool, Clara. So cool."

"I can't do that. Not a whole book." But inside part of me is spinning, floating, dancing, swinging on a trapeze suspended by my imagination. I just thought it, and he just said it. Maybe…maybe it could happen.

He snorts and walks slowly farther down the aisle. "Of course you can."

"No." I look at the stacks of the books and think, *maybe*. Maybe if I really, really, tried.

"I bet you can recite a random poem. That you come up with. Right now. Your brain is amazing."

Now I want to see if I can ruffle him. I bite my lower lip and rest my hands on my hips, letting my shirt ride up to expose my stomach. I tilt a brow and take a step closer to him. "There are a *lot* of amazing things about me…"

He leans forward, touching my exposed side briefly with a finger and letting his lips touch my ear. "Don't I know it."

My cheeks heat up. My heart races. Experiment thwarted. Or failed. Or maybe, with the rush I feel at how close he is, my move worked perfectly. I think about how his friends all said that he liked me. That I could actually have something real with this older, much cooler guy. And that he'd want it for real and not just for distraction. Someone who didn't know me before I got my scars. Someone who met me now, who might *want* me now.

I should not feel so much excitement at the idea of this. It's the *newness* that I crave.

"Poem," he urges. "Spontaneous. Come on."

Rhodes drops his hand and backs up like we didn't just have that moment.

I scramble for a sec, but he's right. I can feel the words forming faster than I can say them out loud.

"There's this really annoying guy.
He's totally bothering me."

I pause just long enough for him to give me a look of mock exasperation. He leans an arm on the bookshelf and watches, waiting for me to continue. The words are there before I open my mouth.

"I stop to wonder why,
but maybe he can't see
that he's the one whose brain
is always a step back.

Oh, how could I train
him to steal a stack
of books from off the floor
as I watch and laugh?
We might run through the door
before we are attacked,
But the old lady here
might not catch us quickly…"

I snort as I try to hold in my laughter, and Rhodes's grin splits his face.

"…stinging bits of fear
that would dissipate so swiftly.
We would be a modern-day
Bonnie and Clyde of books,
listening to the Fray
as our favorites all we took,
And living life as we would be,
careless on the stairs,
With our loot of written word…
We'd run so safely there."

Rhodes blinks a few times as his face softens and he takes a step closer. This is the intense guy I don't know what to do with. The poem was supposed to be silly. Stupid.

He takes another step. Now he's close enough that I can feel his warmth. His breath. I'm waiting for his lips to meet mine or for his hand to slide around my back, but neither happens. "I want you to know what a huge amount of self-restraint I'm using."

"Self-restraint?" I squeak.

"I love how I feel around you. I really do love how your mind works. I'm not lying when I say that I think you could go far."

I swallow hard as he leans almost close enough to kiss me, and it takes everything in me not to move away.

"Thanks for letting me take you out, Clara." He leans away. "Thank you for the poem."

I nod once and clutch Ellen's book tighter to my chest.

"We should go before I do something stupid and make you uncomfortable." His face lightens into a smile. "It's really too bad that I promised to be a gentleman tonight. And too bad we didn't meet in college instead of here."

We walk toward the cash register in silence.

He slides his hands in his pockets and walks with almost a loose swing. Relaxed. "I didn't mean to make you feel weird, just laying out the facts."

I nod and blink a few times, suddenly all out of words. I'm baffled that someone like him would even give me a second glance. I was under the impression that more things make sense as you get older rather than less.

Guess I was wrong.

31

I shove the food around on my plate, hoping that if I spread it out enough, Dad won't notice I've only had a few bites. The deadline for fall admissions hovers. I don't have much time to put down my deposit or defer, and I'm not sure why that decision hasn't come to me.

I've left Elias four messages begging him to let me talk and explain, but silence. He still won't even look at me in the hallways. I tried to give him my half of our joint project for history, and he walked away. It's all even worse because I know it's my fault. So, silence at school. No texting back. No Facebook messaging back. Total lockout. In a way I can't blame him, but it's really messing with my sanity.

The moment Dad and Rhodes start talking airplanes again, I get up from the table. Rhodes gives me a questioning look and I shrug, leaving it up to him as to whether or not he follows me.

The smell of hay tickles my nose as I step through the barn door.

"How are you?" Rhodes asks, making me spin around.

"I…" I need to step up and be honest. "I'm not sure."

Rhodes leans against the stall door. "Elias is being pretty harsh. You deserve better."

"You're jumping right in." I scowl and head for the water to fill buckets before I deal with food. I expected him to be softer or something after the other night.

Rhodes stands next to me and takes the bucket to help. "It seemed stupid to avoid the thing that's obviously still weighing on your mind."

I'm too exhausted over the whole thing to talk about Elias. In some ways, breaking up with him still feels like the stupidest thing I could have done. In other ways, a weight has been lifted, but that comes with guilt I wasn't prepared for.

"I wasn't fair to him. I said yes one minute and no the next, and didn't give him a lot of explanation why." A few more days of school and then I won't have to face him. There's a nudge of sadness at that— maybe Elias can salvage something after this mess. "Mostly because I don't completely understand why, aside from my need to not be tied down."

"Is that what you want?" He takes a step closer, and I can't let myself internalize what he might be implying with that move, because there's a good chance I'd jump on him and make a fool out of myself. "To not be tied down? Does that mean you'll be going to New York?"

"I'm not sure." I head for the ladder that leads to the hayloft, partly to escape Rhodes, because ever since he got here, it's like I've forgotten how to be a regular person when he's around. Not that I seem to be very good at that anyway. "I had a plan, you know? Part of me still wants to stick to that."

The nearest bales are too far against the back wall so I start to slide a few of them forward. They're heavy and I'm distracted to the point of feeling weak. It's not really an important job so I turn around to go back down but pause. "You wanna come up?" I ask.

"Sure."

I sit on the floor of the loft, and Rhodes sits next to me.

"Oh. Hey." My palms are insta-sweaty, and I can't take a deep breath. We're alone. He's close. I'm pretty sure I'm some kind of a bad person because I don't mind. Rhodes and I have done one drive for Taco Bell and the bookstore together. But I'm all fluttery like so much more has happened. Like I'm ready for so much more. Girls like me don't kiss another boy when they're with a boy. They don't immediately want to kiss someone else when they've just broken a guy's heart. And yet… here I am.

"Scoot back?" he asks as he slides against the back wall, stretching his legs out in front of him.

I sit next to him and pull my knees up, wrapping my arms around my legs. Rhodes does the same, and now our legs touch.

"You could do anything, Clara. I don't want to bag on your town, but you're better than this. At least see what the rest of the world has to offer before you settle here."

"I'm not…" But I don't know how to finish because his leg just touched mine and all thoughts ran from my head.

"I probably shouldn't be here," he says quietly.

My hands rest on my knees, but his hand slides up his thigh, touching mine as he moves, shooting jolts of excitement and anticipation through me. He traces the top of my hand with his fingertips, and nothing exists but me and Rhodes and this small space in the barn.

After the energy that has spun between us since he arrived, I want to test it out. Him. Us. That's what not having ties does to people—it leaves them free to try out new things. That's what I wanted. That's why I split with someone I know.

I slip my fingers between his, and the only thing I can think of to do now is kiss him. He must have had the same thought because we meet between us, my lips brushing his in the softest touch. Soft enough to make me ache and soft enough to send shivers through me, making my body crave more of him.

"This isn't smart," he whispers.

"I'm not sure I care." I wrap my arm around his neck and draw him closer. We fall over and are now lying down, tongues tangling. Everything feels so new. Rhodes and I don't have a comfortable rhythm to kissing, and I don't know what he likes or where my hands should be, but it doesn't seem to matter because we're frantic for a moment before he slows down.

Rhodes pulls back and brushes the hair from my face, cradling my head in his two hands. "As stupid as this may be, I've wanted to do that since the first day I saw you."

"Why?"

"Something in your eyes, I think. Some kind of smartness or strength or determination or...maybe the fact that I've felt like we were equals since we met. Maybe just because I saw your scars and thought you might be interesting. Have insights. Thoughts. Experiences."

I breathe in a deep smell of hay and notice the difference between how Elias's body felt next to mine and how Rhodes feels. Because Rhodes is resting his body on mine like he wants it. Like he belongs here. Like it's an okay place to be, which makes me feel much less horrible about our closeness.

"I think you were seeing things you wanted to see," I tease, and the tease feels so good that it starts to fill in the cracks of all the hurting I've done.

"I don't think so." He traces the scars, forcing my eye to close, moving his fingertip over my lip.

And then I ask the question I was always afraid to. Having my eyes closed makes it easier. "Does it feel strange to kiss me?"

The pause is so long I know he's actually thinking about it, and I love that he's taking the time to give me a real answer. I open my eyes to see his thoughtful ones, his body still resting unapologetically on top of mine.

"You're new. *Everyone* feels different." His fingers brush away a few more stray hairs.

"You know what I mean." I stare at his chest instead of looking him in the eye.

His finger traces my lip. "When I kiss you like this"—his lips touch mine in the softest kiss— "I can feel the difference between one side of your mouth and the other, but just barely. You probably have a warped perception of how drastic your scarring is. And I can't believe you're putting me on the spot like this." He grimaces but is smiling, like we've been this intimate a hundred times and not one.

"I've just always wondered."

"And you never asked Elias?"

His name now feels like a language I don't understand—part dread, part relief, part resignation, part missing him…"No. I never asked him."

"Well, when I kiss you harder, like this…" His lips take mine first and then his tongue slides in my mouth again, and I get completely lost in the moment of his warmth and feel and mouth until he pulls away. "Doesn't feel strange at all."

I start to talk, but he puts his fingers over my lips as he smiles. "It's not weird. It's not actually strange. It's just…You're *you*. I've wanted to kiss you since I got here, and since I kissed you that once, I've wanted to kiss you more. Does that answer your question?"

I grab all the courage I can and pull him closer, feeling the shoulders I stared at a little too much when he first arrived, and kiss him again.

As he pushes his hips against mine, I can feel how he's turned on, and instead of scooting away like I probably should, I wrap my leg around him and bring him closer.

"I can't…" I gasp before our mouths come together again. "I can't go too far…"

His tongue swirls in my mouth again. "Okay," he whispers as he grasps my hips and presses us even closer.

"Clara?" Dad's voice rings out in the barn, and I flip over, knocking Rhodes to the floor.

"Up here," I stutter and then stare at Rhodes. "Grab that end of the bale there," I say as if we were just sitting up here moving bales around.

Rhodes scrambles to sitting so close to the edge that I'm sure Dad can see he was lying down a moment ago.

Dread snakes through me because a conversation about sex or Rhodes and kissing in the barn is about the last thing I want to have with my dad in this moment. Or really, in any moment.

"I got the hay bale, but you can't keep knocking me over," he tries to tease in another pathetic attempt to cover up the fact that we were just groping each other in the barn.

"Don't worry with that now," Dad says. "Why don't you two crawl on down."

Rhodes turns to face me and cocks a brow as if questioning what we're about to face.

I shrug, knowing I'm still mostly out of view.

Rhodes pauses at the top of the ladder. "Glad you joined us, Thomas."

And I almost believe him.

A sick kind of dread pools in my stomach as I slide down the ladder in front of Rhodes. The sad, crinkled eyes are all I need to see to know Dad isn't stupid and knows exactly what was going on.

"Well." Rhodes stops at the bottom of the ladder with a small smile, swings his arms forward, and claps his hands together. "It's been fun, but maybe I should head out."

Dad nods a couple times but doesn't speak, and I bite my lip as I step back and lean against the ladder, wondering if I should try to run for it.

"So…" Rhodes pauses. "Dinner on Thursday?" he asks.

"I'll be in touch." Dad gives him the briefest of glances. "We'll see you later, Mr. Kennedy."

Ouch. Total dismissal.

As much as I should keep my eyes on Dad, I see Rhodes pause at the door and give me a soft smile-frown before stepping out.

"So. I have homework." I start for the door, but Dad is between the door and me, and he holds his hand up before I've had a chance to take two steps.

"Clara."

I pause, unsure if breathing would be smart, every nerve ending teetering on edge. "Yeah, Dad?"

His head cocks to the side. "He's four years older than you. And not just a teacher but *your* teacher. Elias has had me nervous since you two started dating, but Rhodes is...I really like him a lot. But..."

"But?" I ask instead of just staying quiet and nodding like I should.

"I worry about his motivation because he's so much older than you. Rhodes isn't the kind of guy who is looking for a relationship, which is fine until my daughter's in the mix."

Oh great. "Thank you for giving me so much credit, Dad."

He sighs. "You're a smart girl, Clara. Think about what you're doing before you do something you regret. *Please.*"

I fold my arms over my chest. "Next year we could be in the same college classes, Dad. And not even next year, but within six months."

"He give you that line?"

Curse my father's ability to see through pretty much everything. "It's not anything serious. It's...Elias is intense, always has been. I'm mixed up. I'll admit it, but Rhodes is easy. There's no pressure or..."

More than anything, being with Rhodes is about what I want right now and nothing else. I need to do what I want on my terms, and that's what I'm doing.

Dad reaches forward and tugs a few strands of hay from my hair. "When you're on the floor with a guy, it's serious."

My throat is swelling again, and heat rushes up my throat and cheeks.

The idea of my dad knowing what I did with Rhodes...or maybe something of how I feel...It's too much.

"I think they're stellar young men for having such good taste, but as someone who is trying to prove himself responsible enough to handle a teaching position, Rhodes definitely should not be starting any kind of a relationship with a student."

I grasp Dad's arm. "You're not going to turn him in, are you? Say something to the school?"

We stare at each other—almost a war of wills—but Dad's too kind to push forward, and we both know it.

"If you're together with him the way you were tonight, then yes. It's my responsibility, Clara. This is serious. If you two..." He coughs once. And again. And then his eyes are on me so hard, I know he's about to really force his point. "For example, you're seventeen and he's twenty-one. He's more than three years older and in a position of authority. That could be considered sexual assault of a minor, or—"

"Oh!" I hold my hands up between us, shame rushing up my neck and over my face in a wave of heat. "Dad. Don't...No. I'm not going to...We're not..."

Dad sighs, and once again his wrinkles look deeper, his skin paler, and worry grips at me.

"I'm okay, Dad. I'm not going to have sex with him."

He tugs me into a half hug, and we start for the barn door together. "I'm not sure that you're okay. You're still...distracted. Please talk to me. Or Suki. Or even Cecily."

There's something off about leaning into my dad so soon after being so...intense with Rhodes, but I do it anyway because I know it'll make Dad feel better. I don't want to internalize how I should or shouldn't have acted with Rhodes, because I don't want to talk myself out of doing it again.

32

I hit the brakes of my four-wheeler in front of Cecily's house and run for the porch steps, heart still thundering after the phone call.

Her door opens, and Cecily steps out with a smile. "I'm not on your way." She laughs.

Laughs!

"Yeah, well. Elias is ignoring me at school, but it's not like I can suddenly tell his mom I can't help her at the warehouse," I protest. "I need you!"

I spin back around, heart still thrumming, and sprint to the wheeler, throwing one leg over the seat and standing with my feet on the pegs, waiting for Cecily.

"And you got me," Cecily climbs on behind me, and I sit on the padded seat so she can hold my waist. "Don't kill us on the way, alright?"

I hit the gas the second she's on, and we tear up the trail that follows the road. "I'm running late," I yell.

"I gathered by the fifty text messages warning me to be ready."

Bringing Cecily to work is like my buffer. I don't want it to be obvious that I need one, so I may have slightly lied and told Elias's mom that a friend was over, and I had to bring her with me.

Instead of the happy tingling in my stomach I used to get when

Motter Construction came into view, my stomach twists, tightens, and rolls over.

I let go of the gas, and the four-wheeler slows down so fast that Cecily runs into my back.

I slump. "I can't do this."

Cecily snorts. "Yes you can, and you will. You two used to be friends, Clara. Maybe try to get some of that back."

"Elias won't talk to me," I protest.

"Well…" She sighs. "I'm here. Let's go."

I tentatively press on the throttle, and we drive into the parking lot. No Elias.

Thank you.

We step off the machine, and I push open the front door to see Elias standing behind his mom.

Stomach. Gone.

"Hey." I wave as my smile trembles.

Elias gives us each a brief nod before turning away and pushing through the doors into the warehouse.

Cecily puts her hand on my back and shoves me forward.

"Just really quick today." Mrs. Motter smiles, but it's a weird, flat, forced kind of smile.

Right. I broke up with her son. Broke his heart. And it's not like she doesn't know.

"Okay." I walk around the counter on shaky legs and flop in the chair next to her.

We stare at each other for a moment, but I don't have words.

"I'll sort nails," Cecily offers as she moves to that part of the store. I swear every one of us has sorted the bins with nails at some point growing up.

"Just an accounting question." Mrs. Motter taps her computer, and I stare for a moment, leaning in and squinting.

"You just have a few things in the wrong column. Ten minutes. Tops." And then I can leave.

"Thank you," she says quietly as she slides her chair back.

I try to focus on the numbers and columns instead of the fact that she's still silent. I move the numbers back over and scroll down to make sure nothing else is amiss.

My phone vibrates in my pocket and I pull it out.

There's a text from Rhodes. I'd like to see you today if you can swing it.

My head swivels both ways, like Elias will suddenly appear and see that Rhodes is writing me. And then my gaze falls on Cecily's back. She's the perfect cover to find a way to spend time with him.

Yeah. I can swing that. At work now. Should be done in fifteen. Where do you want to meet?

I hold my breath waiting for his response.

You're the expert.

I'm the expert? Oh right. I live here. We've spent a lot of time in my barn, and we've hung at the fairground cemetery. School is out. Church is out. Our few restaurants are out because technically I'm still his student, and neither of us wants to deal with the backlash of us being seen together.

I'll pick you up and we can ride the wheeler. Is that okay?

I set my phone in my lap and shuffle a few more numbers on the Motter computer.

With you on the tiny seat of a four-wheeler? I'm in.

Oh crap.

Well. Actually…the idea that we'll be stuck that close together might be fairly awesome. And my chest bunches up in guilt over sitting next to Elias's mother while texting a guy I'm about to go see.

See you in 30 min to an hour.

And now I just need to focus and get these numbers in.

* * *

"You're seriously ditching me?" Cecily says as we pull up to her house.

"It's for a good cause?" I try a sweet smile.

She folds her arms. "I've barely seen you!"

"I'm sorry, but I really, really want to spend a few minutes with Rhodes."

"Fine." Cecily frowns in a fake pout. "Have fun."

"I will." I grin, sit back on the seat, and once again hit the gas. This time for Rhodes. Because with him there's no pressure. No expectations. Just now.

The swirling excitement whips into a near-frenzy as I cruise up the trail to Ms. Bellings's house. I take a sharp left next to a creek that I know flows through her yard, which is better because being on the roads on my way to him might not be the best thing.

I now get why people do things they're not supposed to. My head is light and swimmy, and my stomach is twirling with anticipatory nerves. This is forbidden, but at the same time, we could totally be in the same college classes next year, so it's *fine*.

I'm meeting up with a guy who likes me for my talent. A guy who is older, goes to my dream school, and wants to kiss me even though my lips are scarred.

Rhodes is jogging down the steps before I've even stopped in the yard and slides on behind me. The strong arms I spent so much time watching are now wrapped around my waist.

"Okay, Alaska, take me into the wilderness." His lips touch my neck, sliding a rush of tingles through my core.

I open my mouth to say something but words don't come. Instead I concentrate on the feel of his strong arms and how his chest occasionally bumps against my back and how his thighs rest over my thighs. We drive back toward the creek and about a mile up the trail where I know there's a lookout. My face doesn't matter. Elias doesn't matter. School doesn't matter. We matter.

He stands up behind me as we pull to a stop. "Wow. You can see the canyon both ways from up here. The town…" He points. "The river…Wow…"

I stand up in front of him and nearly reach back to grab his hand, but I'm not sure if I can just do that now or…"Glad you approve."

His arm slips around my side and across my front. "You could turn around."

I turn around, stumbling over the seat before I'm facing him, each of us still with a leg on each side of my four-wheeler.

He kisses me once, sliding his lips across mine and leaving me aching for more. "Let's sit."

Rhodes sits first, and there's really nowhere for my legs to be until he grasps me under my knees, lifts my legs, and wraps them around his body. He holds my waist tightly, sliding us together. A wave of heat spirals through my body as his lips meet mine again.

Arms hold me, a body is pressed against me, lips search for mine. I feel wanted. Sexy. Pretty. Desired.

His hands slide over the back pockets of my jeans, and he chuckles into my mouth when his fingers slide over my notebook. "Can I see?"

"Nope," I tease as I nip at his lip.

"Tease." He nips me back.

I run my tongue across his lower lip before leaning away from him. "Yep."

He slides his hands up my back, bringing me closer still. "Being alone with you is so, so perfect," he mumbles into my neck before kissing me again.

His warm hands slide under my shirt and up my back. Will he touch my bra? Want something else I'm not ready for? "Not too far," I whisper as my body tenses.

Rhodes grasps my sides, hands still under my shirt. "You feel amazing."

I rest my forehead against his, practically panting for air after so much kissing.

"The Mormon thing, yeah? Why you don't want to move fast?" he asks.

The "Mormon thing" would probably keep me from wrapping my legs around him and wanting his hands on my skin, but I can't give that up. Not now. I'm thinking too much again, which is exactly what I don't want. Instead of answering, I tighten my legs and lick his bottom lip until his lips find mine and we once again find a beat to touching and kissing and…and everything that I wanted from him.

33

I'm looking over heads and trying to smile for graduation pictures while searching for Rhodes in the sea of blue robes and hats. Maybe he's not here.

Intoxicating. Burning. Desire. All words that used to make me cringe in their corniness now stir my chest into this fluttery feeling that's thick with anticipation and want.

Esther and Abby come by and give me hugs that feel more genuine than any words we've exchanged. "We would have talked to you more, but you're so…"

"Intimidating," Abby finishes.

I shake my head, totally baffled. "Me?"

They both nod. "You always seem to know what you want, and you're always so focused and driven." Esther folds her arms. "So…um… good luck in school and everything."

"Where you going?" Abby asks, but I'm not sure what to say.

"University of Alaska this year and then…maybe New York."

Maybe.

I sent in my deferment letter. This gives me a year of…a year of *whatever I want*. Visiting the plastic surgeon in Alaska. Going back to Seattle for my first surgery. Really, it just bought me time. I need time. And hopefully they'll accept my deferment, and I can start next fall. Hopefully.

I mumble, "Congratulations," as they move away. How could I possibly be any kind of intimidating? How can I not just say yes or no about leaving for college? People do it every year. Lots of them. My plan just got shattered with Cecily going early and the plastic surgeon. I had to have some part of my plan intact.

Elias and his parents stop next to Dad. I hold my breath. The boy whose ring I wore is shifting his weight and moving his hands in and out of his pockets while our parents nod, smile, chat. We haven't given each other more than a glance of acknowledgment in the two weeks since we split, so I'm sure he hates this as much as I do. I think about all the love he's given me that I've done a terrible job of returning. I step next to him and slide my arm through his before I lose my courage.

"Congrats." I give him a squeeze.

He leans over like he's going to kiss my head, but stops because we're not like that anymore. I'm waiting for him to tell me how awkward and weird and horrible this is, but we both know it.

"You too." He gives me a quick one-armed hug before walking away.

I watch him go. His walk is more familiar than maybe anyone else's but Dad's. My heart cracks, but I can't be held to what Elias wants. I can only be held to what I want. I'm just not sure what that is yet. So, my revelation in New York about making decisions that only had to do with me was a good one, but I still have no idea what I want to do with myself.

Cecily pushes her way through the crowd and grabs me in a tight hug.

Dad snaps a few pictures before sliding his phone back into his shirt pocket. "What are your plans tonight?"

"Hang with Cecily." I shrug. Even though that's just part of my plans.

"No one else?"

"Nope." I've spent a lot of fake time with Cecily over the past week, which has been used to spend time with Rhodes—especially since Dad's suddenly claiming to be too busy to have him over for dinner.

I shrug. "In a graduating class of thirty, not many of whom I have a lot in common with…"

"Okay." Dad gives me another pat. "Be safe. We'll see you tomorrow."

"Of course."

It's Dad's turn to walk away but I slide my arm through Cecily's, ready to plan my night.

"Did you want to see me, or am I just your excuse to be out of the house?" Cecily's eyebrows rise. "Yet again."

"Both?" I give her a hopeful smile.

Cecily pulls me into a tight hug. "Be careful, Clara. I like Rhodes okay, but he's no Elias."

I pull back. "Was it you or not you who asked me almost every time we talked why I was still with Elias?"

She folds her arms and leans against her doorframe. "Only because you always seemed lukewarm. But he's a lot safer, and you have this reckless look about you."

"What does that even mean?" I throw my hands in the air, immediately frustrated. "I'm still me. What do you think I could possibly do? You're the one who said I should be out having fun."

"I don't know, okay?" She tightens her arms. "I just don't want you to do anything you'll regret."

I'm not sure what I'm after tonight. I just know I'm tired of being so careful all the time. That I've always done the right thing and the safe thing, and turning down Elias wasn't safe. At all. It opened up anything. Everything. Tonight I get to be selfish.

* * *

"You made it." Rhodes smiles widely as I step into his aunt's house. Soft guitar music's playing and the lighting is dim. I'm wondering how much of it is just the atmosphere he likes and how much of it is atmosphere he created. For me. Or us. Or...I don't know what.

Wow. Me being here is really real.

"Can I get you something?" he asks.

The energy crackles and bounces between us, and I'm wondering how long I should wait before I touch him or move to feel his lips on mine or slide my arms around his waist.

"I'm good."

"I was reading. Just sort of waiting." He shrugs. "Hoping you'd make it by."

"I made it."

"I see." He leans in so close that I think we might kiss, but pulls away and sits on the large sectional. The thing is so deep it's almost a bed, and I'm a bit surprised that Ms. Bellings has such modern furniture in her house.

"This guy's lyrics are amazing." He leans back.

"Bobby Long, huh?" I ask. "Are you trying to make a move?"

"Now that we've established...whatever this is between us." His eyes don't waver, and my nerves kick into overdrive as my throat does that really horrible swell-up thing that happens whenever I really need for it not to. "Yes. I'm trying to make a move."

Instead of waiting for him, I decide the best reaction is first action, whatever that means. Anyway, I move in first. I expect him to kiss me like he did in the barn—hungrily. Like he couldn't get enough. But instead my lips barely touch his and the faint touch sparks between us.

"There's some pretty mean chemistry at work here," he whispers.

I feel his smile as he kisses me again.

I couldn't agree more.

Somewhere between one and forty minutes (time sort of gets wonky when I'm kissing Rhodes), he's on top of me and the couch is feeling a little like heaven.

He's turned on and I'm turned on, and I also understand that phrase a little better because it feels like with the smallest touch I could explode.

His tongue traces over my lips before his kiss deepens again, and then he trails kisses down my neck. He tugs my collar to the side and kisses my collarbone, past my bra strap, and to my shoulder.

No guy has ever touched me like he's not afraid to. Elias would never have tugged at my clothes to feel more skin.

"Let's get you out of this."

I'm about to ask, "Out of what?" when his fingers slide up my sides and lift the shirt over my head.

Oh. Wow. Okay. I've never been so…exposed.

"You're gorgeous." His mouth is nowhere near mine now, and I'm not sure what to do. Do I touch his hair? His back? He kisses between my breasts and I can barely breathe, waiting to see what will happen next. How will I know what he thinks? If this is good or not good?

His fingers follow the scar lines over my shoulder and down my back. His lips find the scars on my side, and normally I'm ticklish there, but everywhere his mouth touches me drives an intense need in my body to breaking point.

He reaches around to my back and unclasps my bra, making me gasp.

"This okay?" he asks as he slowly pulls it off.

It doesn't feel like much of a question, so I stay silent as he slides the straps down my arms, and now there's a guy, a man, lying on top of me and I have no shirt on and no bra on, and this is feeling very real and maybe a little scary, and maybe like it would be better if I had been the one to push this instead of him.

And then Rhodes sits up and slides his T-shirt off, revealing the shoulders, abs, and arms I've watched since he arrived.

Emotions crash into the rhythm of want, intensifying all of the burning that makes me need to feel him.

He lowers himself on top of me again, and in about three seconds the heat of him and the feel of his mouth on my mouth fuzzes out everything else. All of the undressing was maybe a fantastic idea. His fingers massage my sides, and I'm pressing my hips up toward his because I can't imagine not feeling his hardness between my legs like in the loft of the barn, and I think about how much better it will be now because his skin is against my skin.

His fingers dance around the top of my jeans and I'm gasping for air as we kiss and I pull on him and my heart hammers and my body just wants, wants, wants.

I don't realize my pants are unbuttoned until his hand slides under the edge of my panties. He's seriously moving his hand down...

Oh.

Wow.

All I can think as his mouth moves over my chest and his tongue teases me and his fingers slide over my skin, on me, under my underwear, is that I get why people like sex. I get why people do this. Why they don't mind being naked because it leads them to this, and I'm whimpering and trying not to, only I'm worried if I don't whimper that I'll moan or worse, and I can't have that. It seems to be encouraging him because his movements are getting more frantic, which is making my body more frantic.

This time I do make an embarrassing noise, which is followed by total...shock.

And not the good kind. It's a shaky, weak, pulsing rush of goose bumps and a fear I've never experienced.

I don't really even know Rhodes, and I'm half naked on a couch in a house I've never been in before—and I maybe shouldn't be with him like this. As the pieces continue to crash down, he continues to tug down on my pants and to unbutton his pants, and for as much as I wanted more of Elias, I'm not ready. Not with Rhodes. Not right now.

"Wait. Stop." I'm out of breath, and I'm not sure he can hear me.

This is so weird. Real but not real. Surreal. How did I get here? How did I end up in this weird place of nakedness with an almost-stranger?

Okay. Not almost-stranger. But almost-stranger compared to most of the people I know. My heart pounds so hard that I swear it's blurring my vision. How could I have let this happen? My decisions. My way. For me. That's what I decided. But this…? I'm not sure how my decisions led me here, even though I was a part of all of them.

"Rhodes." I skitter away from him, my pants now below my hips, and frantically pull on them until I realize my shirt and bra are gone and I'm so exposed. So insanely, ridiculously exposed and I want it over, to be done, for me to be home and in my own bed and far from him and this and everything, and I can't make it happen fast enough.

Nothing I can do will magically transport me somewhere safe. I clutch my chest with one arm while I reach around in the dim light for my shirt or my bra or anything.

I wanted this.

I just don't know why in this moment. Why?

I slide my shirt on and stuff my bra in my pants pocket.

The look on his face is blank…stunned. "Clara…I don't—"

"I'm an idiot. I'm sorry." And I stand up as he kneels on the couch, his pants undone, his shirt on the floor, and it hits me that I don't know who he is. Not really. I know some of him, but not enough for what we're doing here. Not for me.

"Clara?" There's a tinge of worry in his voice, and I don't need anything else to make me feel stupid so I open the door, shove my boots on, and run for my truck.

I need home.

I need safe.

I need to figure out how to turn off whatever kind of crazy brought me here tonight.

As I drive home I feel…gross. Grosser than my face, my scars. Dirtier than I've ever felt before in a way that crawls over me from inside. For so long I always knew my firsts would be with Elias, and now…

I wonder if I should be trying to be with anyone. I wonder if a miracle could possibly happen and I'll wake up any second to realize this was just a dream. A really stupid, bad dream. The spidering guilt over what I did with Elias is nothing compared to the thick blackness spreading through me now. There was a reason I didn't want to go too far before I was married. How did I forget that? How did I let myself go so far with someone I don't know? What was I trying to prove? Who was I trying to prove it to?

By the time I pull into my driveway, it's evident my dream scenario won't become a reality. And that I just ran away from Rhodes in the middle of…whatever that was. And when all I want is my bed, I feel so disgusting and I'm afraid Dad will know what I just did if he sees me, so I slide lower down in my truck and let the tears fall.

34

The doctor's office in Anchorage is completely opposite in feel from the office in Seattle. The desk is cluttered with papers, pens, and several stacks of books. There are diplomas on the walls, but these walls are painted an odd shade of peach and are smudged and scratched.

My chair wobbles, and I shift my weight back and forth. Back and forth. Back and forth.

Why am I even here?

This is so stupid. I already know how little I can be helped. I catch my reflection in a tiny mirror, and I stare at the welts on my face. At the corner of my eye that leads to my thickest scar. At the twist on my mouth.

I'm not sure whose idea it was to put my doctor's appointment the day after graduation, but it was a stupid one.

Every decision I've made since coming home from Seattle smashes into my head like a brick. Saying yes to Elias, stupid. Saying yes to going to Columbia for the weekend, smart. Sending Columbia a deferment letter? Stupid. Saying no to Elias, gut-wrenching. Saying yes to Rhodes, foolish.

How can I explain the trail of rash decisions?

Yes, Elias pushed me too far emotionally—asking me for forever when I wasn't ready to give him that. And Rhodes wanted so much physically—making me realize I didn't want that with a guy as much as I thought. What does that make me? A horrible tease? At the very least, a girl who shouldn't be trusted, not even with herself.

Just getting out of the house alone this morning was a chore because Dad has been treading strangely around me and asking way more questions than normal. I had to leave him home with a baffled look on his face because I can't deal with him being at the doctor's appointment with me.

There was no time to shower this morning, and my skin pricks and crawls with the places I was touched by Rhodes.

I was raised differently. I thought I *believed* differently. I'm so ready for this wretched, swimming pit of dread in my stomach and heart and head to be *over* before I go completely insane.

My stomach rolls. I grab the trash can and lose the oatmeal I ate for breakfast.

"Oh," a woman says. "I'm not this kind of doctor."

And then she laughs.

I cough again, my face still buried in the trash can.

"Did we party a little too hard after graduation last night?" she asks.

I slowly lower the can with shaky fingers to see a young woman with pale skin and spiky pixie hair. Not what I was expecting after the too-quiet doughy man in Seattle.

"No," I groan. "I don't do that." I also am not the kind of girl to let a guy do…whatever Rhodes and I did last night. Only I did, so maybe I can't say I'm not that kind of girl anymore.

Tears press at the back of my eyes. I *do* want to be the girl that applies to—the girl who is careful with boys and about how she dresses and acts and the language she uses and who doesn't drink…all of those things…

And.

Am I?

"Oh dear." The woman slides her chair around her desk and sits facing me, holding out tissues and wet wipes. I grab the wet wipes first and rub around my mouth, and then two handfuls of tissues and press them against my eyes. Maybe if I push hard enough I can force myself to stop crying.

"I'm not this kind of doctor either." She chuckles while readjusting her glasses.

I finally look up. "Rough...couple weeks."

Her eyes narrow and she leans in, scanning over my scars. "Why haven't I seen you until now?" she asks.

Why hasn't she? "I'm not sure," I say. "I've had the same family doctor since...forever. He said something about growing up and letting the scars heal, and my dad was on board with that, so..."

"Still." She bobs her head from side to side. "I could have maybe helped them heal a little smoother. Maybe not. But maybe."

My stomach drops. She could have helped. Before now.

I should have pushed harder. Wanted more. Researched more. Questioned more.

"I can't do this today." I lean back over the garbage can, waiting for the next protest.

She laughs again. "Well, Clara. I'm going to clean a few creams out of my sample cabinet. I have one that might slowly lessen the discoloration a little more than the one you said you've been using. We can do some laser treatments, but your scars aren't as bad as I guessed by reading your file. They're significant, for sure, but still...I don't think you'll gain anything by going back to Dr. Breckman instead of working with me, but that'll be up to you."

Her voice is so...no big deal. "You see a lot of this?" I gesture in a circle pointing to my face.

"Nope. Not so much." She shakes her head. "You're my first facial bear scars, but not my first bear scars."

"Oh."

"I'm from Florida, so I've seen a few gator marks as well."

"Oh," I say again.

"But"—she shrugs—"I don't think you're really in the mood to discuss our long-term goals for you at the moment, and that's totally fine. I'll squeeze you in when you're not feeling like you need to use my trash can to throw up in. Sound good?"

I push out of the chair and slowly set down the can, my hands still shaking, totally unsure what to do with this unexpected woman.

She slides open a cabinet door and hands me two small boxes. "Read the directions. If this feels weird on your skin or scar tissue, rinse it off. This is mild, but it might help you feel like you're doing something more than what your family doctor prescribed. Should bleach you out a little, and this other one might smooth them over a little. The silicone oil here..."

I stare but can't really absorb her words.

"Never mind." She chuckles again. "You call me if you have any questions and do a tiny test area on the back of your hand before applying this to your face. When you first apply something new to your face, only pick one small portion of a scar to make sure you don't react."

I nod numbly.

"And whatever's on your mind? That's what we have friends for, Clara. Go find a friend. Then call me and we'll reschedule you."

"Okay."

I stare at her for a moment longer, and I think that something else to do with my scars has shifted. I came here. I'm talking to her. I'm moving forward or not moving forward on my own terms. That's...something.

As mortifyingly ridiculous as this all is, I nod again and stumble out of her office toward my truck, the final bits of vomit sticking like slime in my mouth and throat.

The first thing I do when I leave her office is get a soda to rid my mouth of the taste of death. I drive past the massive bookstore in Anchorage, but I just can't bring myself to stop. My phone buzzes in what I'm sure are texts from my father, maybe Cecily, maybe Rhodes...

Find a friend, she said. Maybe. Or maybe I just need to find a place to be alone.

With my eyes still swollen and blurry I finally make it back to Knik. I hit the gas too hard as another round of tears falls, and the messes I've made hit me over and over.

At the last second, I jerk the steering wheel and start toward the house Elias is building.

So much for alone. I must be going for another round of torture. I'm pretty sure confronting Elias isn't the same as finding a friend.

Maybe I'll understand the decision to walk away from him again if I see the house. I panicked in that house, and I want to remember the panicking so I'll remember why I made the first decision that put me on the path that led me to throwing up in a doctor's office this morning. That decision was the one to break up with Elias. Time to face it in a better way than shoving a ring in his hand and driving away.

I grasp my stomach with one hand, in hope it'll settle, and then stop at the end of the driveway when I see not only Elias's truck, but two others as well.

This was stupid.

But the second I slide the truck in Park, I get out instead of driving away.

They're on the roof today, but Elias isn't laughing or shoving anyone or anything. Just slapping down the shingles and nailing them to the roof. My chest cracks a bit at his total lack of…anything.

What did I do?

He's been not just my boyfriend but my best friend for way too long for me to see him this way and not hurt because of it. My knees nearly buckle under the stress coursing through me. I tap my back pocket for my notebook, even though I don't really feel like writing anything. It's there. So is the memory of how I threw up and cried at my doctor's appointment this morning.

"Elias!" I call.

But no one answers. The sound of the generator and two nail guns sort of drowns out everything else.

"Elias!" I yell again and pull in a shaking breath.

Why did I think this was a good idea? I'm bothering him at work, and for what? So I can feel better about breaking up with him?

He peers over the edge and stares at me blankly for a moment. "Just a sec," he calls, but there's no tone of voice or anything for me to go on. It's all just flat.

I lean against the front of my truck as he climbs down the tall extension ladder. As I watch his T-shirt pull on him and the way his work pants hug him just right, I think about how careful he is with me...and I start to wonder if I was right in walking away from him.

"What can I do for you?" Elias asks as he shoves his hands in his pockets.

"I..."

His brows go up and his shoulders stiffen. He's trying to show that he doesn't care and I'm interrupting him, but I know him too well.

"I hate that we don't talk and it's making me crazy, and I'm sorry and—"

"Do you want me to ease your conscience?" Elias spits. "Lie to you and tell you I'm great?"

I step back, blinking, bile once again rising up my throat.

"I told you I'd do anything for you. That I'd wait for you while you went to school, that I'd help you if you decided to stay here, and you still walked away. How am I supposed to feel about you being here right now?"

"I don't know," I mumble.

"Because it feels shitty to know how thoroughly I was dumped."

My eyes snap toward his because I don't think I've ever heard Elias curse. Ever.

"I'm sorry," I mumble again, and all the things I've wanted to say to him have seeped out of my brain leaving mooshy nothingness.

"And now there's rumors flying around about you and Rhodes, and I asked you about him, Clara. I *asked* you, and you played it off, but obviously…" He blinks and stops talking. He swallows and then again.

He rubs his forehead and stares at the ground for a moment, and I'm shattering. Again. I did this. Me. I broke it off with him in a horrible way, and then—

He takes a step back and shoves his hands in his pockets. "I'm just… I'm wondering if you're the girl I thought you were."

"I…" But I have no idea if I am or not. "I'm probably not." That's the harsh reality. Elias thought I was someone good and kind and… I'm not.

"Please go, Clara. I can't…I'm at work." He turns and walks away.

Elias has never walked away from me. Not like this. I've known him since I was a kid and now…the hollow pit of loss I carry with me just grew. And this time it's completely my fault.

As I drive away from Elias's house, I finally slide out my phone.

Three missed calls from Dad.

Two texts from Cecily.

One text from Rhodes. I got a call this morning. We need to talk.

He is the last thing I need, but since I'm already on a roll with tor-
turing myself, I know where I'm headed next. It's not like the berating
won't be deserved.

* * *

My insides shake as I wait for Rhodes to open the door, and when he
appears, humiliation weakens me so fast that I lose my words.

"So we need to talk…" He trails off, running a hand over his
unkempt, touchable, blond hair.

"Why me?" I blurt. *Okay, this was not part of my plan of things to say
to him…*

His brows furrow. "What?"

"Why were you interested in me?" I ask.

"I still am." He cocks his head to the side and licks his lips a few
times. I get the impression he's nervous, but I'm not positive. "Stupid as
it is of me. I like you."

"It's just that…"

Rhodes scratches his forehead a few times. "It's that I read a few
things you'd written and thought, 'This girl is pretty cool,' and then I
met you. Half-confident and half-shy or embarrassed as you were cooking, and that's when I realized you might be as interesting as I wanted
you to be. And then other times all that shyness flipped into a strength
that I wish I had."

"But I'm not strong. I'm…"

Rhodes presses his fingers to my lips, and instead of the flutters that
used to pass through me, I get a cold wash of uncertainty. I should have
slowed us down. Last night was definitely too much, too fast.

He stopped the second I said "stop," but I waited too long, and now
I'm faced with the knowledge that maybe we both screwed up—at least
to some degree.

"You *are* that girl. I want you, Clara. All of you. I want to kiss every inch of your body and feel myself inside you, and I want to read together and find new authors together and write and laugh and be…I like you. A lot. I guess I'm not supposed to, but I can also see far enough into the future to know that four years' separation is nothing."

The cold disappears as heat flushes my body, and I stare at the porch.

"I can't. I'm not ready. For…for that…" Maybe I'm also a complete moron.

"It's just because you're so sheltered." He sounds impatient again. "And you've got that whole Mormon thing—"

I hold my hand up to silence him and find the strength to look him in the eye. "Don't you dare bring up my religion if you're going to do it in that voice."

"It's just—"

"No. Here's the thing. I get that you think my walking away was stupid. I get that. I'm sure we could have stopped what we were doing and watched a movie or something, but…" I'm not sure what else to say because humiliation ran me out that door. I can't imagine what it would have been like to sit and watch a movie with him after having my shirt off.

"You can be angry at God or the world or whatever that your brother died, and I could do the same with my mother. Instead I'm going to do what I *feel* is right. I'm seventeen. I don't believe people should have sex before they're married—even if there are times when I wish I didn't believe that. If you think how I feel is brainwashing, fine. But give me a little credit for being smart, okay?"

"Okay." He leans back with a faint smile. "This is the strength I was talking about."

I step back, not expecting a compliment from him after that.

"Anyway." He sighs. "I got an email from the principal this morning. My guess is that either your father called them or someone from the school said something about us maybe being inappropriate. Nothing serious at this point, but him questioning me officially is enough to mark my record."

My gut drops. "I'm so sorry." I rub my forehead. What a mess—another Clara special. "I'll write a letter or something if it comes to that. Talk to my dad."

"Whatever. I mean, it sucks, but I'll deal…" He shakes his head and sighs again. "Please don't stay here. Please go to school. Whatever you do…just…please."

Now he's trying to tell me what to do again. Trying to make me feel stupid if I want to be here. "If I'm so talented, I can use it anywhere, Rhodes. I gotta go."

Part of me, surprised as I am that he was interested in the first place, expects him to argue or to beg me to stay or to pull me into his arms.

"Stay in touch, Clara. I still want to say I knew you when." He chews on his bottom lip for a moment before stepping back and shutting the door between us.

I stare at the door for a moment. Being here doesn't make sense. I don't understand where any of my decisions are coming from right now. At all.

My phone rings and I snatch it as I walk back toward my truck because if I'm going to get lectured, I might as well get it from all sides. "Hey, Dad. What's up?"

"I feel…" His words come out weird and slow, and I leap into the driver's seat and start the car.

"Dad?"

"I think…Clara…I think…" His voice slows down like it's warped.

A wave of ice passes through me, leaving fear prickling my skin. "Dad! Where are you?"

"I...home...I..."

As much as I want to keep him on the line, I flip over and dial 911. I can't take something else falling apart. I just can't.

36

I'm numb and in shock and terrified as I sit in the hospital with Dad. They're calling it a mild stroke. I'm calling it something that could have taken my last parent away from me. He fell on the stairs when he had his stroke, and they seem to be more worried about that than the stroke. He hit his back. He can't feel his legs.

A day later, I've had no sleep, and numerous tests have led to no good answers as to how much damage was done to Dad's spine.

Tears slowly roll down my face as I sit in the corner and hold Dad's hand while he naps. Cecily stayed here half the night with me. We slept on the vinyl couches in the waiting area and watched HGTV until she had to run home this morning—an hour away.

Dad keeps insisting he's fine. But people who are fine don't pass out and don't ride in ambulances and don't have doctors prescribing them medications so hopefully they won't have to do all of those things again. They can feel their legs.

I can't leave Alaska. I was stupid. I made all the wrong decisions about everything. If I'd stayed on my first path, I'd be marrying Elias this winter. I'd have a house. A family. I could be around for Dad. If Dad died, I'd have someone. Even just thinking "Dad" and "die" in the same sentence chokes up my chest and makes it hard to breathe.

After an hour, when the sleepy numbness spreads from my hand to my elbow, I finally let go of Dad's hand.

I curl up in the small chair and close my eyes. I can't leave here. Not this room. Not my town. Not this state.

The wall comes in and out of focus as I stare at the whiteboard with Dad's nurses' and doctors' names. Exhaustion seeps into every pore as I slump lower in the chair.

A clicking noise and the soft pad of the hospital door closing make my body jump. Did I drift off?

Suki pauses with bags of lunch.

"Your dad's been sleeping a while?" she asks quietly.

I nod.

"Good. His body needs the rest. That man is so stubborn that even now he's trying to say he's just fine." She rolls her eyes with her classic Suki smile.

"But he's not." I stare at Suki, waiting for her to contradict me or feed me some BS line.

"No." She sits next to me and sets our bags of takeout on the small table as her smile fades. "No, he's not. But right now I think the worst-case scenario is that he'll be in a wheelchair. That's rough, but it could be worse."

"He could have another stroke," I say. "He could forget who he is…" My throat swells. "Who I am."

Suki frowns. "And I could have gotten hit by a semi when I went out for lunch."

I rub my face with both hands. "I'm glad he has you."

Suki pulls me into a sideways hug. "I'm glad I have him too." She plants a kiss on my head. "And you."

With those two words my throat swells again.

"He'll be okay," I whisper to myself.

"I know you don't want to leave, Clara." She pauses. "But you really should go home and try to get some actual sleep."

I start to open my bag, but I'm so tired I can't imagine eating.

"Yeah." I let out a sigh. "Cecily will be back soon, I think."

"I'll call you if anything changes," Suki assures me.

I walk toward the door but pause before leaving. "Suki?"

"Yes?" She smiles her classic wide smile.

"Thanks…" I hold up my bag and nod toward Dad. "For all this."

"Take care of yourself, Clara."

And I would if I had any idea how. I stumble toward the front door of the hospital, and Cecily steps inside just before I make it outside.

"Kind of a crazy couple of months for you, huh?" she asks as she changes direction, walking outside with me.

I lean into her. "Yeah. And so much has been going on with me that I feel like I know nothing about what you're up to anymore."

"Taking pictures," Cecily says. "Hanging with my dad. Counting days until I go to school."

"Oh."

"And Rhodes is going to take off tomorrow, so I got the gig of taking care of Ms. Bellings's house."

I stop in the parking lot. "He *what?*"

"He accepted an offer to spend the summer in Greece, got a lecture from the principal about boundaries with students, and…I can hardly blame him for taking off."

I close my eyes briefly before I start walking again. "I'm not surprised. Yesterday I sort of told him that he was too much for me right now."

"I see."

"What happened between us wasn't really his fault. I let him think I was ready for more when I wasn't, and he stopped the second I said 'stop.'"

There's a swirl of sadness that I wasn't expecting at the news of him leaving.

"I have to stay at Ms. Bellings's house tonight because Rhodes is crashing in Anchorage to catch his morning flight. Wanna come?"

"No," I say, not wanting to relive that memory of what happened in that house on top of the worry that comes with almost losing Dad. "Just home and sleep right now."

"I can do that."

"You're awesome, Cee. Thanks." I give her a lazy half hug and hope that I can turn off my brain when I get home.

"I'm the best." Cecily sighs as we climb in her car and head for my house. "So, you sort of skimmed over Rhodes, but how are you really?"

One second I'm staring out the window of her car, and the next moment everything I'm thinking and feeling all spills out in a mess.

How my face can't be fixed after all the years of hope. How Elias should have been the perfect-feeling solution to that, but how I freaked out over starting our forever now. How Rhodes liked me even though I'm so ugly, and how I ran from him when I panicked. I tell her how far we went, and how I wish I hadn't. How stupid I feel over the whole situation. How I told Columbia I wasn't coming and was sad about that, but am now glad about that. How I threw up in the local plastic surgeon's office. And I can't be fixed, which brings me back to the beginning again.

Cecily's arms are around me before I see her coming through the faucet my eyes have become. We're in my driveway, and I have no idea how long we've been here.

"I've been a terrible friend," I say as I tighten my hold on Cecily. "I'm so sorry."

"No, you've been a *distracted* friend." She grips my shoulders and leans back, studying my face. "And there's something I should have done a long time ago. It just felt awkward."

"What are you talking about?"

She climbs out of the car, runs to my side, clasps her hand in mine, and starts pulling. I follow her through the living room of my house and into the bathroom. She tugs on me until I'm standing in front of her facing the mirror.

I swallow the familiar threat of bile as I stare at my marred face and turn my gaze to the floor.

"No. No way." Cecily's hands are in my hair, pulling it back, and the rubber band snaps as she settles it into place.

"I'm already having a pretty terrible day, Cee. I can't eat. Dad's in the hospital. I've lost two great guys in a couple weeks. I let Columbia slip. What are we doing?"

Her fingers grasp my chin lightly. "Look up."

I obey, but tears press against the back of my eyes as we look at one another in the mirror, and as I try to look at her smooth skin instead of my gashes.

She runs a tanned finger over the scar that took some of my eyebrow. "You have a line here."

"I know." Why is she making me stare at the thing I hate most about myself?

Then her finger touches next to my eye, following that scar into my hairline. "You have a red line here"—then she touches the one from my nose—"and here"—and then from my mouth—"and here."

My short, shallow breaths echo in the small bathroom. Having Lachelle put makeup on my face was exposing, but not like this. Now it's almost like the welted marks are being etched into me all over again.

"They are just lines on your face. They say nothing about who you are as a person. They say that you were part of a huge experience. I don't notice your scars anymore. I see them, but they're just lines. Why are you letting lines skew your perception of who you are? You're amazing. Funny. Wicked smart. Loyal. Sweet. Your writing blows me away. Your mad skills on your horses and four-wheel are practically *legendary*," she teases. "This is one thing. One thing about you. Not everything. Not anything that defines who you are—"

"But they do," I argue. "They define a *lot* of who I am and how I think. How can they not?"

"Only if you let them. This is you, Clara. You're my best friend. You're a million things that have nothing to do with those scars, and a million tiny character traits that *do* have to do with those scars. I get that they're significant, and I get that you hate the fact they'll always be there in some form or another. I would too. I just want you to make sure they're not swaying your opinions or your decisions when they shouldn't."

"What you're really trying to say is don't let them stop me from going to New York." I push out a weird laugh as I stare at the lines on my face.

Cecily snorts. "Of course that."

I roll my eyes. "Of course."

"But don't be surprised when guys like you *despite* your scars. It's not *despite* anything. People like you because you're you. Don't let Elias stop being your friend, and don't jump in with Rhodes again, or someone like him, if you're letting your warped perception of how you look change how you act."

My heart is squeezing in my chest. "Embrace it, right? Like Dad says?" *I don't know how.*

Cecily shrugs and steps next to me. "I don't know if I'd be able to *embrace* my scars if our positions were reversed. I just don't want you to think that the scarring on your face detracts from who you are."

"But they detract from how I look."

"Or maybe they add to it, because as much as I don't see them anymore, I know you do. Maybe it's just time to let that go. To find a way to not care. Elias really doesn't care about the lines on your face. Rhodes probably liked you more for them. Everyone is going to see you differently, Clara, and honestly? I think it'll help you sort out the not-so-great people from the great people in a much simpler way."

The familiar heat of worry and frustration and embarrassment rushes up my neck and over my face. A few tears escape down my cheeks. "I don't know how to feel okay about how I look."

"You will." Cecily rests her chin on my shoulder, still staring at me in the mirror.

I want it. I want to feel that so badly—to let go and just be. "I like the surgeon in Anchorage."

"The one you barely saw?" she teases.

"Yeah…I think…I don't know. I'll go back, and maybe this time be more prepared."

"Stay and talk longer than last time?" she suggests with a smile. "Maybe not throw up in her trash can?"

"Yeah." And as I stare at myself in the mirror, I know I will. But this time, I can go in to see her knowing she'll be limited. Knowing I'll always have marks. The thought still swells in my throat, but at least I can think around that lump. Around the idea that I'll never look the way I would have if I hadn't taken a walk that day.

I blink a few times. "I miss my mom."

"I can't even imagine," Cecily whispers.

Lines. I'm not sure I'll ever see my face as just having a few lines.

"Let's get you food and find all the blankets in the house before I go, okay?" She finally releases me and walks out of the bathroom.

"You know you're like the bestest friend of all best friends, right?" I call after her. Not a replacement for Mom, but then no one would be. Still…still, I have people.

"Of course I know that! Which is why even if you can't come with me to New York this year, I'm gonna *drag* you next year."

Right now I just want to get through the next few weeks with my dad. Next year might as well be a lifetime away.

37

Yeah. My brain? Not so cooperative. It's spinning. The house feels weird without Dad. I can't write, which is killing me because I feel like if I could get it all out, I'd be able to sleep. Instead of turning on the TV, I pull out my computer to check email. The first one is from Rhodes. Checking email was a really stupid idea.

Clara—

I know how news travels in that tiny town, and I also know I should have told you myself. I'm sorry about the way things worked out, or didn't work out, between us. No hard feelings. It was easy to forget how young you are. I hope we stay in touch, at least a little. My hotel in Anchorage sucks, but Greece will be amazing. Put it on your bucket list, okay?

Rhodes

I'm sure I should respond in some way, so I just write back a quick line telling him to have fun, biting my tongue over his age comment and saying I'll put Greece on my list. Done. Over. Still feels weird. At least he bothered to drop me a line.

I can't sit here. Shoving on my boots, I move for the back door, and instead of heading for the barn, I go left toward the trail where I got my scars. Where I lost Mom. We don't use this trail anymore, and the dried grass and leaves from the past few years have made the wide path harder to pick out.

The forest closes in around me as the light diminishes—partly from the dense trees and partly from the slowly setting midnight sun. What am I doing with myself? Why don't I know how to move forward? Every decision I've made has been wrong. Staying here makes me feel like I can't breathe, but so does leaving. A shiver runs down my spine, and I grasp my arms and start walking. This is the shortest path to the river from my house. Maybe the walk will clear my head.

I tap my phone in my pocket and my notebook, which hasn't done me so much good lately. And then I round the corner and stop. This is where Mom was killed—or not far from here. I turn back toward the house, which I can only barely see through the trees. How did Dad know we were here and needed help? Were we screaming? Was I? Mom?

My gut tightens, and my throat fills with the awful slime, making me swallow again and again. How did Dad know to save me? Maybe that's where my miracle that day was—in Dad being prepared enough to save my life.

As I pull in a long breath the thought hits me. *I'm so very lucky to be alive.* I am. I was smaller and not as fast and…it's a miracle I lived, and now I'm messing that all up.

My fingers tremble and I shiver again. This is not the time of year to be wandering around in the woods alone—too many moose headed back to the mountains and too many bears waking up after a long winter.

I walk toward the house, heart thumping, and break into a jog. But now my footsteps and breathing are so loud that I wouldn't be able to hear anything in the woods. I turn back to scan the trees around me as I run, but the forest is too dense to see anything but odd shadows, and I push harder. Harder. Heart pounds harder.

The second I break into the clearing behind the house, I gasp for air and rest my hands on shaky knees. What's wrong with me?

"Are you okay?" Elias is running from the driveway to where I stand.

Elias.

Is here.

I stand and shake out my hands. "Okay," I wheeze.

A corner of his mouth tilts up. "Freak yourself out in the woods?"

"I was on…" I gasp in a few more breaths. "I was on the old trail."

His half smile pulls into a frown. I don't have to explain with him. Elias knows what that place means to us. Because he knows me. My history. My family.

"I'm so lucky."

His brows twitch in confusion. "I've heard you snap back at that comment too many times for it to not sound completely strange coming from your lips."

"I could have died," I say. "*Died.*"

Like Mom.

"Yeah, I know." He wraps an arm over my shoulders. "Let's get you inside."

The familiarity of him spirals around me in comfortable warmth, and I follow him onto the porch.

Elias pauses before stepping into my house, and everything about him looks uncertain.

"I'm sorry," I start, emotion welling inside me again. "I don't know how to choose anything right anymore."

Elias shoves his hands in his pockets as we stand just inside the door.

"Is this totally weird?" I ask.

He rubs his forehead. "I'm just…"

I'm trying to breathe. "Do you still hate me?"

"Clara." His voice is pained. "I couldn't hate you."

My heart warms at the devotion because that's really what it is. "But I hurt you."

He nods, and I step into him, wrapping my arms around his waist.

"I'm so sorry. I was so stupid. I just…I don't know how to explain. It was too much. The wedding and everything, and I panicked. I wasn't ready to start a forever."

"Are you okay?" he asks quietly.

"I don't know."

"I'm sorry."

"I'm still just…" I back up to look at him. Elias is everything good and sweet and known and safe. "I'm glad you're here. Come in?"

He kicks off his shoes and walks through my dining room into the TV room. I might get back some of my stability, and I need it so bad.

We sit on the couch, close but not so close we'd accidentally touch— but not on opposite sides either, so we might be getting *something* back. He's been my friend for too long for me to give up on us completely.

"Do you need to talk? About being lucky or your dad or…"

"No." I shake my head. "Not right now. I can piece that together later. What…what do you want to know? I'm guessing you have questions for me." And how many times will I hate myself for asking?

"I need to know what happened. With you. Me. Why we split for real. What happened when we were apart." Elias leans back and turns his head toward me, almost resigned. "This is horrible, *horrible* timing. So we can do this later. I thought I could come and be here with you just to make sure you weren't alone, but…I don't think I can without answers."

What I'm about to do to him claws at me, and my chest aches because I know everything I tell him about Rhodes will make him feel as horrible as I do—or worse.

Elias's sad features deepen when I don't say anything so I just start. I tell him about how Rhodes came for dinner before that first day of him substituting in school and how he stood too close and made me confused, and Elias's brows rise in surprise that it all started so soon, which makes me feel worse, which makes me talk faster.

I tell him about Rhodes and my writing and college and how I got so mixed up in what I thought I wanted. And how part of me was sad Elias wouldn't break the rules for me. How it was so amazing when Rhodes did and wanted to, until it actually happened. I don't give Elias specifics, but I do tell him we went too far but didn't have sex, and that's when I knew I'd done everything wrong and backward and horribly. Then Dad had his stroke and I needed to reevaluate everything I'd been thinking because I was doing it all wrong, and when I was with Elias, I was doing it all right because I was in the right place.

I'm not only crying, but I'm crying so hard I'm snotty and probably gross, and Elias does the most perfect, most amazing thing.

He raises his arm for me to snuggle in, and I practically leap across the couch to nestle my head on his chest.

"I didn't want to hurt you, Elias. I didn't. I wasn't ready to wear your ring, that's all. I'm not ready for forever. Columbia is…I want it so bad I dream about it at night, and trying to split my head and heart between what I need for myself and you…It wasn't fair to you or me. I'm sorry I broke things off in such an awful way. I could have said this in the beginning. I just didn't know how. Or I was afraid, or…"

He rubs his hand up and down my arm a few times as I get my breathing under control.

All I want to do is tell him I'm sorry over and over and over and over, but I pull away a little. "I can't take back what I did with Rhodes and how I handled things with you, and I hate that I can't."

He blinks a few times and a tear falls down his cheek.

I did this.

I wipe it away, and we sit in silence long enough that I'm not crying anymore and long enough that I sort of know Elias and I have broken down the awful barrier of not talking to each other, and maybe more than that.

He nods and then pats his chest again so I go back to resting my head on him.

I don't know what we are now, but it doesn't matter. I take my first long breath in two days.

38

"You gonna get that?" A voice jolts me from sleep.

"Huh?" I blink a few times when I realize I'm still on the couch.

"Your phone." Elias grins as he hands it to me. "It's been dinging every five to ten minutes for over an hour."

"Oh." I sit up and a blanket falls off my shoulder and onto my lap. "What time is it? Did you stay? How long was I out?"

"Shhh." Elias chuckles. "You crashed last night. I stayed. I slept on the love seat. Suki called to say your dad is doing fantastic and will be coming home within the next few days, and Lachelle's name keeps coming up on your phone's screen. I'd love to stay, but I gotta get to work."

"Lachelle?" I wake up my phone.

Elias gives my shoulder a squeeze before walking around the sofa and toward the front door. "Suki will be back to bring you to your dad shortly. Okay?"

"Yeah." I'm staring at the text on my phone, but the words aren't making sense. When I hear the front door open, I realize Elias is leaving. "Thank you!"

"Yep," he answers before the door closes behind him.

Summer writing workshop got two last-minute dropouts. I called you the second I found out. I know you missed enrollment for fall, but so many people go straight from the workshop into classes. Maybe you could take back your deferment letter if you were here to talk to them in person? I have room in my place. Remember how close to campus I am? Please come. Please.

My fingers start to shake so badly that I can barely hold my phone. This isn't how it was supposed to happen. I'm not…attached, I don't think, but there's no way I could leave Dad or…

"Clara?" Suki calls as the front door pushes open. "You here?"

"Yeah…" I squeak before clearing my throat. "Yeah. Here."

"Would you like to go see your dad? He'll probably be home to-morrow or the next day. We'll have a nurse here, but he'll be glad to be out. Wheelchair for a while until the swelling goes down, but nothing we can't handle, right?"

The words print across my brain but don't stick.

"Your neighbors are taking care of the horses, so we don't have to go deal with them." Another pause. "You coming?"

I push off the blanket and stumble toward the front door. I'll worry about hair and breakfast later. I'm too…What do I even tell Lachelle? What do I *want?*

I could just go for the summer. That would be fine. I mean, doable maybe if it weren't for Dad. I can't leave him right now. Not like this.

"You got a lot of waking up to do," Suki teases as I step through the door, still staring at Lachelle's text.

"Hmm."

"Your dad and I have a few things we want to run by you, and we've got a drive ahead of us, so scoot in and let's get moving."

My legs are heavy and feel weird as I make my way to her car. I type Lachelle a text once I'm buckled.

Not sure what to think yet.

She replies immediately. **No thought necessary. Come.**

What she doesn't realize is that it's never this easy. I push my hair back and lean my head on the headrest.

"What are you intent on over there?" Suki chuckles as she pulls out of the driveway.

"Columbia. It's sort of been a thing of mine." I drop the phone in my lap and close my eyes.

"A *thing?*"

"Salinger, Welty…I mean the list of writers who went there is…"

"Impressive," she finishes. "And you had a good time when you went."

"Amazing." There's no other way to describe it. "I never told Dad, but it's *the* school, you know? Mom went there, then she got me started on a few authors who went there, and if someone were to ask which school I'd take above all others—"

"That's what you'd say."

I open my eyes and stare at the trees. "That's what I'd say." Except I didn't want to go until my scars were fixed, and now I can't be fixed in the way I thought, but maybe…I'm not on a cliff. I'm on a tightrope. Believing that I could ever be okay with how I look is like starting across that rope, a precarious balance, but…what if I could make it out the other side? What if I could do the small fixes—bleach, maybe some shots or grafts or…whatever is suggested, and then be okay with what's left? Part of me doesn't *want* to want that because I want to feel pretty again, and part of me is desperate for it.

She frowns. "I don't think your father knows Columbia is such a big deal for you. I got the impression he sent you just to show you how big the world is and because Rhodes has a friend there."

I bite my thumbnail. "I'd be surprised if he knows how huge it is for me." I've been afraid to speak the words for too long.

"Hmmm."

"They have two openings in the summer workshop program, and I could probably snag one of them."

"And from there, you could probably start classes in the fall."

"Yeah, maybe. But I asked to defer. I didn't give them my deposit…" I pull in the deepest breath I can like it'll somehow make me feel less…stressed. But the maybe could be a yes because even though I told myself I wasn't going, I told them I'm coming next fall. Maybe I knew all along.

"Everything else aside, is that what you want?"

What I want. Tears spring to my eyes immediately. "I don't know anything. Every time I make a choice, it's the wrong one. I don't trust myself anymore."

Suki gives my knee a squeeze. "That feeling won't last forever. And you know what your dad would say."

"He'd tell me to spend more time on my knees praying." The problem is that there's a whole practical side, and I'm not sure how to reconcile that yet. "It's so expensive, and I'd be so far…"

She chuckles. "I can see that smile trying to break through already."

I press my fingers all around my eyes trying to get rid of any hint of tears. "Please don't say anything to anyone, okay?"

"Summer program has to start soon."

So soon. Too soon. "Three days. I need to tell them tomorrow."

"Well." Suki smiles widely again. "That means you got twenty-four whole hours to let this sit in your brain, but while it sits, can I tell you something?"

"Sure."

"Don't you dare stay here because of your dad. He'll be okay. Don't stay here because of Elias, whatever's going on between you two. And don't go because Rhodes obviously wants you to. This is the time in your life when you're putting together *your* life. It's way too early to wrap yourself around what anyone else wants for you. Your decisions right now aren't forever ones unless you get knocked up." She winks.

I shake my head. "It's not that easy. Everything I decide could have lasting consequences I haven't even thought of yet."

"It *is* that easy." Suki's voice is stern. "It would break your dad's heart if he thought you gave up on something you wanted because of him. And any boy who loves you? It should break his heart too."

"Well, I don't have any boy." *Three days...three days...three days...* Can I pick up and leave in three days?

Dear Heavenly Father,

I know my bargains haven't gone so well, but if you'd leave a note in my room or give me some lightning or some kind of answer, I promise I'll find a way to pay you back.

Thank you,

Clara

* * *

I stand, stunned, in Dad's hospital room. "I'm sorry, what?"

Dad chuckles. "Married. You know. Wedding bells, white dresses, big cake, only..."

"Without all of those things," Suki says. "And at the courthouse."

"And we're doing it tomorrow," Dad adds.

"Dad." I widen my eyes. "I just...It's just..."

He reaches out and grasps my hand. "Life can be short. I love her in a way I didn't think I'd love another woman. I've been afraid to move forward for a thousand different reasons, none of which felt important when I sat here in the hospital realizing what I might miss out on."

I want to harass him more, but it's not crazy. He and Suki together make complete and total perfect sense. Like two love poems—totally different in rhythm and style, but both ending in happily-ever-afters.

"Tell me where to be and what to wear, and..." I shrug but the smile is starting to take over.

I throw my arms around Suki who lets out a small "oh" and hugs me back.

"My girls." Dad grins. "I'm one lucky man."

I glance back and forth between him and Suki a few times. She's already so much a part of our family that everything feels…right. Now I need to find that same feeling about whatever I decide to do. The problem is that every time I close my eyes or let a decision creep in, I hear the same word whispered somewhere so deep inside that I don't know if it's just something in me that wants it, or if it really is what I should do, but it says the same thing every time.

Go.

39

The musty smell of the old courthouse pinches at my nose, and I smooth my hands over the silkiness of my dress again. Dad isn't patient enough for a full-on Mormon temple forever-wedding, if that's what they decide to do. He wanted to be married to Suki now.

The wooden walls and benches are worn, but so is almost everything in Knik.

Elias takes my breath away when he steps into the courtroom in a dark gray suit. It cuts perfectly over his strong shoulders and nips in at his narrow waist. His eyes meet mine and my insides pool into warmth.

"Wow." Cecily nudges me.

"He always will be."

"Always will be," she agrees.

"Okay!" Dad claps his hands, his wheelchair and hospital stay only slowing him a little. He's already twitching his feet. His road to walking will be long, but it'll happen. And he'll have Suki.

Her sister flew down from Nome, and both women are tsking and fussing over lapels and flowers and lipstick—both wearing the same startling shade of pink.

Elias sticks his head between me and Cecily and steps forward until he's standing between us. He holds out his arms and we each take one. The relief that comes from talking to Elias again is something so huge that I can't measure it—a piece of my life has settled back into place, which makes moving forward a lot easier.

The ceremony is brief and to the point and, with a bit of a naughty kiss considering their age, it's done.

Elias gives me a quick peck on the cheek and then gives Cecily a quick peck on the cheek.

Cecily cocks a brow as she leans away with a smile.

"Didn't want you to feel left out." He grins.

I squeeze Elias's arm tighter. "I'm leaving," I say tightly.

"What do you mean?" He pulls back.

"For Columbia." I push out a breath. "I told them this morning. The program starts in two days, so I'm gone—"

"Late tonight," Cecily interrupts. "And I'm stuck here for the rest of the summer. But we'll be catching up in the fall!"

"If I'm there in the fall. They sent out letters to wait-listed students, but I talked to admissions and if someone says no, I can maybe have their spot. I sort of fudged timelines around Dad being in the hospital, so Columbia allowed me to cancel my deferment. But for now, New York." And I'm okay with only knowing what will happen over the next couple months. The rest I can decide later. "I might be home to get my lip fixed between summer and fall or maybe not until Christmas break. But I'm going."

"Clara…" Elias's jaw drops before he grabs me and pulls me into a tight hug. "I'm shocked but happy and so, so proud of you. This is so much to take in. Your mom…You know how amazed she'd be, right?"

I nod as I tighten my arms around him.

"You're going to be fantastic," he says.

"'Course she is." Dad laughs as he swats Elias's leg playfully. "My Ivy League girl. Everyone, load up because I just got married and now I need a steak."

I give Suki a tight hug before she pushes Dad out of the courtroom. *Ivy League Girl.*

It's real. Columbia is *real.*

Goose bumps break out across my skin, and there's no lightning or note or whatever I asked for in my last bargain-prayer, but my decision finally feels right. I'm going to take that feeling with me all the way to New York.

40

"I have to say I'm a little jealous of Cecily," Elias teases as he rests his arms on Snoopy's stall.

I breathe in the smell of the barn knowing how desperately I'm going to miss being out here. Between Suki and Cecily and the neighbors, my horses will be taken care of, but I'll miss my time with the wood and warmth and smells. Some of my best memories of Mom are in here, and the loss of her will follow me, but the memories will too.

"NYU is still many blocks away."

He turns sideways and leans against the stall so he's facing me. "Closer than here."

"Closer than here," I agree.

I'm not sure what Elias is getting at. I don't know what I want. I do know that I miss him. That I miss the easy way we were together until I got crazy on both of us.

He steps closer to me and turns toward Snoopy again, letting our arms touch. I don't think, just rest my head on his shoulder. There's so much between us, and I'm glad there is, but I also wish there wasn't. I'm conflicted, like I seem to be all the time.

"What are we, Elias?"

"I don't know."

I rest my chin on his shoulder and watch him. "Are you okay with that?"

He laughs lightly and I know he's about to tease, which is sort of perfect. "It's better than being dumped by you."

I kiss his shoulder before resting my cheek against it again. "Sorry," I whisper. "I panicked."

"I love you." Elias says it like he knows it. And he does. He loves me in a lot of different ways, I think.

"Yes, I know," I say. I'm just not in a place where I can say it back. I love him as a friend and as the boy who sat next to me when Mom died, but more than that? It's too much to think about, and I don't know what it means to love him or to *say* I love him. I said it to him too many times without meaning the words in the same way he meant them. That's not going to happen again.

"Okay," he says. "I'm going to answer your question."

I stand silently and slide my hand around the arm I'm leaning on.

"I don't know what we are, but I'm also okay with that. Weird, considering that the label of us, of going steady, of being engaged felt so comforting. But now…it's different because I know how I feel about you and that's enough. And I couldn't be more proud. I know someone won't take their spot at your school, and you'll end up staying there in the fall and wowing the crap out of them. I want that for you. So bad."

I give his arm a squeeze. "Thanks."

"I'd like to kiss you before you leave. Am I overstepping?"

"Does…" I swallow hard as I raise my head from his arm. I want to see how he reacts to my question. To me. "Does it feel weird to kiss me? Are my scars…" I swallow again. "Are they as gross to you as they are to me?"

"What?" His brows scrunch in confusion. "What are you talking about?"

I touch my lip. Point to my eye, my cheek.

A small smile tugs at the corner of his mouth. "You are beautiful, Clara. Inside and out. I look at your scars and all I see is strength. I see beauty and *strength*, and how amazing you are to have come out the other side of something that could have taken your life."

His words knock into my heart, lightening, pushing, comforting. "You see the beauty in everyone."

"Not Rhodes," he teases. "I don't think he's beautiful."

I laugh. An honest, real laugh. "You didn't answer my question."

"You." He tilts his head until our faces nearly touch. "You have always been perfect to me, Clara. Always."

I close my eyes and ache at the nearness of him.

His lips touch mine so softly I barely feel him, and a small *hmm* slides up my throat.

"You're complicating things," I say.

Elias laughs once. "I'm not sorry. We both agree we don't know what we are, right? You're leaving. I'm staying. We both have lives to live right now. And after what we've been though together, I think that's a good thing."

"Yes," I agree. "It is."

Elias pulls me to his chest. "You have fun in New York, Clara. I love you."

"And you have fun finishing your house." I don't know what else to tell him because the thought of letting him down again is unacceptable. No pretenses. No idea what we are. No label. Just…whatever is, is.

His hands rest on my biceps and give me another squeeze. He leans down and kisses my cheek before resting his face against mine. "Bye, Clara," he whispers.

I open my mouth to tell him good-bye, but he drops his arms and walks out of the barn before I can speak.

I start for the door but a thought slams into me so hard that I freeze. My decision to leave in two days isn't a forever decision. Leaving for New York is life changing, but it's not *everything*. Suki was right. It's *not* forever. It's not permanent. And suddenly I'm okay with whatever Elias and I are. I don't have to make the forever decisions now. I have to make the now decisions now. And I have.

I. Clara Fielding. Am following my dreams and going to New York.

Holy. Crap.

41

As I sit on the plane by myself, the layers of guilt and not belonging and fear begin to peel away. With every minute I'm lighter and know even more that I'm doing the right thing.

Rhodes wrote back a *Woot!* when I told him my plans, even though he's in Greece and maybe seducing some poor, sweet Greek girl. So, there's this welcome relief that we can talk and be friends.

Lachelle gave my eardrum permanent damage with her scream of *Yes!* when I called to see if she still had room for me. So we'll be roomies—hopefully for the whole year. Or she might end up in Paris. If we're not roommates all year, that's fine. I may end up back in Alaska in the fall, or maybe I'll stay in New York. Cecily is all for the last option. I'm okay with making decisions as they come.

I walk out the doors of LaGuardia and climb into my first-ever taxicab. The moment I'm sitting I have a text from Elias.

So proud of you, Clara. Stay in touch.

I tear up immediately at the many ways I miss him: our history, the amazing person he is, what he's done for me. Even at what I'm doing for myself right now. I wouldn't trade having him in my life for anything.

I hit Reply and send him four short words that I finally feel with everything in me.

I love you too.

Acknowledgments

My daughter was born with Moebius Syndrome, so ever since I started writing, I've wanted to explore writing a girl with some sort of facial difference. When my editor, Wendy, said it might be fun to work on a book set in Alaska, I thought…huh…And the idea of my scarred Clara was born. In my mind, this book takes place near Sutton, Alaska, one of the most beautiful places on earth. The river is massive, the glacier is stunning, and the canyon is terrifying to drive in the winter.

There is no way I'd have finished *Has to Be Love* without my husband, Mike, totally cheering me on and making sure I got some nice long writing stints with peppermint hot chocolates at Kaladi Bros in Wasilla. And when I told Christa Desir what I was thinking of doing with this story, she was like, "Yes. We need more of this." And because Christa is wise in all things, of course I had to move forward.

Massive thank-you to Cassie Mae who inspired me to end the book the way I did (and to add more kissing). Another massive thank-you to Ruthanne Frost, who had some great insights. And to Melanie Jacobson, who is so incredibly brilliant at reading a story with her supah smarts and giving fantastic advice. Kaylee Baldwin gave me some insights that led to some fantastic "duh" moments, and I'm pretty sure I flooded her inbox with questions about poetry.

My agent, Jane Dystel, is a for-real rock star. I'm in such good hands. I'm so incredibly grateful for the hours and hours of work she's done for me with this book, my random author meltdowns, and everything else I drop her emails about.

I have nothing but fantastic things to say about Albert Whitman. Once I started this project, I couldn't wait for Wendy McClure to read it, and her notes had me so excited that I'd accomplished what I'd imagined for this story from the beginning. Kristin Zelazko is amazing. Everyone at AW is just made of awesome.

Every time I step back and realize again that I have for-real books on for-real bookshelves, it's incredibly humbling. I am so, so, so grateful to be able to make up stories and have people read them.

Readers are the very best kind of people. It is always this final moment of a story when I realize how I could never hope to write and publish alone and that I'd never want to. For me, books are, and always should be, a group production.